Enjoy!

PASSE PARTOUT

Sam Wharton

Passe Partout

SAM
WHARTON

libros libertad
2008

First published by
Libros Libertad Publishing Ltd.
PO Box 45089
12851 16th Avenue, Surrey, BC, v4a 9l1
Ph. (604) 838-8796
Fax (604) 536-6819
www.libroslibertad.ca

Library and Archives Cataloguing in Publication

Wharton, Sam, 1937–
　　Passe partout / Sam Wharton.

isbn 978-0-9808979-6-8

　　1. Title.
ps8645.h37p38 2008　　　c813'.6　　　c2008-901688-2

Design and layout by Vancouver Desktop Publishing Centre
Printed in Canada by Printorium Bookworks

Acknowledgements

A first-time novel doesn't drop off the end of a pen; it requires help and advice from many people.

I thank my wife Jackie for her enduring support throughout the difficult process of writing something readable. She listened to my rough draft ideas and read several preliminary versions with love and patience.

I was fortunate to have friends who had been English teachers who read different early versions and offered such valuable advice. What would I have done without Carol Miller, Carolyn Crosby and Joan Parolin. Michael Linggard contributed some excellent suggestions.

Needless to say an author needs the professional advice and support of a publisher and I owe such a debt to Manolis at Libros Libertad.

The style of 'Passe Partout' was stimulated in part by the Flashman novels by George Macdonald Fraser. I enjoyed these books because while they were clearly outrageous fabrications, they were always based on historical truths. As an example 'Flashman at the Charge' gave an accurate picture of the circumstances surrounding the Charge of the Light Brigade even if Flashman's role will never be found in the official records.

The technical description of how safes with combination locks are opened comes from a diplomatic briefing given in a secret location in London in 1967 prior to my posting to the United States. I am grateful for the multifaceted experiences that my military service afforded me from 1956 to 1974.

Contents

ONE

Arrival

On a sultry June evening in 1954 a young man was waiting for the fast train to London. His name was Jonathan Hare and he was impatient to get away, looking up and down the rails that stretched to London one way and to Bristol the other. His mother had insisted on seeing him off and stood there stoically but Jonathan knew she was holding back tears. He prayed that she wouldn't embarrass him.

Suddenly she hugged him, saying, "I shall miss you Jonathan, it seems that you are never at home these days."

She turned and walked away down the platform.

He was by now used to her manner of speech, but it had set them far apart from the people in the down-at-heels railway town. She had drummed into him and her pupils the importance of the King's English and he had received the same discipline at his first boarding school. But such niceties were largely lost on the working class people that drove the trains and carried out the support functions that a major railway junction requires.

He was wearing his St. Eligius blazer and grey flannels, the only presentable outfit he had. He supposed he should have been grateful for what the clothing stores at his boarding schools provided, but each time he had to draw from them it had seemed like another case of charity.

A scruffy leather suitcase lay at his feet, while he held a bright metal case in one hand.

The train arrived and the beautiful Castle class engine at the head of the train rumbled past him, its curved nameplate reading 'Isambard Kingdom Brunel'.

He smiled, thinking it was a good omen, for it commemorated the famous engineer who had designed and constructed this very stretch of railway. He got into a carriage and hoisted the suitcase onto the overhead rack. He held the silver-sided case firmly on his lap.

He had found the case in the XLCR military surplus store run out of an old railway carriage up on blocks on a vacant lot near the station. The case had sturdy cantilevered fastenings that needed a good tug to open. Inside was a doctor's wartime field kit consisting of an old stethoscope and several fine probes, which he had supplemented with new tools and a special piece of test equipment.

He knew the case would arouse suspicion if the police ever saw inside it, so he had installed small combination locks. He had smiled at the time, wondering how many people there were who could open the case without having the right numbers.

As the train got underway he dug out his Assignment Instructions and read them once more. He was to present himself at Harry Sparrow's house, situated in an area of London not too far from Tower Bridge but little visited by tourists.

The Assignment signalled the completion of his two years at St. Eligius Hall, so far ahead academically of his fellow students that the St. Eligius staff assumed that he would pass his University entrance exams with flying colours and be awarded a University Scholarship. But St. Eligius had far different expectations of its students. He shrugged; the school had served his purposes and he had enjoyed the 'supplementals', those additional and mandatory subjects that were part of the curriculum. All in all, having to endure the frequent left-wing tirades from earnest and long-haired visiting lecturers about the importance of the Movement was a small price to pay.

The train clattered across the rails and into the great arched railway terminus of Paddington. He jumped down and walked to the head of the train where the great engine hissed with escaping steam. He stopped for a moment and grinned at the driver and fireman in the cab, giving them credit for the graceful and speedy run. Like most of the passengers, he was unaware that all along the train's pathway it had been directed by unseen and unheralded hands switching the points and turning the signals.

At the gate he asked the ticket collector how to get to Tower Hill station.

"Easy, mate, just follow the colours," the man said cheerfully, nodding his head at a white tiled map of the Underground.

Jonathan bought a ticket and examined the map. The intricate looping of coloured lines held no mystery for him, for he loved all maps and pictures. He walked down the tiled corridor to the platform and got on a Circle Line train.

The 'Tube' train lurched from station to station, sparking its way across the rails. He kept an eye on the overhead map, ticking off each intermediate stop. He looked again at his directions realizing he'd have to ask someone when he got to Tower Hill; he couldn't expect Harry to meet him.

He thought back to that day when Harry turned up at St. Eligius, a 'spiv' if ever he saw one, thin fox's face, loud tie, and cockney accent. But he was good, Jonathan remembered, for Harry had made that afternoon one of the few that had caught his interest.

Harry had been introduced as a Visitor in Supplementals. He had shown a grainy eight-millimetre film of a street in London called Leather Lane. He had been smiling crookedly as he suggested that the class observe and comment in writing.

The opening scene had a policeman strolling amiably along nodding occasionally to the stall-keepers. As soon as he was far enough away, a street vendor appeared with a heavy suitcase, which he placed on the ground and opened, displaying the sparkling jewellery, all the while glancing furtively in the direction of the retreating bobby. A small crowd assembled and money changed hands with astonishing speed. Suddenly the vendor closed the suitcase and disappeared around the corner as the policeman returned, at which point the movie ended.

Harry had handed out a quiz sheet that contained questions such as 'Comment on the contents of the suitcase'.

Jonathan had completed the sheet, which was gathered up with all the others. He had been surprised to see many puzzled faces in the room. Only one had returned Jonathan's grin; it was Charles Barnes, a boy somewhat older than Jonathan, and, while not a friend, not an enemy either. On the way from the room, Charles had come alongside, "Interesting show, eh, Hare?"

Jonathan smiled, "Tricks of the trade, I think."

So began a friendship that would see many challenges in the years to come.

Harry had read Jonathan's response to the Headmaster.

'The case is full of paste jewellery, which the pigeons will find out soon enough. They buy it because they think they're getting something for nothing.'

"This lad is good," said Harry, "he understands why a con works!"

The Headmaster nodded, "And he opened the old Champion safe, too. He'll make someone a good apprentice."

Harry's eyebrows shot up. "I'll take him then." Harry had a clientele that would appreciate such skills.

By the time the tube train arrived at Tower Hill, it was getting dark outside, and to make things worse, fog had rolled in from the Thames. Smoke from coal fires had turned the fog an orangey brown and it was difficult to make out any landmarks. Jonathan put down his cases and scratched his head.

As his eyes grew accustomed to the gloom, he saw a dim light. It came from a window in a corner shop and as he got nearer he saw that it was crammed with musical instruments, men's clothes, table lamps, fishing rods, and other odds and ends. He looked up and saw the three brass balls, recognizing the first pawnshop he'd seen other than in photographs. It boasted the name 'I. Bronsky'. He was sure they'd know where Harry lived.

As he pushed through the door, a bell jangled somewhere deep within and he heard a loud and angry voice. He pushed further through the jumbled assortment of stuff. Turning towards the voice, he saw a large, red-faced man leaning over the counter, grasping the shirt of a much older man who was trying to keep a black hat from falling off his head.

"What yer mean, sold it, it's mine, you stupid old Yid," the heavy-set man was bellowing. The shop owner was unable to respond, his face turning a worrying grey.

Not knowing what to do, Jonathan took a step forward and bumped into a Victorian tailor's dummy, which fell sideways, bringing down a large set of fireside tools and then a ratty bag of golf clubs. The noise was deafening, dust rising in clouds.

"What the?" started the heavy-set man, "Who're you?" He was directing his fury at Jonathan, but at the same time was looking past him at the door. The shop owner was rubbing his neck.

"I'm just looking for directions," said Jonathan softly.

There was a pause. When the angry man turned back, the shop owner had stepped out of reach and a young girl had appeared at his side.

The man kept glancing out of the window into the street; he was getting agitated.

"I'll get you for this," he yelled at Jonathan, and stormed out of the shop.

The young girl spoke in a strange tongue to the old man. He responded shakily, pointing at Jonathan. Jonathan started to say that all he wanted was directions, but was cut short by the girl.

"You saved my father?" Her voice was slightly accented.

Jonathan shrugged. "I did nothing, really."

"If you hadn't interrupted, that pig would have hurt my father." There was little gratitude, just a statement of fact.

"Now, now," rasped the old man, "Tell the young man how grateful we are."

"You do it, father," the girl said, turning and disappearing through heavy brown curtains draped over a doorway.

"I'm sorry, young man, for my daughter's manners. Tell me your name, please."

"Um," hesitated Jonathan, not sure that he was on safe ground.

The old man was peering at him through wire-framed spectacles, his black hat tipped back from his face at an odd angle.

"Could you help me, please?" asked Jonathan politely, "I'm looking for Harry Sparrow's house."

"Tell me your name first," smiled the old man. The smile had transformed his face.

Jonathan gave way. "Jonathan."

The smile deepened. "A good name, my son."

Jonathan had no idea why his name should be so important.

"I need to get to Harry Sparrow's house, please."

"Such a hurry, such a hurry!" intoned the old man with a sigh.

Jonathan had been subconsciously listening to the way that the shopkeeper's voice stressed syllables in an unusual singsong. It dawned on him that the old man was Jewish. He had never met a Jew before.

"Come, my boy, choose something for yourself."

"But why?"

The old man looked surprised. "You have done me a great service, and at risk to yourself. I must reward you."

There was an air of finality about this statement. Jonathan, being anxious to leave, decided to humour the shopkeeper. He looked around and spotted a charcoal grey suit draped over an impressive wooden clothes stand.

"May I have the suit?"

The old man looked even harder at Jonathan.

"And good taste too," he smiled. "Will it fit you?"

Jonathan hadn't thought this far ahead.

"Try it on, my son."

Jonathan was alarmed.

"Where can I change, then?"

"Come with me."

The old man parted the brown curtains and opened a door into a small room. Jonathan carried his luggage and suit into the closet, not seeing the amusement on the old man's face. He tried on the trousers. They were a bit too long in the leg, and tight at the waist, but Jonathan shouted to the old man through the door that they were a good fit, and packed the suit in his case.

He stepped out from the closet to find the young girl waiting for him holding a silver tray. There was a glass with a dark brown liquid. Jonathan felt embarrassed.

The girl refused to meet his eyes. "Take it, please, and go back to the shop."

Jonathan, not sure why, lifted the glass in the direction of the girl and smiled.

"Thank you."

She turned abruptly and retreated, leaving Jonathan to return to the shop.

"You have the suit, then," the old man rasped, eyes twinkling behind his spectacles.

"Yes, thank you."

"Such a polite young man!" Jonathan wondered why this was said in a louder voice than usual.

"And now we will celebrate!" He raised his glass and Jonathan hurriedly did the same.

The old man, with his eyes closed, spoke words in a language that Jonathan found harsh and guttural. He had no idea what had been said, and the old man didn't enlighten him. The wine was far too sweet and strong.

"So, you're one of Harry's boys?"

"I'm not his *boy!*" This sounded too impolite, so he added, "I'm just staying with him for a short while."

The old man nodded. "He has a house two turnings on the left from here, going that way."

Jonathan took his leave, closing the door gently. Behind him, the old man was talking to the girl, wagging his finger.

Jonathan had a feeling he was being watched. A black Wolsley car was parked and might have someone in it. He shrugged and made his way to Harry's house where the door was opened by a woman who sniffed, "You'll be Jonathan Hare, then."

There isn't much welcome here, thought Jonathan.

"Well, you'd better come in, I suppose, Harry's out looking for you."

The tone was accusatory. Jonathan felt obliged to respond.

"I found it rather difficult to navigate in the fog."

It was immediately clear that he had said the wrong thing, although he didn't understand why.

Before the woman could respond the door opened and Harry came in.

"Oh, you made it then. Welcome, welcome to me 'umble abode! You've met me trouble and strife then?"

"My name is Rita, as you well know, Harry Sparrow," she said, tossing her head and leaving the room.

"What's got into her, then?" grinned Harry.

"I'm sorry, Mr. Sparrow, if I've caused you any trouble," said Jonathan.

"How did you find yer way, then?"

"I got directions from Mr. Bronsky."

Harry shrugged and gave him a handful of business cards that carried the grand wording:

'Harry Sparrow & Company', and represented Jonathan as 'Samuel Ward'.

"But Harry, that's not my name!"

"Look, yer second name is Samuel and yer me ward, ain't yer?" grinned Harry.

Jonathan examined the cards. "So this is your business?"

Harry tensed. "Sharp, ain't yer, then," he said, "Solve other people's problems, don't I."

Harry tried to move on, but Jonathan persisted.

"So you get paid for what I do?"

"That's for me to know and you to mind yer own business!" said Harry, curtly, "Well, I expect you're tired. Yer room's on the top floor."

TWO

Mountbeck

Far to the north of London the great house called Mountbeck glared sullenly down over the lawns and across the man-made lakes. It was a huge but undistinguished building with scores of rooms spread over the three upper floors. It had not endeared itself to the many generations of the Bellestream family. They had built a fortune in international commerce by employing methods that in later years would have landed them in jail. They had donated wisely to royal causes. The first Duke chose the title 'Hawksmoore' in recognition of his passion for falconry with his coat of arms a single gauntlet holding a tethered falcon.

They had prospered in society by educating themselves in the numberless arcane rituals of the aristocracy and had made many successful alliances through marriage. The Bellestreams also maintained social ties with many European families that had earned their status by similar commercial practices, and it was from them that they invited their most important guests.

The twentieth century had not been kind to the Bellestreams. When the thirteenth Duke died it exposed the family to the recently introduced Death Duties. In 1952, his heir William, together with his wife and child disappeared on a sailing holiday to Biarritz.

It fell to the younger brother, Edward, Lord Erinmore, to take control of the family affairs, but it proved to be a legal and emotional task that Edward found overwhelming. He was so traumatised that caring for William's daughter Jane was all he could manage. As for the financial acumen that had driven the family success for so many generations, it had passed him by.

To make matters worse, the huge working capital of liquid and untraceable assets stored in the specially built Champion safe were impossible to get at, for the combination, so fanatically guarded, had gone down with William into the cold Atlantic somewhere off the west coast of France. And the Champion Safe Company was only one of many factories that had been annihilated during the London Blitz, depriving the Bellestreams of any company experts to open the safe. The few freelancers that Edward had felt able to call in after Williams's disappearance had given up in disgust, defeated by the special fabrication that the Bellestreams had ordered.

The income from the estate was miniscule compared to the clandestine profits made by the family's financial support of enterprises far from the public domain. It was quite insufficient to sustain the cost of keeping Mountbeck in its former manner. Servants were let go and economies made everywhere, and now a complete wing was closed.

In the massive study, Edward was looking at the envelope containing the weekly duty letter from his niece Jane. As usual he was filled with despair. Writing from Oxenham College for Ladies on paper headed "Lady Jane Temple Bellestream" she would pour out her unhappiness. She hated the place, and had made few friends. Edward may not have inherited the family financial brains but he knew enough about people to know that Jane's problems were of her own making. He might excuse her for suffering from the loss of her family when only thirteen and then being sent to Oxenham, but he knew she was also arrogant and selfish and uncaring towards those she deemed inferior in station.

A door opened silently and Travis, the Bellestream Butler, materialised from thin air. Edward was lost in his reverie and looked up, startled; he should have got used to it by now, for there were passageways within Mountbeck, as in all great houses, that permitted servants to appear suddenly in the most useful places.

Travis coughed. "Good morning, my Lord, the Steward is here

with the weekly report. Is there anything you need before I show him in?"

"Can't you get rid of him, Travis?" growled Edward.

As he spoke, he realized that this was not appropriate.

"Excuse me, Travis, please show him in."

Travis was used to these sudden mood swings.

Mr. Obadiah Hawthorne, Steward to the Bellestream family, was waiting nervously outside Edward's study. The great oak door opened silently and Travis nodded politely.

"You may go in now."

The Steward, his throat dry, approached the elegant desk at which Edward was seated.

"Good morning, my Lord."

Edward looked up, his prematurely greying hair cut immaculately to flow around his ears.

"Ah, Steward, good morning to you."

Hawthorne placed the leather-bound portfolio in front of Edward, his hand not quite steady.

He had rehearsed this speech a dozen times, but was still uncomfortable.

"I am afraid, my Lord, that the news is bad. I have listed the additional assets of which you informed me at our last meeting. They have been assessed for realizable value, shown in the right hand column," he added, knowing Edward's difficulty with balance sheets. "Taken all together, however, the estate is, um," he hesitated.

"Stony broke?" interceded Edward, noticing the Steward's dismay.

"Indeed, my Lord."

"What's the damage?"

"I'm afraid the situation is not remediable with any temporary infusion of capital."

The Steward had recently attended a professional meeting of his financial colleagues and had been impressed with this phrase.

"Why not?" A note of irritation had entered Edward's voice.

"Well, my Lord, as you will see from the projections on the next page," he prompted, "the estate's running costs have increased so much that, each year, we will be in deficit by several thousand pounds, with no foreseeable gains in income."

Despite his distaste for figures and balance sheets, Edward was an intelligent man.

"What I don't understand, Steward, is how we can have gone so quickly to the dogs."

The Steward had anticipated this.

"If you will look at the wages column, my Lord, you will see that recent legislation that established the minimum that we may pay has most seriously elevated these costs."

"But we have already sent half of the staff away, closed a complete wing of the house, all at your suggestion." There was a certain chill to his tone.

"Indeed, my Lord, but you will recall that the government's nationalization programmes have deprived us of much of the income that supported the previous level of staffing."

"What are the options then?" sighed Edward.

"There must be some way to increase the estate's income," murmured the Steward almost to himself.

"And I suppose you have an idea?"

"Well, my Lord, there is the possibility of drawing considerable income from the development of the Abercorn."

The Steward was doing what his obligation to the Movement had demanded, raising the difficult issue of the beautiful lands adjacent to the Village. It had, in the past, provoked a thunderous rebuke. Today, Edward merely looked defeated, but recovered quickly.

"Steward, I thank you for the excellent work you do, but I will have to give some thought to the matter."

The interview had come to an abrupt end. From somewhere, Travis materialised and escorted the Steward from the room.

Edward stared at the letter from Jane, quite incapable of opening it. He thought about the future; he would have to deal with his brother's disappearance and face the awesome responsibilities of becoming the fifteenth Duke of Hawksmoore. All around him the estate was deteriorating and he could see no way out. He sighed, waiting for the depression to deepen and the dark shadows to slide across his peripheral vision.

Safely at home, Mr. Hawthorne stared for a long time at the telephone before he asked for the number that he had committed to memory.

"Bessemer Foundry," said a rather common voice.

"This is Hawthorne, and it is exactly 12:03."

There was a prolonged silence.

Finally a strongly accented voice responded.

"Well?"

"I have performed the Veronica," said Mr. Hawthorne, as if reading a script.

"Good. Your service has been noted."

The telephone, clammy from Mr. Hawthorne's grip, had gone dead.

THREE

Getting Settled

Jonathan went up two flights of stairs to his room in the attic; it was somewhat like his room at home although the furnishings were in much better taste. It was welcoming and comfortable, which fitted with what he had already observed about Harry's house, set back in a quiet circle with a small green area in the middle. Harry must do well even if his cockney accent and flamboyant dress placed him well out-side polite society. Jonathan smiled at that, remembering again the unnerving emphasis on the King's English at Standish College, his first boarding school. He hadn't had any difficulty there, his mother had seen to that.

"We may be poor, Jonathan," she had often remarked, "but at least we were raised properly."

He dropped his tool case onto the single bed and unpacked his suitcase, grimacing at how shabby it looked. He hung up the suit that the old man had pushed on to him. He'd have to get the trou-sers altered, he thought, but the jacket and waistcoat had felt good on him. When he fitted the suit onto a hanger, it seemed to flow from the shoulders, everything smooth, the lining must be silk. It would make a change from his boarding school blazer and flannels, at least. This thought stayed with him as he unpacked the rest of his belongings, aware once more that virtually everything was out of one school clothing store or another.

He sat down on the single bed thinking it was a bit like those in the dormitories, but this one was made of wood, not steel. St. Eligius had been a bit more comfortable than Standish, the dormitories were smaller, five or six to a room, rather than twenty. He ran his hand over his tool case with pride. He smiled as he thought of that old Champion safe in the Workshop at St. Eligius. There had been such a ceremony when he had opened it, the Headmaster himself coming down from his Study to congratulate him. Some of the boys had complained that he had used his stethoscope, but they were rudely put in their place by the Workshop Master, Mr. Harris, always known as 'Tweedy', who pointed out that being prepared was essential.

Tweedy had taken him on one side afterwards and told him about the bombing of the Champion factory.

"Flattened, young Hare, absolutely flattened, nothing left at all except some old hulks. All the designs burned to a cinder, bits of charred paper floating around for ages."

He had paused, looking at Jonathan with vacant eyes. He had taken a breath and continued, "Most of the staff went up in smoke, too, so there's lots of Champions still in use, but with no-one to look after them."

He had thought Tweedy was going to add something, but the master had turned away rather abruptly and left the room.

He decided that he'd better go down and be polite to Harry and Rita. They were sitting in front of a massive black and white television set. There was some inane variety show on and Harry jumped up at once. He seemed to relish the opportunity to get away from it. Rita never stirred, but Jonathan had a peculiar feeling that she was very much aware of what was going on between him and Harry.

Harry was spelling out the timetable for tomorrow; a few minor jobs, show him around the manor, get a pie and a pint somewhere. He was a bit too animated; Jonathan felt as if he was constantly getting an elbow dug into his ribs, although Harry never touched him.

It was a bit overpowering at first; boarding school life, even at St. Eligius, frowned on any show of emotion.

Harry wondered what Jonathan had to wear, and was pleased to hear that he had brought the khaki smock coat that was the uniform in the Workshop.

"Got a business suit, then?" asked Harry, raising his expressive eyebrows, "We may have some special jobs, never can tell who'll call on old Harry's services. Did a job for the British Museum last week, filing cabinet jammed solid. Those old geysers haven't got a clue, could have used one of the janitors, but it was something special they said, sounded like higher griffins, but what do I know?"

Jonathan was stumped for a moment, then said "Well, actually my suit needs a bit of alteration, the trouser legs are a bit too long."

Harry slapped his thigh. "Hear that, Rita? Right up your street, darlin'!" and to Jonathan, without waiting for Rita's response, "Give them to Rita first thing tomorrow."

Jonathan went to bed feeling that Harry had made him feel at home even if Rita had been strangely hostile. He had almost no experience of how married couples related to each other; his mother simply wouldn't talk about his father. He knew a bit about cockney slang and supposed that 'trouble and strife' for wife was normal for this part of the world, and yet Rita's response had been really snotty. He shrugged, lost in this new world of relationships.

FOUR

Battle Lines

Jonathan remembered the War well; the gap-teeth rows of houses where bombs had fallen, the planes fighting like dogs overhead and the air raid sirens. Like all boys born just before the War, he accepted that it was simply the way life was, along with the rationing and the propaganda slogans such as 'Make do and Mend' and 'Dig for Victory'. When the War ended he was still too young to comprehend the social watershed that occurred when England elected a left-wing government.

Those in the 'Establishment', accustomed as they were to centuries of power, were shocked and dismayed at this sudden political shift. They could claim that they had led the nation through the expansion of the Empire and the industrial revolution and deserved their privileges. But the obligatory left-wing lectures at St. Eligius made it clear that among the working classes who had provided the manpower for this progress there were militants strongly opposed to the social imbalances. The militancy had matured and now called itself the 'Bessemer Movement'.

The lectures had left him unconvinced to the point of boredom. He accepted that those who toiled in the mines, railway workshops and especially steel mills could claim that they were put in danger merely to 'line the pockets of the rich'. But privately he remained uninvolved, avoiding as many of the marches and demonstrations and youth meetings as he could.

He had realised quite early on that his Scholarship to St. Eligius was because someone had spotted his special talents and that they fitted well with the Movement's plan for a more aggressive agenda. It had to be one of the masters at Standish, but he would never know who it was.

Eventually the Bessemer strategy had become clear; power came from placing supporters within the existing system. Candidates would have to be selected, groomed and educated, and this was where St. Eligius came in. The Movement had acquired what was once the country home of a family that had failed to protect itself against the ravages of Death Duties and this had become "St. Eligius Hall". Over time its graduates obtained University degrees and membership in professional institutions and were fed into prepared positions within the Establishment. But those who graced the hallways of St. Eligius were equipped with certain clandestine skills far outside the pale of polite society.

The Establishment grew increasingly alarmed at the number of landed families that had to sell up or open their previously private houses and lands to the public. One of the most senior peers went so far as to establish a wild animal park in his grounds as a means of staving off the increasingly onerous effects of Death Duties. Many grand and historic houses were handed over to the National Trust and so became public property. And they could see that their domain was being slowly invaded by people outside the accepted social milieu. 'Not people like us' became a common complaint amongst those used to power, but in the new order there was officially nothing that they could do about it. They realised that the Bessemer Movement was determined to undermine the very Establishment system that they cherished, using techniques that were only tolerated in agencies that were never found on any government rolls. Some sort of counter attack was clearly essential.

So they created an agency that would defend them against the less acceptable tactics of the Movement. It would appear to be an apparently legitimate organization – the Royal Horological Society – dedicated to the study of all things related to the measurement of time and the associated sciences, including a specialized museum housing appropriate national treasures. It was set up outside the regular police and other intelligence departments and absorbed dozens of wartime units, still largely intact but forgotten by the departments that had created them. The fact that the Society received Royal approval indicated how seriously the threat was taken. Parliamentary scrutiny was clearly not an option, so funds were channelled from many different sources into one of London's private Banks and from there to the Director of the Society.

A magnificent house was found south of the river, not far from the Royal Naval College and the Greenwich Observatory and just across the Thames from the Isle of Dogs. It became a favourite place for high-level meetings that would have attracted too much attention if held in the City. Choosing the Director, who went by the rather mundane title of 'Curator of the Royal Horological Society', was relatively easy. There were families that had gained financial independence through the expansion of the Empire and which had subsequently served the country with complete dedication and with little public reward. One of these was the de Quincy family who could trace their ancestry back to the Conqueror, and it was Sir Roger de Quincy who was selected as the Director. The Establishment considered it more than fortunate that his brother, Sir Hubert de Quincy was presently the Commissioner of the Metropolitan Police.

FIVE

The Wasteland

A few miles east of the Tower of London the Thames suddenly turns south and then abruptly north again, creating a peninsula called 'The Isle of Dogs'. It has the attraction of a lengthy river frontage and over the years became the natural home for a variety of marine industries. It also served as a focal point for the nefarious activities that go on in any port city, and so became a magnet for the criminal fraternity.

As the Port of London grew, a canal was built across the north end to provide a shortcut. It was never a success, and was eventually converted into the West India Docks, which ran east and west and virtually cut off the peninsula from the rest of London. Extensive shipbuilding facilities developed, including heavy steel mills, and the Champion Safe Factory found it convenient to locate close to the mills to meet its specialised and confidential requirements. Unfortunately the Dockyards became one of Hitler's main targets and night after night during the Blitz, incendiary and high explosive bombs were dropped from fleets of warplanes. Acres of the docks were flattened and deemed uninhabitable due to the unexploded munitions that were known to be there. The Champion Safe Factory had been located in one of the most devastated areas.

The Isle of Dogs remained desolate for years after the end of the war. The task of recreating its commercial vitality was beyond the energies of Councils and Commerce and this created a vacuum that was filled by various enterprises that found it convenient to carry on their activities untroubled by the usual authorities. As often happens in similar lawless situations, the brutal and sadistic rose to the top. In this case it was the twin brothers, Ronnie and Reggie Grey[1] who became pre-eminent and soon ruled an empire that extended over some fourteen square miles of the East End.

The virtual annexation of much of east London by the Grey gang should have come as no surprise to the police, since they had been unable to react to the efficiency and brutality of the Grey's campaign. By 1954, the Isle of Dogs had become almost impossible to police, since access to it was so constrained at the north end and the rest was a maze of apparently derelict warehouses and other facilities that fronted onto the river and where it was not unusual to find streets as narrow and disgraceful as they had been three hundred years earlier. In practical terms, the authorities were forced to turn a blind eye to the activities of the unlicensed companies that provided so much income to the Grey twins. Such was their control over the area that many pubs and billiard halls were safe havens for their people, where they met openly.

The Metropolitan Police Force acquired the world famous name of 'Scotland Yard' because its first home was a small building in Whitehall in a courtyard that had once been owned by the Kings of Scotland. The Commissioner of the Metropolitan Police is one of many senior positions in the civil service where the incumbent is honoured with a Knighthood for 'Service to the Nation'. It carries with it immense power far beyond the scope of crime fighting and demands a grasp of political realities. To be appointed, a candidate must have developed connections that tie him firmly to the Establishment, and yet must appear to be entirely impartial in the administration of his functions.

The glaring embarrassment of the Dockland situation grated for years on the Commissioner's nerves, but he was limited to keeping watch at the perimeters, hoping to catch one of the Grey leaders in a moment of carelessness.

---

1 In real life, these were the Kray twins.

Scotland Yard had built its reputation in large part on the excellence of its record-keeping system, which was housed in the basement of the building and became a world of its own, inhabited and understood by only a handful of dedicated clerical staff, some of whom, it was said, spent their entire careers manning a single cell in a particular section.

The post-war years had seen a growth in crime and a gradual increase in its seriousness, so the Commissioner decided to create a Serious Crimes Record Section, staffed with the ablest and most dedicated of these unknown civil servants. The principal target was to be the Grey gang. A reward of a thousand pounds, a huge sum in those days, was offered, without much hope that any of the gang would be tempted. But there might be some in the wings that could offer valuable information.

Up in his attic room, Jonathan was thinking about the cold shoulder that Rita had given him so obviously. He lay on his bed wondering why he had gone through life with so few friends, not that he had ever seemed to need them. He was an only child; his mother had run a Montessori Kindergarten School and had made him join in when he was at least a year younger than the others. He had developed visual and mechanical skills that few recognised, although their neighbour Monsieur Renaud, a Belgian more prescient than some of his countrymen, had told his mother about the Chinese puzzle box that Jonathan had opened, "Your boy einserted his little finker so quickly onto the secret part; unlocked it straight away, he did!".

Jonathan read voraciously and had discovered the joys of the Library at Standish College after he had won that Scholarship. A boys' Boarding School can only survive if the masters maintain a certain distance from their pupils, and Jonathan was content with that remoteness. Other boys who might have been his friends were frustrated at his attitude "You should have been a Prince," one of them had once hissed. His scholastic progress was far ahead of the others, although his term reports consistently carried remarks such as "Jonathan leaves the impression that he knows more than his Teacher." His mother, so absorbed in trying to make ends meet, hardly noted these comments; Jonathan would not have known how to change in any case.

It is hardly possible at an all-male boarding school to foster a relationship with a girl, and Jonathan found that the girls in his working class town saw no future in a young man who only appeared on holidays every few months and then for only a week or so.

Ah, but then there was Victoria. He brightened at that thought; how had he met her? Oh yes, he had been going to the Town Library when a huge Rolls Royce eased up to the curb and a young girl in riding attire rushed out, slipped on the wet pavement and fell with a thump onto her backside. Books had flown everywhere, and Jonathan had moved to pick them up. But she had said with such haughtiness, "Leave them and help me up!"

He had been instantly angry at her tone, but his mother's insistence on good manners had obliged him to hold out his hand to her. And when she was on her feet, she had simply stood there looking at the books until he scooped them up. "Come on," he said and opened the door for her. Dumping the books on the return desk, he stalked away to the shelves. Spotting an illustrated book on the Oxford Clay Vale he sat down at a reading table, flipping through until he found a page describing the Uffington White Horse. Absorbed in the photograph of the stylistic galloping horse carved into the chalk hillside, he didn't sense the girl standing next to him.

"Oh," she whispered, "that's the White Horse, we can see it from our place."

She had taken off her riding helmet and was much less imposing.

"Really?" Jonathan responded icily, then realized that this sounded ungracious; his mother would have had something to say had she heard.

He produced a smile. "I was thinking of riding up there before I go back to College."

The girl was immediately excited, "Oh, it's the most wonderful place to ride. There's always a wind up there and the horses love the turf."

She was looking at him appraisingly. "Where do you go to School?"

Jonathan told her.

She frowned and then brightened. "I knew you weren't a town boy. You do ride?"

"Only my bicycle!" he said hurriedly.

"Oh, you don't know what you're missing!" she exclaimed. "Do you know Frodsham Grange? My family has our stables there. Why don't you come for a ride?"

Jonathan was about to say that his experience was limited to the old plough horses that worked the farm in Cornwall, when he realized where this might place him socially. He had never been on a horse, and had no particular urge to do so. For a moment, he could think of nothing sensible to say, but she *had* invited him.

"Perhaps I will," was all he could manage. She looked at her watch, and told him she must rush. As he followed her progress, she turned and smiled and walked back, thrusting her hand at him.

"My name is Victoria de Quincy."

She waited expectantly. Jonathan rose and took her hand. Nothing else for it, he thought.

"Mine is Jonathan."

There was a momentary pause; neither of them seemed able to fill it.

"Must go!" she said, turning away.

They had become, well, friends he supposed, although her mother had soon put an end to that. But at least he had received those letters with the de Quincy crest when he got back to Standish and didn't mind the teasing, "Hare's got a girl friend, she must be blind or something!"

He felt a bit brighter at these thoughts, and drifted off to sleep. He dreamed that he was back in the tiny Cornish village, where they had lived just after the War, wrestling with Tony using a style peculiar to Cornwall, where the object was to use the hip as a fulcrum to bring the opponent to the ground. It was almost an obsession with the boys; whole play periods could pass while a boy would struggle to get the other off-balance and then jam the hip into him, pulling down on the arm at the same time. After a while it became almost second nature to most boys, and if they were particularly good, it could lead them into competitions right across that ancient county.

SIX

Home Sweet Home

Lady Jane Bellestream had found a friend at Oxenham, or perhaps the friend had found her. Germaine Boisin possessed a warmly foreign accent that Lady Jane found sympathetic. She confided that her family estate was spread over many 'ectaires' in Normandy, where they had stables and grooms that were, in Germaine's words, 'super dishy'. Lady Jane had no idea what 'super dishy' meant, but had made the appropriate noises. Her own equestrian pursuits had barely satisfied Edward; she had no love for the huge beasts, or for the disgusting maintenance chores. The friendship between the two fifteen year old girls was fuelled more by Lady Jane's loneliness than by any sense of generosity, but Germaine provided an ebullient presence that carried their relationship forward. As the school year ended, and the summer holidays came closer, Germaine dropped several hints that eventually prompted Lady Jane to invite her to Mountbeck; Germaine accepted graciously.

Germaine had a strange effect upon Edward. He had seen to it that the girls ate at the high table with him. Lady Jane was self-absorbed and uncommunicative, while Germaine's vibrancy elevated her far beyond her years. Edward was at first unsettled, but began to look forward to Germaine's company at the table, thinking that he hadn't felt like this for years, and then paled, filled with sadness at the thought of William and Marguerite, so badly missed.

"Must do something about it," said Edward to himself. He sat up straighter, surprised at the surge of decisiveness.

"Come on, Jane," laughed Germaine, "Let's go and ride!" She stopped and looked at Edward.

"I regret, your Lordship," she said demurely, "Will you excuse us, please?"

Edward, emerging from his reverie, produced a broad smile, which caught Lady Jane by surprise.

"Of course, my dears"

The girls went quickly, leaving Edward sitting alone. Travis materialised.

"Will that be all, your Lordship?"

"I will be in my study, and please make sure I am not disturbed, Travis."

Travis escorted Edward to the main door of the dining room. As soon as it closed, he snapped his fingers. Young Daisy appeared as if by magic, although it didn't surprise Travis, since the design of the room permitted servants to come and go silently without using the main door reserved for the family. The serving table was placed against a section of the wall that extended into the room by a couple of feet. The end furthest from the head of the table was open, permitting direct access to the stairs that came up from the kitchen. This architectural feature is common to virtually all great houses and is known by the strange name of 'Passe Partout'.

When Jonathan came downstairs the next day, Harry and Rita had gone out, so he had a chance to examine the house. Although it fitted well into the terrace, it was laid out much better than he expected. There was a good flow through the rooms and the furniture was all in good taste. To his surprise, there was a telephone[2] which meant that Harry must know what he was doing, have some inside contacts somewhere.

Just then, Harry returned and took him across the East End to a client's house. The front door lock was jammed, with the remains of the key wedged into the tumblers.

---

2   It was almost impossible for a private person to get a telephone in those days.

Jonathan looked at Harry.

"Is that all?"

"Well, show us yer mettle, then," said Harry.

Jonathan assumed this meant that he was to demonstrate one of the St. Eligius supplementals. He took a hand drill and fitted a specially tempered bit. He drilled into the broken key, turning the handle one way then the other until the bit broke through. He reversed the drill, and the now hollow key collapsed under the pressure of the tumbler springs.

"Spare key?" he asked.

Harry handed it over, and Jonathan slid it through the lock pushing out the broken key.

"Didn't touch the sides, then." Harry was grinning.

Jonathan had come across this expression, which has its roots in the billiard parlour and which signifies a smooth piece of handiwork.

They went into a pub for lunch. It was crowded and noisy and everyone seemed to be having a good time. Beer was flowing copiously.

Harry forced their way to the bar. "Hey, Rosie!"

Rosie looked their way. She was a plump blonde of a certain age with her hair piled up and wearing lipstick in a pronounced cupid's bow. She had a mascara beauty spot on one heavily powdered cheek and was wearing a transparent nylon blouse with a multitude of shoulder straps beneath. A cigarette was dangling from her lower lip and she was squinting through the smoke.

"Well, hallo stranger, what yer having, then?" she said in a tobacco baritone.

Harry ordered two pints and two pork pies. They forced their way to a table, where Jonathan looked suspiciously at his pie. Harry simply picked his up and bit into it with gusto, so Jonathan took a bite; it was remarkably fresh and very good. He said as much to Harry.

"Better be, this close to Smithfield!"

Jonathan recalled that the huge London meat market was not far away.

"Probably fell off the back of a lorry," Harry winked.

After lunch, they did a couple of jobs. One was at a down-at-heels terraced house, where the woman had lost the key to the front door; she was "ever so grateful" to Harry and pleaded with him not to tell 'me hubby'.

"Slap me around something terrible, he will," she said with conviction.

The lock had to be picked, and Jonathan felt his way quickly through the tumblers, disengaging them one by one. The door opened and they replaced the barrel of the lock from Harry's toolbox. Harry didn't take any money this time. "Do me a favour, love, just pass the word!"

Working with Harry turned out to be good fun, although Jonathan was at first stumped by the Cockney dialect used by the people living around the London docks. While basically English, it was almost entirely colloquial, and could be, and often was used to confound those unfamiliar with it. Jonathan was fascinated with the technicalities. He noticed that the sound for a short "u" was a short "a", and the ending "tter" in words like "gutter" and "letter" was replaced by a swallowed "huh" sound, so that a Cockney would say "ga-huh" and "le-huh."

Swear words laced every sentence and vulgarities that would have been cause for severe discipline at Standish went un-remarked. And then there was the rhyming slang. Some of it has passed into everyday humour; "trouble and strife" for "wife"; "apples and pears" for stairs.

Despite these difficulties, Jonathan recognised that there was a special atmosphere here, with a refreshing openness. In quite a short time, Jonathan was able to understand enough Cockney to get by, and to parrot a good deal of it. It seemed to give Harry great amusement. But Harry had recorded another skill for future reference.

The next job was more interesting. They entered an old theatre called the Alhambra, and went to the stage manager's cubbyhole.

"Thank God you're here, come with me, quickly please."

The cabinet was centre stage; all the house lights were on.

"Lousy doors are jammed, see!" said the sweating little man, "only three hours to curtain." He was almost wailing.

Jonathan looked at Harry, who shrugged, "Not my cup o' tea!"

The escape door to the rear of the cabinet was a modification of the split wall. From the audience's view the door looked solid, but it was hinged at one end and in the middle. When the beautiful assistant was inside the cabinet the smallest nudge opened the door and, once behind it, she could close it as simply. Jonathan examined it; it resisted all his attempts to open it. After a while, he asked for a step-ladder, and used it to peer at the top corner of the door.

"Torch, Harry, please." He shone it into the crack at the top of the doorway. "Ah!" he said with satisfaction.

"What?" asked Harry.

"These things have an emergency release. If the door jams, the magician can free it by pressing on this panel, here," he pointed. "Normally, it releases a plunger that forces the door open. But the plunger's embedded itself into the doorframe."

Harry scratched his head. "How yer going to fix it then?"

"Get me some butter, please."

There was much laughter and not a few coarse jokes peculiar to the stage. Then they realised that he was serious. The stage manager produced a sandwich and Jonathan laughed as he scraped some butter off the bread and smoothed it around what he could see of the plunger.

"Now what?" asked Harry.

"Cigarette lighter?"

Harry grunted and flicked one alight, and Jonathan applied the heat to the wood around the plunger.

"Now we wait," Jonathan grinned.

A comedian and his stooge started to rehearse. The jokes were pretty awful, but Music Hall audiences never seemed to mind – a groan was as good as a laugh.

"Did you hear about the riot at Hampton Court Maze?"

"No, what happened at Hampton Court Maze?"

"A crowd of Irish tourists couldn't find their way *in*!"

There were a couple of dull thuds from a drum in the orchestra pit.

Jonathan thought his life was like that, hard to get started and impossible to see ahead.

After a few minutes, there was a click, the plunger withdrew and the door folded outwards. There was a small round of applause.

"Better put a dowel in that hole, stop the plunger getting back into the wood," said Jonathan with satisfaction.

"And where did you learn that magic stuff?" asked Harry, pursing his lips.

Jonathan explained about his interest in stage effects and about the Standish Library. He had found so much there that was far more interesting than the duty lessons needed to pass Ordinary Levels. He told Harry about the Caligula project; he had constructed a working model of the famous cabinet used in the best magic acts; it is placed centre stage under spotlights, with a black curtain behind it to add drama. The beautiful blonde assistant enters from the front, and, after some stage business, an explosion of flash-powder momentarily blinds the audience. An invisible rope lifts the top off the cabinet; the sides fall down to reveal – nothing!

The cabinet has two rear walls, each slightly over half-width and displaced by a foot or so. The assistant has slipped through the invisible passage, sliding behind the curtain while the flash occupies the audience.

Harry shook his head, but Jonathan had gone up a few notches in his estimation; perhaps he could use him after he graduated, he might make an excellent con man, or ideas man more like, we always need more of them, work out all the wrinkles behind the scenes, don't they? Nothing better than a good con, Harry thought.

On the way back to Harry's, Jonathan wanted to know when he would get paid. Harry stared at him. "Paid? What for?" Jonathan explained that he was doing all the work.

"Hey, don't think you're the expert here!" The subject appeared to be closed but Jonathan decided that Harry wasn't going to get away with it.

SEVEN

How the Mighty Have Fallen

When they got back to Harry's, Rita was in a bad mood.
"I suppose you'll want me to feed you now?"

Harry was quick on his feet. "Nah, let's go darn the old loaf of bread, have a few, wadyersay?"

Jonathan was confused, "Loaf of Bread, funny name for a pub isn't it?"

There was a small silence until Harry and Rita started laughing.

"That's the King's Head; you know, big pub on the corner, not far from Bronsky's."

The pub was busy when the three of them entered; Jonathan found the noise deafening. Harry pulled some notes from a back pocket and slipped them to Jonathan, with a wink.

"Advance on your earnings, old boy," he said in a fake upper class accent.

He lifted three fingers to the barman and drew a circle around the group with his other hand. The barman raised his thumb.

"Go and get the drinks," said Harry to Jonathan, "your round!"

Jonathan, extremely possessive of his money, glared at Harry, but saw no real alternative. He fought his way to the bar, where three pint glasses sat on a tray, wooden skewers containing various bits of fruit and leaves added for decoration. When the barman told him the price, his anger at Harry increased. The drinks were expensive.

"Pimm's is always that much," said the barman. His accent was certainly not cockney.

Jonathan didn't want to display ignorance, so he carried the tray back to their table.

"Harry always drinks Pimm's," said Rita, smugly.

"Had one before?" asked Harry.

"Not at these prices!"

"Well, yer in our league now," laughed Harry, then stood up and shouted "Heh, Charmaine!"

Rita, focussing over Jonathan's shoulder, said acidly, "And doesn't she look the part!"

Jonathan turned and saw a tall young woman of about Rita's age coming towards them. She was wearing a black strapless dress with a skirt that flowed silkily around her calves. Her hair was drawn back from her face.

Jonathan thought that she was a bit overdressed for a pub.

Harry did the introductions.

Charmaine looked directly at him. "You are Jonathan? I am called Charmaine." She offered her hand. Jonathan recognized from her speech that she must have been born in France. He took her hand in the continental style, bowing over it. "Enchanté!" came automatically to his lips. There was a small silence.

"Well," said Harry, "would yer look at that, proper little frog, ain't he?

Jonathan recognized the centuries-old English tendency to look down on all things French, and released Charmaine's hand. There was a faint blush at her neck.

"Vous êtês française, je crois," said Jonathan.

"I thought I spoke very good English," she said stiffly.

Harry jumped in. "You do, love, you do, only Jonathan here has a special ear for accents."

Jonathan realised that Harry didn't miss much.

Rita said rather too quickly, "Charmaine runs the Palais de Dance, just down the street."

Charmaine's eyes were certainly her best feature, and she used them to effect. In her homeland she would have been called "jolie-laide", which can be only roughly translated as 'someone who might not be pretty but who has that special warmth that can so attract a man'.

"You dance, Jonathan?" asked Charmaine, raising an eyebrow.

The look of dismay that spread over Jonathan's face was due to his irrational fear of the dance floor. It is akin to the debilitating fear of heights known as acrophobia, but Jonathan's condition has no scientific name.

In his last year at Standish, all boys were required to attend an organized dance, with girls imported from a nearby Academy. It had been a nightmare for Jonathan, who had tried to sneak out as soon as the music began. He had walked straight into a master known to all as "the Toad", who was about to read the riot act, when he saw the sweat on Jonathan's face.

"Problems, Hare?"

"Yes, sir."

"The girls are probably as scared as you."

Jonathan slumped down onto a low brick wall, his head in his hands. The Toad relented.

"Ah, I see that you have a bad headache, better go up to your dormitory and lie down."

"Yes, sir," Jonathan had said, much relieved. The Toad smiled at Jonathan's back thinking how much the candidate was prized by Bessemer. Everything was going according to plan, but setting up the transfer to St. Eligius might be tricky.

Before anyone could comment on Jonathan's dismay, there was a commotion at the pub door. A large red-faced man barged in, shouldering people out of his way. There were two other equally large men with him. The barman looked up and reached beneath the bar. Jonathan turned towards the noise and saw the man coming towards him. It was the heavy set man from Bronsky's. The crowd parted in a small panic as the man pushed in towards their group, spitting into the palms of his hands.

"Gonna teach yer to mind yer own business!"

Harry had moved quickly in front of Jonathan.

"Now then, Ronnie, we don't want trouble."

But he might as well have saved his breath, the man shoved him aside and Harry fell backwards over the low table, crashing onto the floor. He seemed content to stay there. Rita was screaming. The barman was moving from behind the bar.

Ronnie poked a massive forefinger towards Jonathan's chest. Jonathan reacted instinctively to the threat just as he had in hundreds of schoolyard raggings. He grabbed the arm and turned anti-clockwise, thrusting his hip hard into the man's belly, at the same time pulling down on the arm. As generations of Cornish wrestlers know, the man had nowhere to go but down hard onto the floor, his weight adding to the effectiveness. He lay there stunned, trying to get his breath.

The barman arrived stripping off his tie, which he wrapped quickly around Ronnie's ankles.

The door burst open and a squad of police rushed in. The Sergeant looked down with a huge grin, "Ronnie Grey, got you at last! Take him away lads."

Behind the Sergeant's back, Harry was signalling to Jonathan, pointing to himself and miming that he would do the talking.

The Sergeant turned to the group. Charmaine was hugging Rita.

"OK, let's have it, Harry!" he demanded, taking out his notebook.

Harry grabbed the spotlight. "That Ronnie was out to get my apprentice, here," he said, pointing to Jonathan.

"Why?"

"Seems he stepped in between Ronnie and old Bronsky the other night."

"Why?"

Harry shrugged. "Old man sold off something that Ronnie had popped, I suppose."

"Name?" said the Sergeant, turning to Jonathan.

Before Jonathan could speak, Harry said, "Give him yer card, boy!"

Jonathan fished a card out of his pocket and handed it to the Sergeant.

"Staying at your place, Harry?" Harry nodded.

Thus it was that the police report of the famous re-capture of Ronnie Grey placed Harry at the centre of the action, with only a passing reference to the apprentice Samuel Ward. There was no mention of the incident at Bronsky's.

Charmaine was almost hopping with excitement. She lapsed into her native tongue.

"Formidable, Jonathan, c'etait formidable!"

Jonathan was embarrassed by her effusiveness.

"C'est rien," he muttered.

Charmaine recovered herself.

"Where did you learn to do that?" She swivelled her hips, mimicking the hip throw. It was at once humorous and suggestive.

Jonathan, taken aback, hurried to explain that it was 'just part of Cornish wrestling'.

Charmaine laughed, with a twinkle in her eye. "So you like to wrestle, Jonathan?"

Rita and Harry spluttered with laughter. Jonathan was left to wonder what was so funny.

"Oh, it is time to commence the dancing!" Charmaine was preparing to leave. She glanced over her shoulder. "Come for luncheon on the next Monday, if it pleases you."

The invitation had included them all, but Rita wasn't fooled.

When they got home, Rita sent Harry out to get fish and chips. She waited for a while, looking sideways at Jonathan. She finally made up her mind. Jonathan was sitting at the kitchen table. She brought the suit old Bronsky had given him and put it on the table.

"You liked Charmaine, didn't you?"

To Jonathan, Charmaine was a woman old enough to be beyond his reach. Whether he liked her or not didn't seem to him to be very important. She was certainly different; that hip movement was something no English girl of Jonathan's limited acquaintance would display in public.

"She's French," he parried, with a Gallic shrug.

Rita sighed. She tried again. "What was all that hand-kissing when you were introduced?"

"I greeted her the continental way, that's all."

"Looked a bit more than that!" Rita snapped.

She regrouped. "Well, she certainly likes you!"

Jonathan shrugged again, not knowing what to say. There was something odd about Rita's accent, he thought, as if she was a stage cockney. He heard overtones of a more cultured background. But she was getting heated, "Just you watch out, young Jonathan, you're too valuable to the Movement to be playing around with older women."

He heard the word 'Movement' with dismay, surely she wasn't another of those hysterical socialists?

He was even more taken aback when she snarled "And where does someone like you get a Chaseman suit?" pointing at the table. Before he could explain, Harry arrived with a huge package wrapped in newspaper, accompanied by the enticing aroma of fish and chips.

Later that night they watched the BBC's Nine O'clock News in amazement as the Commissioner of the Metropolitan Police took all the credit for the re-capture of Ronnie Grey. Members of the gang had busted Ronnie out of Pentonville a month earlier by parking a furniture van alongside the great wall; some well-rewarded inmates had boosted Ronnie up. Several prison guards had been injured in a small riot designed as a diversion. The caption under the Commissioner's head read 'Sir Hubert de Quincy'. Before Jonathan could take it in, Rita was snarling "Pompous bourgeois oaf, I suppose you'll take the reward for yourself too!"

Jonathan looked up sharply, "There's a reward?" he asked.

Harry grinned, "A thousand smackers, not that any of the likes of us'll ever see it."

Jonathan hoped Harry and Rita wouldn't have detected his reaction to the possibility of a reward. He had long ago mastered the suppression of any emotion, such a necessary skill in an all-male boarding school, but the thought of a reward of such a size set off some strange signals indeed.

He was lying in bed before the name 'de Quincy' sank in.

EIGHT

On Thin Ice

Jonathan was wondering how common the name 'de Quincy' might be. The letters from Victoria with that crest indicated that she belonged to an important family. He smiled as he remembered how angry he had been at her superior attitude at the Library. But she hadn't been so bad after all.

He tried to recall what made him set off on his bike for the White Horse. It was one of those days in late March when the countryside was almost painfully beautiful. Trees were budding and the hedgerows were alive with early primroses. The air was fresh and yet it carried the sweet and sharp scents of countless emerging leaves and blossoms.

He was nearing the track that climbed up the scarp face to the White Horse when he noticed a fence running along the side of the road. Horses by the score were in the paddocks, some with foals. In the distance he saw a rather grand stone entrance to a long driveway lined with elms. He spotted a sign reading 'The Frodsham Stud' and without a lot of thought turned up the driveway.

In the distance were several buildings, one a wonderfully proportioned and very old house. It was castellated, the walls almost completely covered in ivy.

As he cycled along, a white horse on the other side of the fence came galloping alongside. Jonathan was pedaling fast and the rider was hunched forward over the horse's neck, urging it on. Jonathan was enjoying the race, but all too soon had to slow down. A wide expanse of gravel lay immediately in front of the house, and Jonathan knew the perils of cycling into that. He got off the bike, exhilarated. In the paddock, the rider was turning the horse in circles, patting its neck. She jumped off, and led the horse towards him.

"So you came after all!" Her face was flushed. "Are you going to ride with me?" It was almost a plea.

"Sorry," said Jonathan, "but it's not one of my skills."

For a moment she looked as if she would cry, but recovered.

"Actually, Lucy is tired; I've been riding her all morning. I'll go and put her away."

She turned the horse and walked it towards a rectangle of stables some way off to the side of the house. Jonathan walked with her on the other side of the fence. In the stable area, a short wiry man appeared.

"Let me do that, Miss Victoria."

She shook her head. "I want to check her over first; I'll call you in a minute or two."

Her voice had taken on that tone of command that had so annoyed Jonathan at the library.

She took Lucy into a stall, hooked in the retaining rope across the entrance, put down her riding crop and started undoing various buckles.

She suddenly turned toward him, saying, "If you don't ride, why did you come?"

To Jonathan's surprise and returning anger, her voice was still full of haughtiness.

"You knew I didn't ride a horse. Do you ride a *bike*?"

She unhitched the girth. Glaring at him, she lifted the saddle, not paying attention to the danger of this particular movement. Lucy stepped sideways, pinning her against the stable wall. Jonathan remembered the same thing happening to him in that old barn in Cornwall when big Ben had tried to scrunch him. Dan, the farmer, had prodded Ben sharply in the hindquarters with his stick. Ben had reluctantly moved away, freeing Jonathan.

Victoria was shouting "Get away from me, ow, ow, Lucy, stop it!"

Picking up the riding crop, Jonathan hit the horse sharply on the rump. Lucy squealed and jumped away from Victoria, who collapsed against the wall. Jonathan ran into the stall and wedged his backside against Lucy as he braced his hands against the wall, forcing the horse away. Victoria was gasping for breath.

"Come on, you have to get out of here!" he shouted.

She crawled under the rope just as the groom appeared. "What's up? Are you alright, Miss?"

Jonathan said, "Lucy put the squeeze on her."

Alarmed at her appearance, the groom told them that he would finish things up, and asked Jonathan to take her to the 'big house'. Jonathan turned back to Victoria. He was horrified to see that she was crying. She was holding a handkerchief, which she seemed to be trying to tear apart, her eyes lowered.

She looked up "I could have been hurt in there!"

She shook her head. "And you said you didn't ride! How did you know what to do, then?"

Jonathan looked straight at her. "I didn't say I didn't know horses!"

She tossed her head in annoyance. "I thought we might be friends, but you, you're a liar!"

Jonathan stepped back, angry again. "Can you make it back to the house?"

She nodded defiantly.

He walked over to where he had left his bike, his face hot with anger. "I'll be off, then."

Before he could throw his leg over the saddle, she said in a different voice, "Actually, I don't think I can walk that far."

Jonathan had already lost the edge of his anger and he realized that his mother would be ashamed if he didn't 'respect the wishes of a lady'.

"Look, I'll take you as far as the house, then I'm going."

He took her arm and placed it along his shoulders, putting his other arm round her waist. "Is that all right?"

She nodded, and together they walked slowly to the house and through a side door almost hidden under the ivy.

As they entered, Victoria called out "Mother?" but there was no response.

"In there," she nodded, and they entered an elegantly furnished room.

"I can manage from here, thank you."

But she made no move to disengage, so Jonathan found himself holding a girl with a waist that was slender and taut. For a moment, neither of them moved. Then he guided her to an armchair, where she lowered herself gingerly. She tried to raise her hands to her riding helmet, but gasped with pain.

"What's the matter?" he asked.

"Could you take this thing *off?*"

He leaned over her and fumbled with the straps and buckles. It was more difficult than he thought.

"It's supposed to be tight," she breathed, close to his face.

He peered more closely at the buckle. There was an interesting quick release built into it.

"Ah!" he said. They were very close.

She tried to laugh, and said, "You sound like Sherlock Holmes!"

Jonathan pressed the spring release and the straps flew apart.

"How did you do that?"

Their eyes met, and he was surprised to see admiration there.

"Just one of my many skills," he muttered.

There was a sound of crunching gravel. Through the great bay window, Jonathan saw the Rolls Royce come to a stop.

"Perhaps this is your mother?"

Victoria looked at him with alarm. She whispered, "Look, Jonathan, you may find her a bit," she searched for a word, "protective," she finished.

Jonathan was sure it wasn't the word she had wanted.

"Sit over there, quickly," she continued, nodding at a companion armchair.

Distant voices could be heard, and then footsteps hurried down the hall and the door flew open. A tall, very lovely woman swept in.

"Victoria, what *have* you been up to now? Look at your clothes!"

She stopped abruptly, seeing Jonathan rise from the armchair. "And who are you?"

Victoria's chin was raised defiantly. "Mother, this is my friend Jonathan."

"Jonathan Hare, ma'am"

For some unknown reason, he bent slightly from the waist, lowering his eyes.

Victoria's mother raised a hand to her throat, startled. "Hare?"

Before she could continue, Victoria said, "He's on Spring holidays. He came out for a ride" – her eyes flashed quickly in Jonathan's direction –"and saved me from a nasty injury!"

Jonathan felt both flattered and embarrassed. Even the most heroic exploits would hardly have been mentioned at school, and compliments would always be shunned in favour of insults.

"Injury? Are you quite all right, Victoria? You do look pale."

Victoria's mother turned her beautiful eyes full upon him. "Please ring the bell."

Jonathan had no idea what to do.

Out of her mother's direct gaze, Victoria was looking pointedly at a floor-to-ceiling length of velvet material. He walked over and tugged on it. Somewhere deep inside the house there was a faint tinkle, causing Jonathan to start thinking about the mechanics of such a system within a house as old as this. As he thought about it, mother and daughter were engaged in a conversation that passed him by.

The door opened and a man entered. Jonathan had not heard him approach.

"Yes, Madam?"

"Oh, Thomas, tea with plenty of sugar, I think, for Victoria and bring me an aperitif. Luncheon as usual?"

The man merely bowed and left as silently as he had appeared.

"Have we met before?"

Victoria's mother had begun the inquisition. Out of her sight, Victoria rolled her eyes and smiled sympathetically.

"I don't believe so, ma'am," he parried.

There was a silence. Her mother was waiting, an amused look in her eyes.

She tried again. "Where are your people from, Mr. Hare?" There was a slight stress on his name.

Jonathan thought that a version of the truth would have to do. "Rather out of the way place in Cornwall, I'm afraid."

"And does this place have a name?" She was clearly not going to be diverted.

Jonathan was trapped. Nothing else for it, he thought, and gave the name of the remote farmhouse. "It's Trevidgoe, actually."

He had subconsciously adopted a tone that assumed that everyone, at least in Cornwall, should recognise the name.

Victoria's mother said that she was afraid that she had never visited Cornwall, with the implication that no one in her circle would choose to actually live there.

Jonathan, sensitive to such criticism, rejoined with a smile, "Then you can't know what a beautiful place it is!"

The woman rose with a ravishing smile. "I must change. Perhaps you will join us for luncheon, Mr. Hare?"

It was a command rather than an invitation. He leaned forward from the waist, lowering his eyes, saying "How kind" and looked up to catch the full force of the mother's stare. She turned and swept out of the room.

There was a look of amazement on Victoria's face. "I think she likes you!" she blurted, then left the room.

Finding himself alone, he looked round the room; it was certainly the most beautiful and comfortable he had ever been in. Above the fireplace hung a painting of a field of wild flowers stretching away and up a slope towards a distant house. It was far removed from the traditional Constable prints deemed appropriate for a wall in most English homes. He examined it more closely. It was original, not a print. He was puzzled because it was clearly of the Impressionist school, but far less strident than his favourite, Van Gogh, more like a Monet. He stood there running names from the books in the Standish library through his mind. A couple of names emerged from the fog; one of them was 'Sisley'.

The door opened silently behind him. Jonathan heard a cough, and turned.

"Perhaps the gentleman would like to prepare for luncheon?"

For a moment Jonathan wondered if there was someone else in the room.

Thomas was holding some clothing over his arm.

"Thank you, um, Mr. Thomas."

A ghost of a smile appeared on Thomas's lips. "Just Thomas will do, sir. Please follow me."

Down the hall they went, passing large canvases hung every few feet on either side. They crossed a spacious foyer, light streaming in through a window two storeys high. A magnificent double staircase seemed to hang on the sidewalls, with more paintings lining the stairs. Thomas opened a door into a cloakroom.

"You will find everything you need here, sir. And you may find this jacket and tie will please her ladyship."

The word 'Ladyship' disconcerted Jonathan; absently he picked up a brush and attempted to tidy his hair. He managed the side parting, and eventually got his hair into some sort of shape. He washed his hands and slipped into the jacket, which was incredibly light and seemed to have a life of its own, flowing smoothly over his sturdy build. He buttoned up his shirt and knotted the tie, which was a bit like the one he was required always to wear at school. When he looked in the mirror, he could hardly recognize himself, thinking that he looked like one of those people with their picture in The Tatler[3]. He had found the magazine in the library and discovered a secret fascination with the life that those people led.

Emerging from the cloakroom, he found Thomas still there.

The tiny smile reappeared. "Her ladyship will be pleasantly surprised."

Jonathan detected a note of satisfaction. "Thank you, um, Thomas."

---

3   The Tatler magazine catered to high society. Every issue was full of pictures of the social events of the season. It was essential reading for those with any sort of claim to standing in society and particularly for those temporarily out of touch serving in the military, for instance. No Officers' Mess would be without a copy, and it could be found in some School libraries.

"The ladies will be a while, sir, they ask that you meet them in the Day Room."

Smiling more openly, he added, "Where you were before, sir. Luncheon is cold today, galantine and salad."

Jonathan sensed that this was meant to be helpful. His mother made a grand galantine, although she did so to finish up every last scrap of food, declaring, as she did so often, "Waste not, want not!"

As he crossed the foyer, he noticed a picture of Victoria's mother. It was a posed and rather stiff portrait that didn't capture much of her beauty. Her eyes, especially, seemed bored, without the dazzling directness that she had turned on him. It appeared to be a duty painting to go along with the many others. They all had small gilt plaques; he read 'Lady Antonia de Quincy'. Before he could move away, she came down the stairs, wearing a dress of simple linen. A silk scarf was draped over one shoulder, setting off her eyes.

She reached the foyer. "Oh, Mr. Hare, don't spend your time on that!"

He knew from this formula, so often used by his mother, that she was expecting a compliment.

"It must be hard to capture, um." He stopped, wondering what she expected. She waited, prolonging his anxiety, raising her eyebrows.

He was suddenly inspired. "There, *that* look."

She smiled at him distractedly, taking in the jacket and tie and smoothed hair.

"Come along, we will wait for Victoria in the Day Room. I insisted she take a bath, I expect she will be sore for a day or two."

They were alone in the beautiful room. She was standing looking out of the bay window. Without turning, she said, "Victoria is quite taken with you, you know. But she will be back at school next week, as will you. I doubt if she will still think the same when she returns."

Jonathan was shaken and angry, understanding the real message.

He said, stiffly, "It was Victoria who invited me, Lady de Quincy."

There was a strained silence. He heard her say, more to herself, "And I suppose I *should* be glad that you were here today."

Jonathan's anger reached boiling point. "Perhaps it would be better if I left now."

"Jonathan, please sit down."

He stood defiantly next to the fireplace, and then realized that this was the first time she had used his first name. It was all very confusing. He compromised by perching on the arm of a chair.

She was standing directly in front of him. "Victoria will be starting the Season soon. She will be expected to socialise with people from the highest families in the land. It is you I am trying to protect, you may get hurt."

Suddenly her whole attitude changed. "How old are you, Jonathan?"

"Fifteen, ma'am."

She subsided into an armchair. Presently she took out a handkerchief. "Excuse me, Jonathan, I see I have offended you. It's just that I love Victoria and want so much to see her happy."

Jonathan was still outraged. "She seems very happy to me, especially when she's riding."

"But that's just it, Jonathan, she will have to give that up soon. The Season is very demanding and she will need to spend so much time in Town."

They were not prepared for Victoria's entrance as she stormed in.

"Mother, the Season doesn't start for another eighteen months. Why are you doing this? Why won't you let me have any friends here?"

Lady de Quincy got to her feet, "But it's only –"

She could not continue, and swept out of the room, the handkerchief pressed to her mouth.

Jonathan was hugely embarrassed. "Perhaps I should leave?"

Victoria turned on him. "You stay right there, Jonathan Hare, I haven't finished with Mother yet."

She hurried out of the room. There were voices in the distance.

Victoria returned. "I tried to warn you about her. She was an actress before my father married her. Always makes a scene about everything."

Jonathan looked at her. She was wearing a white dress that flared from her waist. She was really quite pretty.

"What are we going to do, then? I'll be back at school next week" he asked.

"We can write. Here," she snatched up some paper and scribbled an address, "Write to me here."

He nodded and put the paper in the pocket of the jacket.

She came closer. "Thank you for getting that idiot Lucy off me."

There was an awkward moment. He put out his hand.

She pouted, "I liked it better when you put your arm round me."

Jonathan felt a small lurch in the pit of his stomach. He reached out and put his arms round her. It felt good. She leaned back and gave him a peck on the cheek.

"Go home now." Her voice seemed a little weak.

He was half way home before he realized that he was still wearing the jacket and tie.

When Jonathan got home, his mother was waiting. "Where *have* you been all day? And where did this come from?" she asked, fingering the jacket. Jonathan felt the onset of panic; if he told her the truth, he was in for an evening of recriminations and emotion. A version of the truth would have to do.

"I cycled out to White Horse Hill and ran into a friend from College, who lives nearby. I was invited to lunch and they lent me this. I just forgot to give it back."

His mother stared at him. "And did you have a good *time?*" but he was ready for this trap.

"Oh no, Mother, far too fussy, made me feel uncomfortable, not like here!"

"Well, you'll have to take it back, we're not a charity case, yet!"

And, surprisingly, she let it go at that.

He went up to his room and, as he took off the jacket, remembered the note that Victoria had scribbled out. It read "Laurel House, Oxenham College for Ladies" with an address in the Cotswolds. There was no time to take the jacket and tie back before his return to

College, so he hid them in his ugly but functional Edwardian wardrobe.

Back at Standish, he began a strangely bland correspondence with Victoria. He looked forward to her letters perhaps more as symbols of a girlfriend's interest than in anything contained in them. Jonathan began to look forward to the summer holidays; perhaps she would agree to a bike ride. Then he realized that this would commit him to getting on a horse.

"One step at a time," he told himself.

He wrote to tell her that he must return the jacket and tie, and they agreed that they would both be at home during the middle week in June. But, before the term ended, he received another letter. The paper was crumpled and the writing agitated. Victoria would not be at Frodsham 'due to unforeseen circumstances'. This phrase was far more formal than anything she had written before; it sounded to Jonathan as if she had been told to write it.

"Please keep the jacket and tie to remember me by," she had added beneath her signature. There was something decidedly odd about the letter, as if someone had been leaning over her shoulder until she signed it. And, to his amazement, the paper carried a remnant of scent. Jonathan shrugged – at least he wouldn't have to get on a horse.

NINE

The View from the Met

While Jonathan was working with Harry, Jonathan's friend from St. Eligius, Charles Barnes began his Summer Assignment as a 'Cadet Records Assistant' under a program approved by the Commissioner to bolster recruitment.

He was taken under the wing of Clive Atkins the Head of Serious Crimes Records, and quickly demonstrated an unusual ability to associate patterns of behaviour with the records of particular criminals.

Clive did not fit the faceless clerk image. He had risen rapidly to his senior supervisory position, his Welsh fanaticism giving him a drive foreign to the stuffiness of the basement. He supervised his Section with a fervour that threatened trouble for anyone not cooperating fully with his staff. Clive's father was an ex-miner, a quiet man who seldom telephoned the Bessemer number. When he did it was always 12:17.

The morning after the sensational re-capture of Ronnie Grey, Clive called Charles in and gave him a special assignment. He was to gather everything known to Records on Ronnie Grey and his gang. The Third Floor Briefing Room had already been dedicated as a central point to coordinate an all-out attack on the gang.

"Timing, Charlie boy, timing is everything. Feather in our cap if we do this well!"

Charles didn't mind Clive's use of the familiar – his own father sometimes did the same, but only when he was feeling good, thought Charles.

He had been analysing the police report of the re-capture of Ronnie Grey. It didn't fit with any of the others he had read, which were composed in that stilted prose that lower ranking officers used. They never walked, they proceeded; they never saw, they observed. Every arrest was prefaced with "applying reasonable force".

The Ronnie Grey report, although signed by the Squad Sergeant, read like a press release. Charles thought the words flowed naturally and rather elegantly. He had a mental picture of a senior officer dictating it.

"Have you read this, Mr. Atkins?"

Clive frowned. "Need to organize the Room first; come on boyo!" said Clive rushing through the door.

Charles followed at a more leisurely pace. He was tapping the report against his upper lip, deep in thought. What he had learned was that one of the witnesses was named Harry Sparrow.

"Can't be two of them!" he said to himself."

By the following day, the Third Floor Briefing Room had been re-named 'Grey Central'. The furniture consisted of a lectern and a dozen folding chairs around a table. Three of the walls were covered with maps and photographs. Pins connected to coloured ribbons festooned the material. The wall behind the lectern was bare except for a framed print of Her Majesty. It was the much-loved Annigoni portrait. A drop-down screen hung from the ceiling. There were no windows.

Charles and Clive were doing a final check.

"A fine job you've done, Charlie. You're a natural at this. Didn't teach this at school, I bet!" There seemed to be a question hanging on that remark.

Charles wondered how to answer. "Oh yes, it's part of data analysis, you know, the new University craze? Only a couple of us enrolled, though."

Clive nodded, apparently thinking of other things.

"We ready for the big cheese, then?" Clive was referring to the imminent briefing by the Commissioner.

"Unless anything comes up at the last minute."

Clive thought Charles sounded a little too smug, but let it pass.

"If it does, be prepared with a clipboard. Put a heading on it, something like 'Breaking News'.

Charles made a note.

"Have you had a chance to read that Limehouse station report yet?" he asked.

Clive snapped his fingers, a little embarrassed. "On my desk right now!" he parried.

As Sir Hubert de Quincy entered Grey Central, everyone stood. He looked round the room, asserting his presence.

"Please sit," he commanded. "I should first congratulate all who participated in the capture of Ronnie Grey. That was, on the whole, a well run operation. There were one or two points I want to examine, however."

A chill ran through the room; this phrase was usually the prelude to a serious confrontation.

"First, Superintendent, how did we miss Ronnie at Mr. Bronsky's?"

The senior officer stood.

"Commissioner," he began, "we had trailed him from the docks, expecting him to go to one of his usual safe houses, and, to be frank, we had no reason to expect him to go into Bronsky's. The arrest teams were positioned at the three most likely locations. By the time we began the redeployment, Ronnie had left Bronsky's on the run. Something, or someone alerted him to our presence. I believe it may have been the then unidentified suspect who left Bronsky's some time later and entered Harry Sparrow's house."

Charles sat up straighter.

"What then?" asked the Commissioner.

"Ronnie gave us the slip before we had enough men in position.

We put a watch on Harry's house. As you know, sir, we do this quite regularly!"

A knowing chuckle ran round the room.

"The suspect seemed to be nothing other than one of his apprentices. They did the usual service calls, nothing out of the ordinary. But we did learn that the suspect's name is Samuel Ward."

Charles frowned.

"What on earth were they doing in the Alhambra?"

The Commissioner wanted the gathering to know he had read the reports.

"It seems that Ward has some knowledge of magicians' equipment, sir. According to the stage manager, he rescued that night's performance."

Charles relaxed, for he was now certain that 'Ward' was in fact Jonathan.

"Yes; go on."

The superintendent checked his notes. "Later that evening, sir, we had an alert on Ronnie, heading back towards Bronsky's. Sailor Wilson stopped him and they had a brief word. Ronnie changed tack, dived into the King's Head. As you know, sir, we had targeted that and the Palais, as two of his favourite haunts. May I ask Sergeant Dobson to take over from here?"

The Commissioner nodded and Sergeant Dobson stood. It was the barman who mixed the Pimm's.

"Ronnie Grey came in with two others, sir, one was Sailor Wilson. I didn't really see the other. I pushed the alert button immediately. Ronnie went straight for Harry Sparrow, pushed him aside and was yelling at Samuel Ward. Next thing I knew, Ronnie went down like a sack of coals. From where I was, I didn't see how that happened. But I found him semi-conscious on the floor, and secured him just as the arrest team arrived." He closed his notebook.

There was a pause while the Commissioner pursed his lips. "There's a loose end here. Why was Ronnie going for this Ward fellow?"

There was a rustle of discomfort. As usual the Commissioner had asked the awkward question.

"Excuse me, sir, but I think I can add something."

"Ah, it is the lady agent from the Palais de Dance!" observed the Commissioner, with a rather lopsided smile. "Please enlighten us, Miss Montpelier."

She stood; it was Charmaine.

"I was there, sir, saw the whole thing from close up. It looked to me as if Ronnie was out for revenge – his words were 'going to teach you to mind your own business' – then the young man referred to here as Samuel Ward used a kind of unarmed combat throw to bring him down."

"Police throw?"

"No, sir, he said it was a move from Cornish wrestling."

There was some suppressed laughter that received a stern glance from Sir Hubert.

"Please pay attention, gentlemen, this is information about a possible link to the Grey gang."

He turned back to Charmaine. "And what did you mean, *referred* to as Samuel Ward?"

Charmaine was thinking that Sir Hubert certainly hadn't lost his instincts for interrogation.

"I've made friends with Harry and Rita, sir, and Harry introduced him as Jonathan Hare."

The Commissioner turned red. "Let me see that report!"

There was a frosty silence. "Who wrote this?" demanded Sir Hubert.

The superintendent shifted uncomfortably. "The version you have, sir, was prepared in order to support your television appearance. It is perhaps more conscious of the publicity value than the original."

It was clear that the Commissioner was having difficulty restraining his annoyance.

"Superintendent, please see me after this meeting. Meanwhile I want everything we can get on this doppelganger, is that understood. Miss Montpelier, you seem close to him, give him the works, eh?"

There was little doubt what Sir Hubert meant by this, but Charmaine was not to be so easily pushed into action.

"Sir, there is another thing. I am using my French heritage as a cover. Mr. Hare, if I may call him that, spotted it immediately. He reacted impeccably and while his command of the language is more academic than natural, his mannerisms are very, um," she hesitated, "well bred, sir."

Charles was listening in astonishment. Jonathan, a well-bred Frenchman?

"Curiouser and curiouser," the Commissioner mused. He looked at his watch.

"I must close this meeting. I want this handled with great care. We need to neutralize the rest of the Grey gang as soon as possible. They have introduced a level of violence that we have never seen before. Unless we get on top of this, we may never recover, you all understand?"

He rose and with a final word of thanks, left the room.

Charles stood back as the crowd dispersed, and fell in beside Charmaine. He was holding the archive copy of the official file.

"Miss Montpelier, I wonder if you could give me a description of the young man you have just mentioned to the Commissioner? For the files, of course."

Charmaine looked at him. "Are you telling me there isn't one on file?"

Charles explained that the report focused on the capture by the arrest squad. They looked at each other, recognising the danger of further comment.

"He looks quite a bit younger than you, strongly built, a little under six feet. There's something else; he's very serious, he hides his feelings behind," she paused, "behind a mask. Do you know what I mean?"

Charles knew very well what she meant; it was as good a description of Jonathan as he could imagine. He was in a quandary; the rules for summer assignments were clear, there was to be no contact between students. But Jonathan was his friend and surely couldn't be set up for a gang member by mistake.

He decided to keep a watching brief; he could always use the emergency number at St. Eligius if all else failed.

The meeting which had taken Sir Hubert from Grey Central, but which would never be recorded officially, was with his brother, Sir Roger, and took place at the Society. It concerned a report from Sir Roger's agent in place that Harry Sparrow's newest apprentice was not what he seemed to be.

When the name Hare had surfaced during the briefing, it was all Sir Hubert had been able to do to limit himself to a mild rebuke to the Superintendent, for he hated to be fed sloppy information. And now it seemed as if there was indeed more to this Hare character than was apparent from the King's Head incident. And what Sir Hubert now discovered was that Roger had an interest in him as well. Sir Hubert's well honed intuition was now working at full speed.

TEN

Timing is Everything

Harry set up a job that was evidently special because, before they left, Harry told him to wear the suit.

Jonathan stared at him.

"You know, the one old Bronsky gave yer, the one Rita altered for yer, look smart in that, yer do!"

Jonathan recalled that Rita had made the alterations efficiently, but had snapped "And where does someone like you get a Chaseman suit?"

In his room he had looked inside the jacket and eventually found a thin strip of material proclaiming that it had been made by Chaseman and Company. There was a white area for the owner's name but it had been ripped out rather savagely; he had no idea what that meant.

Harry and Jonathan arrived later that morning at a grand Georgian house, bearing a polished brass plate that announced that it was home to the Royal Horological Society.

An elegant older man, wearing a beautiful suit with a gold watch chain strung across his waistcoat, welcomed them. Jonathan thought the suit looked a lot like his.

The Curator handled their cards rather gingerly. Jonathan didn't catch his name.

"Allow me to show you the problem."

Jonathan was struck by the silky speech cadences and slight drawl.

They went into a room with a dark glass wall and a felt-topped table displaying an old mechanism of a sort that Jonathan had only ever seen in text books.

"It is, of course, the famous longitude device, made with so much difficulty by William Harrison. I'm afraid it has stopped working and so we have called you in."

"Valuable, is it?" asked Harry

"Priceless and irreplaceable, one of the nation's treasures."

"Better look at it meself." Harry sat down and probed the device. After a while, he looked at Jonathan, and said grumpily "Can't see anything wrong with it; you have a butchers[4], me boy."

Jonathan had been scrutinizing the glass wall. He turned to the Curator.

"I wonder, sir, whether there are people watching us through the dark glass?"

He had subconsciously adopted a smoother voice not too different from the Curator's and had placed a small stress on the word 'sir'.

Astonished stares from both men met Jonathan's gaze.

The Curator was the first to speak.

"Actually, yes there are some of our experts there. No one is allowed to handle the device without at least one other staff member present as a witness. Security, you understand, I'm sure."

Jonathan shifted uncomfortably. The contents of his tool case could get him into trouble.

"I try to keep my techniques secret, sir."

Harry was trying to intercede, but the Curator held up a commanding hand.

"If I guarantee that my people have been removed, may I stay myself?"

Jonathan smiled. "Of course, sir," he said. He ignored Harry's perplexed stare.

The Curator left the room and the sound of his voice could be heard.

---

4 Butcher's hook, cockney for 'look'.

"What the blazes are yer doing?" Harry was clearly angry. "Worth a bob or two, this is."

"Not to me, Harry, is it?"

Harry glared. "Smart bugger, ain't yer?"

But there was an air of approval somewhere behind his words. The Curator returned and Jonathan thought he detected a hint of a smile.

"How did you know?" he asked Jonathan directly.

"It seemed a sensible precaution, sir, particularly for security reasons."

"I see. Well, shall we continue?"

Jonathan turned his tool case towards him, set the combinations and extracted the stethoscope. He inserted the earpieces and applied the contact piece to the nation's treasure. He wound the spring and listened, frowning.

"Something wrong here," he muttered, and turning to the Curator, "I shall need to use my test equipment."

"Oh Lord, will that be quite safe?"

"Yes, sir, it is designed for non-destructive testing."

Harry's amazement was evident, which amused the Curator.

"Go ahead," he agreed.

Jonathan reached into the case and took out a small black box. Two probes with crocodile clips were connected to one end. There was a toggle switch and a sliding frequency adjuster.

"Battery operated, eh?" breathed the Curator, fascinated.

Jonathan nodded as he attached the clips. He switched it on and applied the stethoscope again, slowly adjusting the frequency.

He stopped and said, "Ah, yes."

The Curator gave a sigh of relief.

Jonathan said, "I think my employer and I would like to confer, before we document the problem and the solution."

"Quite so," smiled the Curator, leaving the room.

"Now what, as if I didn't know?" asked Harry.

"It's only fair, Harry, this time it really was me, wasn't it?"

"OK, OK"

"So how much are we getting?"

"More than a poke up the snoot," grinned Harry, "Tell yer what, I'll give yer five quid."

Jonathan smiled. "More like twenty, I think"

"Cheeky bugger!" exploded Harry, and then subsided. "OK, but this is a one-off."

The Curator returned at Harry's invitation to find that Jonathan had written out an explanation and a set of instructions on replacing the tension keeper.

"You will find, sir, that the keeper looks intact, but is in fact fatigued. After a few seconds it is unable to retain the spring tension."

As they were leaving, the Curator stopped them.

"I am most impressed. May I call on your services if we have further problems?"

Harry beamed. "Of course, sir, you have my card."

Jonathan heard Harry trying to speak a better class of English. It wasn't convincing.

The Curator turned to Jonathan with a twinkle in his eye.

"You must do well, Mr. Ward, isn't that a Chaseman suit?"

For a moment, Jonathan wondered who this Ward was, but recovered quickly.

"Thank you, sir, it is indeed."

"Please take the Society's brochure, with my thanks."

As they walked away, Jonathan wondered why the society's experts couldn't have detected the problem. And why would they have that expensive one-way mirror?

He shrugged. "Worth twenty pounds to me, why should I worry?" he said to himself.

Some way from the Society grounds, Harry said that he was dying for a cuppa. He headed towards a dingy corner café. Jonathan was appalled.

"Not there, Harry, please!"

"You really are a snotty little bugger! Come on, I'm paying"

In fact the café was reasonably clean and the tea was strong and generous.

"Care for a wad?" Harry was nodding in the direction of some heavily sugared doughnuts. Another word slipped into Jonathan's vocabulary.

"Thanks, Harry."

They sat in silence for a while, enjoying the moment.

"If I'm going to pay yer, we'll have to take on some heavy jobs."

"What does that mean?"

Harry chewed for a while on his doughnut.

"Some people have problems they don't want other people to know about." Harry tapped the side of his nose with his finger.

After a moment Jonathan said, "Well, you know best, Harry, it's your company."

No more was said.

When they got back to Harry's house, there were two envelopes addressed to Jonathan. The first contained the results of his University Entrance exams; he had achieved a 'B' in French, an 'A' in Science and a 'Distinction' in Mathematics, a grading rarely given. The other envelope asked him to attend for an interview at an Oxford College, but he didn't immediately recognise the name. There was a possibility of a Galdraith Scholarship – whatever that was. He told Harry, who was full of praise. "Feather in the cap for St. Eligius, eh, me boy?"

Jonathan nodded, thinking, "But what about me?"

Up in his room he took off the suit. The brochure was sticking out of a side pocket. He opened it and a card fell out. It read:

Royal Horological Society
   Sir Roger de Quincy Bt.
   Curator

There was a telephone number that had been circled. Jonathan stared at the name 'de Quincy'. Surely there couldn't be many people with that name, it came as a bit of a shock for it reminded him again of those letters from Victoria written on that blue notepaper that she liked, with just a tiny remnant of perfume. That last one, the words so unlike her, and what looked like tear smudges at the bottom had upset him a bit, not that he let anyone know at Standish. He sighed.

His trousers lay in a heap on the bed, so he started to hang them up.

"That clothes stand would be nice," he said to himself, "wonder what old Bronsky wants for it?"

ELEVEN

Sleight of Hand

A day or two later, Harry took Jonathan on one side. "We have a heavy job tonight. Friend of mine has a safe, forgot the combination, didn't he, silly bugger. Bring your case."

Jonathan was immediately suspicious because this was their first outing at night. He hoped Harry knew what he was doing. Then he brightened; at least it would make a change from that inane television that Rita watched.

As they left the house, he saw a black car, a Wolsley, parked at the end of the approach road and at a slight angle from the curb, perhaps ready for a quick get away. There was something odd about it. He took another look as they came closer. The rear of the car was raised noticeably higher than others of that run of the mill saloon. He nudged Harry.

"Could that be a police car?"

Harry laughed. "Why would they be interested in us, me boy? They'll be chasing after Ronnie's gang!"

Nevertheless, Jonathan stopped by the rear wheel to tie his shoelace and used his door key on the wheel housing to make a scratch that gleamed white under the streetlight. Harry sighed and rolled his eyes. Just then a double-decker bus came along, which Harry succeeded in flagging down, much to Jonathan's surprise. Harry must indeed be well connected if a bus driver would pick him up between bus stops.

The bus rattled along Commercial Road for a while. They got off and went into a non-descript pub immediately north of the West

India Docks. Harry passed a note to the barman, who scribbled something on it.

Jonathan wanted to know what it was all about.

Harry took him outside and whispered, "We're in gang territory here, we need clearance to go any further, lucky they know me, we'd never get far otherwise."

They walked for some while, taking several side turnings and came to an apparently derelict warehouse. Harry tried the side door. It was locked.

"Funny," said Harry. They walked around the building and came to a loading dock. The Thames was making oily noises nearby.

A voice came out of the darkness. "In here, Harry!"

They went through a small door. Jonathan was suddenly nervous; surely Harry hadn't gone on the wrong side of the law? The few lectures on 'field craft' at St. Eligius that had interested him had emphasized that the risk was not one they should take lightly.

They climbed stairs in the dark and reached a surprisingly orderly office. There was some light from outside filtering in.

A small balding man was waiting nervously, "Blimey, Harry, where've you been, you won't tell Arthur, he'd sack me, soon as look at me" he breathed.

Harry reassured him. "Show us the beast, then!" he whispered.

Jonathan looked at the safe, which was of the standard combination type found in all businesses that handle a lot of cash and securities. It had a central combination dial and a simple handle. He saw that there were a hundred gradations, rather than the usual fifty. There would be five numbers to set, alternating clockwise and anticlockwise.

Harry motioned Jonathan forward. "Try yer stuff on this ugly bugger, then!" he challenged.

Jonathan stared at Harry. "Tell me who this is," he said, pointing to the bald man.

"It's Bert Coleman, Arthur Salmon's manager, friend of mine."

"Just as long as this is above board, Harry."

He set to work, ignoring Harry's protestations. He took the

stethoscope out of the case and applied it to the combination housing. Spinning the dial clockwise and anticlockwise while listening to the clicking, he quickly determined that the sequence started anticlockwise.

"This will take a while, Harry," he cautioned. Bert and Harry went and made some tea.

But it was easier than he had expected, the combination appeared never to have been changed, and wear had set in. About thirty minutes later, he pushed down on the handle and the door opened. Jonathan saw several dispatch boxes; they each had a distinctive aniline scarlet label that announced, 'Banco Internationale, San Marino'.

On an impulse he pulled a box open and found it stuffed with what looked like expensive vouchers. The wording was Italian, but seemed to say that the voucher was worth One Thousand Pounds Sterling. Jonathan whistled under his breath, for this was at least twice what his mother earned in a year as a senior teacher. He closed the box and stepped away from the safe, calling for Harry and Bert; Bert was so relieved that he patted Jonathan repeatedly on the back. Jonathan told him the combination, and stressed the need to change it. He showed Bert a trick to remember the combination. It involved telephone numbers on the office filing system.

"Got to look legitimate, Bert," he cautioned, "somewhere in Glasgow is always a good bet."

They left through the side door, accompanied by protestations of lifelong gratitude from Bert. Jonathan was feeling good as they made their way back to the pub. Harry handed in the note and they left through the front door. As they made their way to the bus stop, headlights suddenly blazed at them.

Harry said out of the corner of his mouth, "Let me handle this."

Heavy footsteps came towards them. "Oh, it's you, Harry. What're you up to at this time of night, I shouldn't wonder?"

Harry laughed, "Just doing a job, old Bert really messed up, mustn't let Arthur know, eh?"

The interrogator, in plain clothes, peered at Jonathan. "Who's this then?"

"This is me new boy, Samuel Ward." And to Jonathan, "This is Sergeant Davies."

Sergeant Davies, whose reporting lines were not what Harry may have assumed, stared harder at Jonathan.

"You the one brought down Ronnie?"

Jonathan couldn't now escape. "Well, just luck really, more like instinct."

To Harry's surprise, Jonathan had spoken in passable cockney, swallowing the 'l's and modifying the vowels.

"Well, on your way, then. And Harry, stay on our side, there's a good lad!"

It was a scarcely disguised threat.

Arthur Salmon had worked his way up the Grey gang hierarchy as a result of his financial acumen. The twins were brutal and ruthless, but understood that they needed his help, for the flow of contraband depended on the efficient payment of their suppliers.

With the government's attempts to control the exchange of Sterling, Arthur had had to devise a way to circumvent the controls. He had done so through a complex arrangement with a commercial Bank in the tax haven of San Marino. Suppliers were paid with Bearer Bonds, which he kept in the warehouse safe, well out of the twins' sight.

His personal rake-off was so well disguised that only a disaster would ever bring it to their attention, but that was a risk he couldn't take, for he knew what sort of punishment they would mete out. Even from jail, their reach could be remarkably effective.

So, when he had discovered Bert Coleman's stupidity and that a stranger had had sight of the contents of his safe, he realised that he could be in danger, and that he would have to contain it by getting his hands on Harry's apprentice. He could disguise this as revenge for the capture of Ronnie, he thought, and perhaps throw in some other smoke screen.

Several days after the job in the warehouse the Thames Police recovered a body from the river. It was one of the least identifiable that the authorities had ever seen, but recent advances in forensic science would eventually enable them to put a name to it. When they did, it was Bert Coleman.

Arthur Salmon had called a meeting of the remnants of the Grey gang. They met in one of the gang's safe houses, and all were nervous; their tyrannical leaders, Ronnie and Reggie were both 'inside', and the gang's future looked dim. Arthur had been determined to get his revenge.

"We all know what happened, the filth put out bait and Ronnie took it. Never could resist it, could Ronnie, fists first, think later. So who was that springer[5] that hit Bronsky's?" There was a silence; no one seemed to want to risk retribution.

Finally Sailor Wilson said, "All I know, Arthur, is how Ronnie described him, young, well built, not local, spoke proper. So when I saw someone like that on his way with Harry to the Loaf, I got on to Ronnie. Never saw Ronnie so worked up, just went bonkers, took Freddy and me and rushed into the pub, straight into a trap, like you said. Me and Freddy just got out before the squad arrived."

Arthur frowned, "Ronnie told me he never heard the springer come in to Bronsky's, first he knew there's a lot of noise, things pushed over, usual stuff to cause panic, so he got out of there fast, saw a watcher in a car, but got away. Next thing I know, they've got Ronnie trussed up in the Loaf and then in the van. Damn Commissioner boasting on the telly, put the skids under our manor all right."

The other members had already realised that, with both the brothers put away, their hold on the territory had been seriously weakened. Arthur sighed, "I never was one for having that Harry Sparrow operating freelance, don't know why they allowed it, Harry's good, but he's not one of us, useful maybe, but knows too much. Too many friends on both sides, that's why we put you in, Blondie."

---

5   an agent put in to flush out someone into the arms of the police.

There was an angry snort.

"My name is Rita, Arthur, as you well know! If Ronnie never explained things to you, that's your bad luck. I keep Harry in line with the movement's goals, just lucky for you if I can help. Harry runs a summer school for promising operators. Your so-called springer is just the latest."

Arthur wasn't convinced, "Oh, yeah, so he just happened to come by Bronsky's when Ronnie was in there?"

"The lad said he went in to get directions, pea-souper that night, remember, Harry had to go and look for him. Lad arrived before Harry got back."

"What did he have with him?"

"If you mean luggage, he had a ropey old suitcase, seen better days, and a small case, takes it everywhere on the job."

Arthur wanted to know how big the case was.

Rita held up her hands, "About so, and so, Arthur."

Arthur looked at Sailor, "Sound familiar?"

Sailor nodded, "Could be, Arthur, but I'd need to see it for meself."

Arthur sucked his teeth, "We'll arrange that. Now, anyone know how come Ronnie got clobbered in the Loaf?"

Rita responded with, "I was there when he attacked the lad, bad luck for Ronnie that he ran into someone who could look after himself."

"What do you mean?"

She shrugged, "Used a hip throw on him, never seen it before. Lad said it was out of Cornish Wrestling."

There was some rumbling from the members, in which the words 'combat training' could be heard.

Rita was getting angry, "He's just a lad, only seventeen. You've got it wrong, he isn't anything to do with the police. Mind you, he is a strange one, not like the others Harry gets. Hasn't got a farthing, but acts like a toff[6] and talks like one, as Sailor said. And another thing, he speaks good French, spotted Charmaine right away, talked to her

---

6   A derogatory term (from toffee-nosed) that describes a member of high society.

in her lingo, she had to put the kibosh[7] on him. Mind you, he was really charming to her; I think he fancies her, cheeky bugger. You know how she flirts, maybe she fancies him."

There were some salacious comments around the room.

Arthur was angry. "That's all well and good, Rita, but look at it this way. Everything going according to plan, pull off that Hatton Garden heist, before we can fence the diamonds, your lad appears, flushes Ronnie out of Bronsky's, gets Ronnie that angry and lures him right into a set up. Comes out of Bronsky's with a case like we used to heist the diamonds. Sorry, but I think he's fooling you. And another thing, did you know there's a minder on him and Harry?"

Rita laughed, "Oh, they're always putting a watch on Harry, gives them something to do!"

Arthur glared at Rita, "You're not listening, Rita, this ain't a watcher, it's a minder, brought in special, I should think."

"Who do you think he's minding then, Arthur?" asked Rita.

"Well, it ain't Harry, so work it out for yourself!"

Rita was taken aback by Arthur's bad temper. "Arthur, you know Bessemer doesn't use heavies, so who are you saying is doing the minding?"

Arthur shook his head, "Don't know for sure, but it puts your lad well in the frame."

The members left understanding that Arthur believed Jonathan was the prime cause of the trouble they were in.

---

7 Another imported word (from Egypt?). 'To put the kibosh on' means 'to silence permanently'.

TWELVE
A Sea Change

There is a tide in the affairs of men,
Which, taken at the flood, leads on to fortune;
Omitted, all the voyage of their life
Is bound in shallows and in miseries.
On such a full sea are we now afloat;
And we must take the current when it serves,
Or lose our ventures.

—Brutus' speech, in Julius Caesar

Edward, Lord Erinmore had placed a call to Felix Sandbourne his solicitor in London. He waited impatiently in his newfound mood of decisiveness. The telephone rang.

"I have Mr. Felix for you, your Lordship"

"Thank you, Travis."

"Good morning, my Lord," laughed Felix.

"Oh, stop that, Felix!" Felix was one of only a few outside the Bellestream's commercial network on first name terms. They were at School together.

"Your summons sounded urgent, Edward."

"It's a delicate matter. Perhaps I should wait until I come to Town?"

Felix hesitated, mentally scanning what subjects Edward would call 'delicate'. It came to him.

"Is this about William and Marguerite?"

"Yes it is. What should I do about it?"

"You should do what I recommended some time ago, Edward, start proceedings."

"Will it be a scandal?"

"Not now, old boy, we've done all that we can to find them."

"So they will all be, well, declared dead?"

Edward was surprised that his voice had remained level.

"Indeed."

There was a pause.

"Look, Edward, I'll have the papers prepared for you to sign when you come down."

The conversation ended with Edward staring vacantly out of the immense and rather ugly window that filled the north end of the study.

The most senior levels of the Establishment conducted their business in a manner which had evolved over time and had been reduced to a fine art. They preferred to meet in private clubs founded in previous centuries to provide a safe haven in London for those with particular interests.

The Atheneum Club was founded in 1823 'for the Association of individuals known for their literary or scientific attainments, artists of eminence in any class of the Fine Arts, and noblemen and gentlemen distinguished as liberal patrons of Science, Literature and the Arts'.

One of the first members was that amazing engineer Isambard Kingdom Brunel famed for his construction of the Great Western Railway line that links London to Bristol. The line was planned and engineered to run through the railway town that Jonathan was too proud to call home and terminated in London at the famous arched station of Paddington.

Sir Roger, as Curator of the Royal Horological Society, found it convenient to be a member of the Club, which is located at the southern end of Pall Mall. A Messenger from the Palace would only have to take a noontime stroll down the Mall and walk up a set of steps to slip unnoticed into the Club. The Porter, who guarded the entrance with military authority was selected and trained to recognise, but never recall the presence of the most senior and influential men in the land.

It was over luncheon that Sir Roger learned how much concern there was that the Bellestream family was under attack. The Messenger frowned, "I suspect that your last report touched a nerve; the Bellestream's recent tragedies were a matter of some distress, I remember. The point is, Roger, that it would not be well received if you failed to intercede."

This remark was so unusually blunt that Sir Roger knew immediately that he should take urgent action to prevent further damage to this particular family.

A few days after the night job, Harry announced that he had to go out of town. It was clear that it didn't include Jonathan.

"And where are you going, Harry Sparrow?" asked Rita, with her hands on her hips.

"Brighton!" laughed Harry giving Jonathan a salacious grin.

"You're a pig," shrieked Rita, "if you're going there, I'm going to Harrods!"

"Just pulling yer leg!" shouted Harry after her retreating figure.

Jonathan knew that Brighton was the traditional resort for 'dirty weekends' and the hotels there ran a profitable business catering to those wanting a divorce, for which the only viable legal method was to prove adultery. Certain hotels made sure that black-uniformed chambermaids were available to testify that "Mr. Smith was in bed with this woman when I entered the room to draw the curtains." The fact that the evidence was trotted out in the same manner case after case did not seem to worry the Courts, provided the case was uncontested.

Harry, having provided a neat diversion, chose not to enlighten Jonathan, apart from a hint that there may be a heavy job coming up. He passed his forefinger across his throat and said, "Shtumm!"

Jonathan didn't think that Rita meant what she had threatened, but she stormed out of the house, dressed smartly, which made him think that perhaps she *was* going to Harrods.

Left to his own devices, he was surprised when the telephone rang.

The voice demanded, "Mr. Samuel Ward, please."

He was momentarily at a loss.

"Who wants him, please," he said, letting some cockney looseness into his voice.

"Sir Roger de Quincy," the voice said grandly.

Jonathan allowed a few seconds to pass.

"This is Samuel Ward," he said with considerable disdain, matching as nearly as he could the snootiness at the other end of the line. There was a click.

Sir Roger's smooth tones emerged from the earpiece. "Mr. Ward, I was hoping you might call me privately. Is Mr. Sparrow there?"

"No, sir, he is away on business."

There was a pause.

"Then may we meet for luncheon today? We do an excellent buffet here at the Society."

Jonathan was relieved not to have to get his own meal, and made his way to the grand house, wearing his Chaseman suit. As he entered, Sir Roger smiled warmly and shook Jonathan's hand.

"Would you mind if my daughter joined us for lunch, she is helping us here during her summer holidays?"

Jonathan saw no reason to object.

They went into the dining room, and towards a table set in a bay window overlooking the garden. A young woman was sitting there. When she looked up, he saw that it was Victoria.

As their eyes met, she stood up abruptly, the water glass in front of her spilling over. She picked up a linen napkin and dabbed at herself, which seemed odd to Jonathan, since the water did not appear to have reached her.

"Oh, look at the mess, please excuse me, Father," and she departed. Her father was looking strangely at Jonathan.

"Well, Mr. Ward, perhaps we should start – there is something I want to talk to you about later."

Jonathan was hungry enough to overcome the strange feeling that the sight of Victoria had aroused. She was plainly but elegantly dressed, and wore make-up, which he had never seen her do before. It made her look prettier, he thought, not slathered on like some of the girls at home.

Sir Roger led him to the buffet; the food was good in the best British tradition of institutional catering, plain and filling with no sense of subtlety. Jonathan watched what Sir Roger did and helped himself in much the same way. They ate their meal accompanied by Sir Roger's attempts to put Jonathan at his ease, although he got the feeling that there was more stress on the name "Ward" than might be warranted. Jonathan adopted his usual neutral expression, waiting for the real issue to be raised. Victoria did not reappear.

Sir Roger summoned a waiter. "Has Sir Hubert arrived yet?"

"He is waiting in your study, sir."

"Shall we?" said Sir Roger, leading them out of the dining room and into a magnificent panelled room. As they entered, a tall man got to his feet.

"This is the young man I spoke to you about, Samuel Ward, and this is my brother Hubert."

Jonathan shook Hubert's hand. "I'm honoured, Commissioner."

Both men seemed startled.

"I saw you telling that story about Ronnie Grey. On the television," he added.

The men exchanged glances.

"Please have a seat," Sir Roger invited, gesturing to a chair in front of the desk. He walked round and sat down, opening a file.

"Forgive me for coming straight to the point, but your name is not Samuel Ward, is it?"

If Sir Roger thought this would unsettle Jonathan, he underestimated how well Jonathan had learned to shield his emotions.

"It's just a name on a business card." Jonathan attempted a smile.

The Commissioner growled from his corner, but Sir Roger raised a quieting hand.

"But you do work for Harry Sparrow under an assumed name?"

"It's just Harry's penny-pinching; he uses those cards for all his apprentices."

"I see. Would you tell us your real name?"

Jonathan, without being aware of it, hesitated too long, expressing the thought that this was none of their business. The Commissioner was making more aggressive noises, but Sir Roger assumed command. Jonathan found this odd; his reading in the Library left him with the impression that the Commissioner of the Metropolitan Police was about as senior and powerful a position as there was in England.

"It's Jonathan Hare, isn't it?"

This finally unseated Jonathan's composure and he had difficulty maintaining his stoic expression.

"Is that what Victoria told you, with that act at the table?"

The men sat forward.

"I see that you are not to be underestimated, Jonathan."

There was a smile on Sir Roger's face.

"She caught sight of you when you were here last, recognised you immediately. Said some quite flattering things about you, actually, something about saving her from a horse?"

"I'm glad I was there," said Jonathan.

"So am I!" laughed Sir Roger.

The Commissioner could contain himself no longer. "So you are Jonathan Hare, and you work for Harry Sparrow, doing all sorts of nefarious deeds, what?"

"Nefarious, sir?" asked Jonathan, wondering what was meant.

"Locksmithing, safe-cracking, breaking in, things like that?"

"Oh, sir, please, everything we do is a service requested by others through Harry – just like the job we did on the Harrison longitude device," he said, looking at Sir Roger.

"Got you there, Hubert!"

"He's very good!" the Commissioner allowed. There was a pause.

"Come on, Roger," growled the Commissioner, "Get on with it."

Sir Roger leaned back, placing his fingers together like a church steeple.

"You have a gift, Jonathan that we would like to make use of from time to time. It wouldn't be a full time job, just to meet certain emergencies. It would not, ah, be assigned to you through Harry. Which brings me to the next point. What are your plans for the future?"

Jonathan was feeling both complimented and threatened. A version of the truth would have to suffice.

"Actually, I've just passed my 'A' levels and am being considered for a Scholarship at an Oxford College. After that, well –," he shrugged.

"Scholarship? What Scholarship?" demanded the Commissioner.

"I believe it is, um." He pulled out the letter, "Galdraith."

The Commissioner asked if he might see the letter. "Must be a new one, never heard of it!" he barked, as if that condemned it to worthlessness.

But Sir Roger's eyebrows were now well raised. "May I see?"

He made a note and handed the letter back to Jonathan.

"You must have done well at 'A' levels!"

The telephone made a discreet buzz. Sir Roger excused himself and picked up the handset. After a short pause he told the Commissioner "Your chariot of fire awaits."

The Commissioner let a profanity escape from his lips, then sighed, "No peace for the wicked!" and left at what seemed almost a trot to Jonathan.

"Sir Hubert has been called away on an emergency requiring flashing lights and great speed," laughed Sir Roger. He was examining Jonathan closely.

"May I ask you something rather personal?"

Jonathan shrugged.

"Would it help you to have a source of funds to supplement your Scholarship?"

"I haven't been awarded it yet, sir, but I certainly don't have a private income like some I've heard about. That would make University life a lot more pleasant!"

"Then what I suggest is this. Only you and I will know of this arrangement. A sum will be paid monthly into your bank by standing order. You will never question the source. When I need your services, I will leave you a message with the Porter to ring this number, but we must disguise the request – can you suggest something that you will remember easily?"

Jonathan thought for a moment. "What about 'Mr. Harrison'?"

Sir Roger snorted with laughter and made a note.

He stood. "Victoria is waiting for you in the garden. She tells me she needs to talk to you, Jonathan; sounds very mysterious to me!"

Jonathan seemed to have been left no options, so he followed Sir Roger through a side door. Victoria was sitting on a lawn chair, under a sun umbrella. It was a pleasant sight and when Jonathan turned to thank the Curator, he had vanished.

She was reading, but sensed his presence, and looked up.

"Did I get you into trouble?"

He looked at her, remembering that strange last letter. He was surprised to find that he was still a little hurt.

"I suppose that your first duty *is* to your father."

This sounded ungracious, so he added, "Actually, it all seems to have worked out for the best."

She relaxed, but her eyes were fixed on him. He waited for her to say something.

She got up. "Walk with me a little, please?"

There was nothing superior in her attitude. They set off on a path through a thicket of rhododendrons. He sensed that she was struggling to find the right words. She suddenly turned and faced him.

"It wasn't my idea to stop writing!"

He smiled. "I realised that. Probably your beautiful mother's influence."

She had turned pale, biting her lip.

Jonathan was still feeling annoyed at her deception so he said, "You could have told me that two weeks ago, when I was here on a job."

She looked bemused. "How could I, I've only just got back from Scotland."

He just managed to control his reaction, wondering who was lying now?

He thought he'd better lay a smoke screen.

"My mistake, I thought I saw a very pretty girl in the garden that time."

She blushed. "You mustn't flirt, Jonathan, we live in such different worlds, remember how difficult it was to find any common ground, me on my horse, you on your bicycle!"

They both smiled.

She suddenly became serious again. "We might have been friends, then."

She had a handkerchief in her hands and was pulling at it. He was reminded of that day at Frodsham.

"Did you know that I am engaged to be married?"

Jonathan felt obliged to say something, so he blurted, "I haven't been keeping up with the Tatler recently, I'm afraid."

She was suddenly furious. "It isn't something to laugh at, Jonathan Hare!"

She moved closer to him, and he thought she was going to slap him. She collected herself, and then turned away from him. To his intense dismay, she was crying.

He had no idea what to do. "I'm sorry if I upset you, it was, um, clumsy of me."

She whirled round, her eyes red with tears.

"It's nothing to do with you, you idiot, it's my life. I hate it! It's all so," she paused, searching for a word, "*arranged*," she finished.

"But you have so much, parents, beautiful homes, horses, a society life, you ought to be happy."

She was gazing at him. "Does it really look like that to you?"

Jonathan shrugged, out of his depth with all this emotion.

She took a deep breath and smiled as best she could. "I've said too much. We should say goodbye."

"Again?" he asked, without thinking.

"Yes, again."

He turned on his heel, anxious to leave, but felt her hand on his arm.

"Don't go yet. Would you say goodbye properly? Put your arms round me just once more, please."

He sighed, feeling desperate to get away. He raised his arms and she moved closer to him. There was that scent that had clung to the letter. He closed his arms, finding that she felt quite different from the girl in the riding outfit at Frodsham. Her face was close to his for a moment, and then she broke free and ran down the path. He stood quite still for a moment, unable to make any sense of this latest venture into that strange territory called 'women'.

Sir Roger was sitting at his desk, drumming his fingers on the table. Perhaps Antonia was right; she had seen Jonathan as a younger boy at Frodsham.

"Spitting image of you, Roger, at that age," she had said.

He wondered whether God would be punishing him after all these years. One drunken moment, one starry night on a boat, a girl carried away by the romantic atmosphere. She had told him later that she was pregnant, but, by the time he had understood all the implications, she had vanished. He had found out that her family had sent her away in disgrace, but that was the end of the trail.

His father had been no help, pointing out that his own future was too important to jeopardise. He had told Antonia after they were married, but with her stage experience she had thought nothing of the affair. "Happens all the time, darling!" was all she had said.

Over time, he had allowed what he now saw as a moral failure to fade into the background. His father had died and he had inherited the title that included such a heavy responsibility to King and Country. And there was always his relationship with his brother, Hubert, which had been so stormy. Hubert had resented his position and title, and had competed fiercely with him. But now they had a common interest in this young lad; Hubert wanted the Grey gang and Roger had to find a way to dampen the effectiveness of the Bessemer movement's attack on the Bellestreams.

Roger wondered what he should do about Jonathan. He had already manipulated him mercilessly, for such a talent couldn't be allowed to operate freely for Bessemer. The agent watching Harry had suggested that Jonathan was different from the other apprentices, advising that the standard compromising techniques that the Service employed might not work. If the young man were to be snared, it would have to be through other means. The Harrison longitude device had been a ploy to gauge the level of his expertise; no one had expected such technical command from someone outside the profession. Harry was good, and the Service kept a close watch on him, but his skills were really quite ordinary compared to Jonathan's.

When the wire recording had picked up Jonathan's negotiation with Harry, and even though twenty pounds seemed a paltry sum to Sir Roger, Jonathan's interest in money had provided the leverage point. And how unscrupulously he had used it, he thought with a grimace.

An image of Victoria in the garden swam across his vision. What was going on there?

A father's perception is never a match for a mother's, but it was clear that Victoria felt something for the young man.

"Oh Lord," he pleaded, "show me the way out of this."

THIRTEEN

The Best Laid Plans

W hen Jonathan got back to Harry's, no one was there. There was a note by the telephone from Rita, telling him that Harry wouldn't be back until tomorrow and she had gone to visit a friend, and wouldn't be back until later. He was wondering what to do about his evening meal, when the telephone rang.

"Allo!" said Charmaine, "Is Rita there?"

When she found out that he was alone, there was a pause.

"Would you like to come for an early supper before the dancing?" she said, "I have pâté de foie, and croissants, and a gateau of cherries. You shall come and help me eat it, oui?"

Since this neatly solved his immediate problem, he agreed.

"Come down the traverse at the side of the Palais, there you will find my door."

When he arrived, Charmaine greeted him with her hand held out. Jonathan didn't know what to do. He looked at Charmaine for guidance. She giggled, and then lifted her hand higher. Jonathan took it and bowed over it allowing his breath to linger there for a second.

"Vous êtês trés gentile."

"Your French is good, Jonathan, where did you obtain it?"

Jonathan explained that in certain schools, there were compulsory lessons leading to certification.

"You are certified?" She collapsed in laughter. Jonathan managed a laugh himself.

"There," she said, raising an eyebrow, "when you laugh you are not so –" She was unable to find the word.

Jonathan felt that he had been caught in a trap, expected to contribute.

"Boring?" he suggested.

"No, no," she frowned. She gave up.

"Defendu? How do you translate, Jonathan?"

He thought for a moment. The word might mean 'defended' or even 'fortified', but that couldn't be it.

"Perhaps you mean, 'guarded'?"

Charmaine shook her head.

From somewhere an image came to him. "How about 'stone faced'?"

She nodded then raised a hand to her mouth.

"Oh, but I have offended you, perhaps? You never seem to be content in my presence."

Jonathan experienced a sense of relief.

He laughed. "Oh, no, it's just my usual face. Nothing personal."

She rested her hand on his chest for a short moment. "Now I understand."

She turned and went ahead of him into a room brightly decorated in yellow and blue. A small palm sat in a black wrought iron stand.

"This is my special place." She turned and caught him examining the room closely.

"You like it?"

Jonathan had been mentally reviewing images found in the Library. He thought he had an appropriate comment.

"It's very Mediterranean."

Charmaine raised an eyebrow. "And what else?"

Still focussing on the decor he said, "It feels a little Spanish."

He sensed that she was still waiting.

"I like it very much!" he said, surprised at his enthusiasm.

"Bravo, Jonathan, you have a good perception. And you have never been to Perpignan?"

Jonathan felt secure enough to admit that he had never been to France at all.

"Where is Perpignan?" he asked.

Charmaine opened a thick book full of colour pictures at a page headed 'Perpignan la catalane'.

She patted the couch. "Come and sit here and we will uncover the secrets of my birthplace."

Jonathan, who loved pictures, sat down with her.

She slid closer to him and began turning the pages, accompanying each picture with a passionate description in her somewhat fractured English. Jonathan found his arm getting in the way as she turned the pages. He rested it on the back of the couch.

He laughed. "If you love your home so much, why do you live here?"

Charmaine closed the book abruptly.

Standing up, she said "But we have not taken our repast!"

She directed Jonathan to a sideboard, where food was covered by a white cloth. When she removed it, Jonathan was taken aback; there appeared to be nothing that he could eat.

English cooking, especially in boarding schools and similar institutions, had suffered so much through the years of rationing that it had now achieved an unappetizing utilitarian blandness. The order of the day was stringy meat, two overcooked vegetables, and lumpy mashed potatoes, the whole swamped in powdery brown gravy.

"Help yourself, please, and sit with me here," she said, gesturing to a tiny table set with yellow and blue china decorated with sprays of black olives. She sliced off a piece of what looked like meat paste, and scooped some runny cheese onto her plate. She added a crescent shaped roll, and went to the table. Jonathan simply copied what she had done. When he sat down, there was not much room for his legs and they brushed against Charmaine's.

When he looked up, she was smiling. "We are too close?" she asked.

He shook his head.

He saw that Charmaine was waiting for him to start eating, so he had to admit defeat. "Um" was all he could manage to say.

She laughed. "You are in difficulties, I perceive, let me aid you."

She broke off some croissant, and placed a small amount of the runny cheese on it. Leaning across the tiny table, she offered it to him.

The croissant was crisp and chewy at the same time, and the cheese had a silky texture with a sharper aroma than Jonathan had expected. The inside of his mouth reacted to the strange tastes. He realised that he was salivating.

"There, wasn't that good? Try the pâté. Oh, I am remiss, I have forgotten the wine."

She returned with a small carafe.

"It has breathed," she commented standing next to Jonathan. She leaned forward, sliding the wine gently into his glass. She was very close, and Jonathan noticed, for the first time, a fragrance. It seemed to be coming from her neck and throat. She moved away and sat down.

Jonathan had never tasted a good wine before, since beer or scrumpy cider was the extent of his repertoire. Charmaine explained that the wine was 'from beside the Rhone'; it was mellow and full of flavours, and by the end of the meal his eyes were sparkling. Charmaine ushered him into the other, much larger room. It had a parquet floor, the only covering a single rug before the fireplace, with two armchairs on either side. Otherwise, there was little in the room.

"I must prepare for the dancing," she laughed.

When she returned, she was wearing the same black dress she had worn before.

"It is my working clothes," she said, pirouetting so that the skirt flared outwards. Jonathan was treated to a glimpse of leg quite far above the knee.

"I love to dance, will you dance with me?" She was putting a record onto a portable gramophone.

"Um," said Jonathan. The expected rush of panic didn't materialise.

"Actually, I can't, I mean I haven't learned, haven't taken lessons." His voice faded away.

Charmaine laughed, "Then I shall be the perfect teacher! Come!" She was standing with her arms open. Jonathan realised that there was nothing else to do, so he moved forward, feeling a little awkward. She took his left hand and moved closer. He detected the scent again; it seemed a bit stronger.

"You must turn a little and let your right side be close to me. Good, now place your hand high on my back. That is it. Oh, your elbow, she must point a little downwards; now listen to the rhythm and let me lead you."

She had become the dancing instructress, which allowed him to relax a little. She cued him to the lilting beat and they glided away, her hands exerting pressure deftly. He responded to her direction and found to his amazement that he was moving lightly with her in a series of circles. She was nodding and smiling. They swooped into a corner, where Charmaine's hands held him still, while she leaned slightly away from him. She was laughing. On the downbeat, she directed them out of the corner. The music ended.

Charmaine was looking at Jonathan; there was something new in her eyes.

"Did you enjoy it?" There was a tightness in her voice.

"Very much," said Jonathan. He was beaming, perhaps more with relief than anything else.

"But Jonathan, you have been telling the lies, I think? You dance too well."

Jonathan grinned wildly. "No, no, it was you, you showed me how!"

She was still examining him. "Then we shall dance a different dance." She put a new record onto the gramophone.

"This is a slow waltz, the sort we have at the Palais at the end of the dancing. It does not require the same amount of movement. Come."

She opened her arms, and Jonathan started to take up the same position.

She dropped her arms. "You must hold me differently for this. Put your right arm here." She moved it round her waist. Taking his other hand and swaying to the luxuriously slow beat, she seemed to simply move her centre of gravity, causing them to step sideways a short distance. With his arm around her waist, she was much closer to him. She freed her hand so that she now had both hands on his shoulders.

"Put your left hand high on my back, yes, just so."

They were very close and she was breathing so heavily that he could feel her breath on his cheek.

"You must get used to this, all the girls will want to have the last dance with you."

Jonathan wondered what girls she was talking about.

There didn't seem much to this dance, he thought, but she felt so good in his arms. A lock of her hair fell loose, and he moved it out of the way, his finger brushing her cheek. Suddenly her mouth was pressing urgently against his. His experience of kisses had been mostly experimental in dark cupboards at otherwise insipid birthday parties during school holidays, but this kiss was altogether different. Her mouth had opened a little and he felt the wetness of her lips. He was dizzy with excitement. Charmaine's hands were at his neck pulling his head towards her. Then she broke away with a wild look in her eyes.

"Who *are* you, Jonathan?" she whispered, "You are too young for this!"

"Can't we dance some more?" he pleaded.

She looked hard at him, biting her lip. "Jonathan, we can't be together again. I have a job to do here and you will be too big a distraction. Now go back to Harry's."

He frowned, trying to understand how he could be a distraction to a dancing teacher.

She touched a finger to his lips. "And, Jonathan, you need to be very careful around Rita."

She hesitated, looking into the distance. "She is not what she seems."

At the side door, Jonathan wanted to embrace her, but she kept him at a distance. Finally, he held out his hand. She shook it firmly.

"Goodbye, Jonathan," she said, turning abruptly away.

He was halfway back to Harry's before he realised that she had spoken without a trace of her French accent.

In late July, Edward had called Travis into the great study at Mountbeck.

"I shall be going up to London tomorrow. Perhaps we can look forward to a better future here."

Travis realised that Edward was preparing himself to sign the documents that would legally declare William and his family dead.

He decided to take a risk.

"And has your Lordship given thought to the opening of the safe?"

"Oh, Travis, one thing at a time, please! Why don't you get someone in?"

Travis suppressed a sigh. The Champion Company had been bombed out of existence and skilled men from security companies had been unable to solve the puzzle.

"Don't understand it," one of them had opined, "bloody thing's as silent as the grave!" Travis had thought this remark more than a little appropriate.

"Certainly, my Lord." But, thought Travis, where am I going to get anyone with such expertise. He had a vision of a burglar wearing a black mask and a cloak. He shook his head as he left the room.

Edward quite enjoyed the journey to Town, even if the train wasn't as clean as it might be and the station staff seemed to be interested only in the Daily Mirrors that stuck out of their back pockets. Not like the old days when staff had pride in their railways, thought Edward. He took a taxi to Mayfair and walked into Felix Sandbourne's quietly luxurious office. The documents on Felix's desk looked impressive. Felix introduced a gaunt and much older man as Lord Justice Steed.

"His Lordship has granted an immediate finding, based on your previous instructions to me, and pending your signature on the documents. Quite a lot of them, I'm afraid, Edward."

Edward overcame a feeling of guilt and signed wherever Felix indicated. The judge added his signature to a surprisingly brief document, which Felix intercepted.

"You may find this a bit painful, Edward."

"Got to go through with it now, old boy."

Edward read the single page. It began "Whereas William Clarence Bellestream, Duke of Hawksmoore, Marguerite de Montpelier Bellestream, Duchess of Hawksmoore, and Clarence Reginald

Bellestream left their normal domestic abode and set sail from Cowes, Isle of Wight . . . ."

It declared that extensive attempts to find them had not been successful and concluded that for all legal and hereditary purposes, they were hereby declared to be deceased. There followed some more legalese concerning the disposition of the estate.

"Is that it? Bit curt, isn't it?" asked Edward.

Felix explained that it was the normal procedure, no different for William and Marguerite than for anyone else.

"And this is the College of Arms document that you must sign. As soon as it receives the Royal Signature, you will become the fifteenth Duke of Hawksmoore."

Edward was past caring, so he signed and took his leave.

Ever since London achieved world domination of the flow of money and securities, those with interests in such matters found the need to come and go with minimal publicity. To cater for them, establishments sprang up and prospered; they appeared to be much the same as any private house, but combined the features of a Gentleman's Club and an exclusive Hotel. They can still be found in quiet squares south of Piccadilly in elegant terraced houses surrounding a central private garden. The Hawksmoore dynasty had long ago obtained the required interest in such an establishment, which they always referred to as the Manse.

Felix's offices were not too far north of the Manse, so he decided to walk. He was surprised at the spring in his step. Coming down Savile Row, he was about to pass Chaseman's when he decided to go in.

"Good morning, my Lord," said Mr. Horne. He had opened the carefully guarded door as soon as he recognised Edward.

"Thought I might have a new suit, I feel like a change."

Mr. Horne cast his expert eye over Edward, whose measurements were written in copperplate in the great ledger, and determined that, for the first fitting, no changes would be necessary. He did note a more upright posture. Mr. Horne thought that Lord Erinmore was looking more like his old self.

"Will that be city or country?"

Edward shrugged. "What about a Prince of Wales check? Something light, I think."

Mr. Horne remarked that it would certainly be appropriate to the season and made notes in the huge ledger. He ushered Edward to the door.

"It will be about a week to the fitting, sir."

Arriving at the Manse, Edward was intercepted by the porter

"From the Count, my Lord," he said proffering a small envelope.

The porter was referring to Count Paolo Passaglietti, known to Edward simply as Paul, the head of one of the many European families with whom the Hawksmoores had built their little known but hugely influential financial empire. Edward had sought the Count's assistance with the Mountbeck accounts.

Sitting in one of the leather armchairs in the lounge, Edward read:

"You must locate the assets listed as 'sequestered'. Your Steward has, quite properly, not included them in the principal accounts. Should that not be possible, other, more periculous (Edward smiled at this Italianisation) avenues must be pursued."

He recalled that the safe still retained its secrets. He went in search of a telephone, which the porter switched into a discreet booth in the hallway.

"Travis? Oh good. Have you got anyone in to open the safe?"

Travis, having no idea, had consulted the Steward, who had paled for a second, then brightened.

"I may be able to assist you, Mr. Travis, but it will take a day or two." He wasn't looking forward to the phone call or that voice that always unnerved him.

Travis took a small gamble.

"Will you be returning soon, my Lord?"

"Here for a week or so, I think."

"We should be ready upon your return, sir."

Word of the need for locksmith expertise at Mountbeck had filtered through the Bessemer network at a senior and confidential level. As soon as the name 'Champion' surfaced, the headmaster at St. Eligius thought of Jonathan's mastery of their rather ancient test model. He phoned Harry Sparrow at the time appointed for urgent call-outs. It seemed to be far too late in the evening.

"Could you be here tomorrow?" he asked.

Harry yawned into the mouthpiece. "Sorry about that. Sure I can. I'll ring you from the station."

Harry was excited. This would be a heavy job, he was sure.

When he arrived at St. Eligius, the headmaster seemed unusually nervous.

"We have a job to do that will tax our resources to the limit, Harry. And it is unusually delicate."

Harry was waiting for the other shoe to drop.

"It's possible that young Hare is the only person who can deal with the technical side."

Harry racked his brains, and recalled the headmaster's almost boyish enthusiasm while recounting Jonathan's success with the Champion.

"Must be a Champion safe that's to be eased."

"Exactly, Harry, but there's more to it. If he succeeds it is probable that one of our longer range strategies will be thwarted."

Harry waited.

"So he will need not only to open it but to sanitize the contents," the headmaster said carefully.

"Sanitize? You mean steal, or what?"

"No, no. He will have to determine whether the contents are what we think they are. If they are, they will have to be replaced. If they are not, there may be no problem."

Harry was perplexed. "And where do I come in?"

The headmaster shifted uncomfortably.

"My instructions are that you are to mentor him from a distance. You can't be seen at the location, you're far too easily traced. We want you to act as support, stay at a hotel near a telephone, dig him out of any trouble, you know." Harry was staring in disbelief.

"Is this my operation or not?"

"You will be in overall command, Harry. But Hare will have to go it alone, I'm afraid. And we can't have Hare traced, should there be trouble."

Harry realised that this must be a really heavy project, and that the movement must know something about Jonathan that he had missed.

"Come on, he's only seventeen, just a boy really."

"Look, Harry, this isn't easy for me to say. Hare will be operating in," – he searched for a way to save Harry's feelings – "in a context where he will be accepted more readily than you would."

Harry sat thinking about this. He had come to like Jonathan and admire his technical skills. But he couldn't seem to get close to him. Just as he was thinking about Jonathan's snooty ways, he recalled the ease with which Jonathan had spoken with the Curator. And there was that thing about the suit, too.

"Stone me!" exclaimed Harry, "You're going to hit one of them toffs."

The headmaster was relieved that Harry had opened the way for him.

"You worked that out quickly," he said, smiling at Harry, "Hare will indeed be operating within a social level far higher than we are used to. Far higher," he added.

"When will I get the details?"

There was another pause.

"Hare will be briefed directly on the specifics of the job. I will be briefing you on the support aspects."

Harry was getting nervous. "You mean I'll not be briefed on what's in that safe?"

"More secure that way, Harry, what you don't know, they can't get out of you."

"They? Are you saying Police or what?" Harry's eyebrows were raised as high as they could go.

"Exactly, Harry, if anything backfires, you would be a prime suspect, wouldn't you?"

"Count Passaglietti has arrived, my Lord."

"Thank you, Albert, ask him to come to the lounge, please."

Paul sat down. He was looking worried. This was so unusual that Edward leaned forward.

"Is everything all right, Paul?"

"I hope so, but we have received word from one of our people that there may be some sort of financial attack being planned against you. Does the name Abercorn mean anything?"

"Well, yes, some people have been after that property for years, but I have refused to sell."

Paul chose his next words delicately.

"The valuation in your accounts is seven years old. Land prices have increased in that time."

Edward thought about it. He had a vague idea that an article in the Times had quoted a figure for land appreciation, but it had not made much impact on him. It was all too complicated. He realised that Paul was waiting for a reply.

"I see. I remember the Steward made a suggestion at our last meeting. All those projections and appendices; didn't make a lot of sense to me!"

Paul tried hard not to smile; he realised that he would have to provide even more support to help Edward out of this mess.

"The High Court judgment must have been painful for you, Edward."

Edward got out a handkerchief and blew his nose rather loudly. The disappearance of William and Marguerite must have been a greater tragedy than Paul had understood.

"Damn pollen, always gives me hay fever," muttered Edward to cover his embarrassment.

Paul leaned forward. "Now, it is most urgent that we locate those assets."

Edward was too embarrassed to admit that the safe was impenetrable.

"I believe I may have them in my possession very soon."

Paul raised an eyebrow. "What good news! You must keep me informed."

But it did not fit at all with the intelligence coming in almost daily now. Edward was so unworldly, thought Paul. It was time to call in a favour and a big one at that.

He decided to change the subject.

"Maria is in town, she wrote to you, but she thinks you are ignoring her."

"Been down here for a few days, perhaps the letter is at Mountbeck."

"She always stays at the Savoy, you remember?"

Edward recalled having a pleasant afternoon tea with Paul and Maria in that room overlooking the Thames.

He made a sudden decision. "Then I must ask her to tea!"

Paul was astonished at this sudden burst of enthusiasm. All those hints and carefully staged meetings, all to no avail, and now this, he thought. He observed that Edward looked quite a bit younger and fitter.

Paul got up. "Why don't we telephone Maria now?"

Charmaine Montpelier had had a sleepless night replaying her failure with Jonathan. She had set out to make him fall for her so she could keep a closer watch on him. He was only seventeen, she ought to have been ashamed, but she had thought it just part of her job. It should have been easy, but as fast as she had made progress he had unsettled her. It had really started when they first met; he had responded so gallantly, his French too schoolboy, but his accent and behaviour definitely haute monde.

Information from the watchers had let her time her invitation precisely and he had seemed eager to come. What had he said when she had made him laugh? It was something to the effect that his face of stone was a mask to hide behind. And, she thought, what a transformation when he relaxed! He had described her décor so accurately as Mediterranean and a little Spanish, about as good a description of Perpignan as one could expect. How could he know that if he had never been there? Was he hiding something?

When she had thought to interest him with the photos, things had started to go wrong. He had slid his arm almost around her shoulders. She should have heeded that warning, she scolded herself. A seducer seduced? But he had been so naïve, so gauche.

She thought she had got the upper hand during their meal. The wine was a nice touch and his apparent inexperience another sign of his innocence. So the dancing should have done the trick. Where had she gone wrong? He hadn't seemed at all eager to dance at first, even after the pirouette; perhaps that had been too much, too soon? And why hadn't he learned to dance before? Or was his reluctance another part of his repertoire?

Her thoughts took a wayward path. As soon as his hand had touched her back, she had felt a frisson that she had overcome by concentrating on the instructions. He had followed her loyally, his sense of rhythm immediately apparent. She had not originally intended to include so advanced a manoeuvre in the corner, but he seemed to find it just another part of the dance.

He had held her so strongly as she leaned away from him, their bodies so close, another warning that she had not heeded. What a fool she had been, indulging herself with that slow waltz, but she was only human. And what technique he had used, his hand brushing across her cheek and against her earlobe! Even now she blushed at the violence of her response. Her kiss was an invitation that he could not refuse, and yet she had given him no chance. Why should she have had that sudden onslaught of guilt? It had come from nowhere and she had sent him away, no closer to finding out what his connection to the Grey gang might be.

FOURTEEN

Get ahead, Get a Hat!

Jonathan came through Harry's front door still thinking about the strange experience with Charmaine to find the telephone ringing. It was Harry.

"Hey, Jonathan, we've got a heavy job coming up. I won't be back tonight. I'll meet you at Paddington, nine o'clock tomorrow morning, Main Buffet, OK? Oh, have you eaten yet?"

Jonathan was just about to say that he was still full from his meal with Charmaine, when he thought better of it. "Perhaps I'll get some of those fish and chips?"

Harry thought this would be a great idea.

"You got a notebook in that case of yours?"

"Of course," Jonathan snorted.

"Bring it with you. See you tomorrow, we'll have time for a bite at the Buffet."

Jonathan was left holding a silent telephone.

There was an envelope lying on the hall floor. It had obviously been delivered by hand. The note asked him to meet Mr. Harrison at the Savoy Hotel at eight o'clock that evening.

He opened the London telephone book. His eye fell on an entry in bold type:

'**Savoy Hotel.**
The Strand, WC2'.

With the twenty pounds he had from Harry, he felt that he could be a little adventurous. Better wear the suit, he thought.

On his way to the tube station, he passed Bronsky's and decided to ask about the clothes stand. Mr. Bronsky was delighted to see him.

"Here he is, our hero, look Rachel, look who's here, it's Jonathan!"

Rachel was standing between the brown curtains. She nodded politely.

"And what can I do for you, my son?"

Jonathan looked around, but the clothes stand was not visible. "I'm really enjoying this suit, but it would benefit from being hung properly on that clothes stand you had."

Mr. Bronsky's face fell. "Only yesterday I sold it," he muttered.

"Just a thought, Mr. Bronsky. I must be off."

"Such a hurry always, Jonathan, and where are you rushing off to now, if you please?"

Jonathan told him about the Savoy Hotel. A look of horror came over the old man's face.

"But you can't go up there without a hat, my son! Come Rachel fetch a," – and here he used a word that Jonathan had never heard.

Rachel glowered as she disappeared through the curtains. She returned with an armful of brown hats and offered one, which fitted him well.

Then she was laughing and dragging him by the arm to a mirror. "Look, father, it's Dick Powell!"

Mr. Bronsky threw up his arms in mock surrender. "No, don't shoot!" he laughed.

Jonathan was looking at the mirror in astonishment. What he saw was a dapper and sophisticated young man, and indeed not a bad likeness of the famous film star.

"Take it, take it, please, with our gratitude!" the old man was slapping his thighs with pleasure.

Jonathan tried to pay, but all his attempts were swept aside.

Rachel approached him shyly. "Would you do something for me before you go?" Jonathan could hardly refuse.

"Would you embrace me like Dick Powell does?"

Mr. Bronsky rushed in. "He is her fantasy man, she is – how you say – crazy about him."

Jonathan wasn't sure what a Dick Powell embrace was all about, but he took Rachel in his arms, looked deeply into her eyes from under the brim of the hat and kissed her lightly. When he started to pull away, he was surprised that she held him a moment longer than necessary. Then she was out of his arms and running through the curtains.

Jonathan looked at the old man, who laughed and shrugged flamboyantly, as if to say "Women!"

All the way up to the Savoy, Jonathan was thinking about the strange way they did behave.

Count Paolo Passaglietti had been forced to call in a favour. He had occasionally used his commercial networks to assist Sir Roger with the intent of maintaining what might be a strategically valuable contact. Merely asking for help in dealing with the Mountbeck safe had been an exercise in diplomacy. He had been surprised at the immediately positive response, almost as if Sir Roger had been expecting the request.

The Savoy Hotel was built when Richard D'Oyly Carte, the impresario, decided that his audiences needed a place to stay after the shows at the Savoy Theatre.

The hotel took five years and vast expense to complete and incorporated unheard of features, including full electric lighting and no less than 67 baths. Its famous front entrance became one of London's landmarks; it was also conveniently close to West End theatres, opera, ballet and shopping.

When Jonathan arrived, the hotel was quietly busy, but he detected a discreet tension in the air. He approached the front desk, large enough to accommodate several small parties of guests.

"I am to meet Mr. Harrison here at eight o'clock," he told the formally dressed attendant.

"Yes, sir, please take a seat in the lounge and I shall page him for you."

Jonathan thought he could get used to such civility. He decided to use the gentlemen's room, which astonished him with its opulence.

Everything was of the highest quality. When he took off the hat, he saw that his hair was a little unruly. There was no comb in evidence, which reminded him of Frodsham. He brushed in a parting and smoothed his hair to one side. Tatleresque images ran through his mind again. The attendant asked him if he would need his hat so he turned it in and got an embossed receipt card that set out elegantly the virtues of the hotel.

In the lounge, a uniformed page approached. "Mr. Hare, sir?"

Jonathan nodded.

"Mr. Harrison awaits you in the Isis Suite, please follow me."

Jonathan followed the page to the bank of lifts. Naturally one lift was waiting with a seated operator wearing white gloves.

"Mr. Hare is for the Isis suite, if you please, Igor."

Jonathan knocked on the door, which was opened by a tall athletic man wearing a rather shiny dark blue suit.

"Mr. Hare?" Jonathan nodded.

"Come with me, sir"

He led Jonathan into the luxurious sitting room. Three men were present, all dressed in quiet but beautifully tailored suits. Jonathan recognised Sir Roger, but not the other two.

"Mr. Hare, Sir Roger," the man announced and withdrew to the doorway.

There was a silence.

Jonathan realised that Sir Roger had been staring at him for rather too long. Sir Roger took out a handkerchief and blew his nose rather pointedly. "May I get you a drink?"

Jonathan said that he had not eaten yet and Sir Roger nodded to the man at the door.

He cleared his throat. "Jonathan, these gentlemen have a delicate problem that you may be able to resolve. Would you mind if I don't introduce them at this stage?"

"I quite understand, sir," he said quietly, modulating his voice to match that of Sir Roger. The two strangers exchanged glances, which Jonathan pretended not to notice.

Sir Roger explained that very important papers were located in a safe, the combination to which had been mislaid. It was of national importance that the documents were taken into proper custody, but very discreetly.

Jonathan had listened with interest, but it now seemed as if he was expected to respond.

"Surely, sir, this is a job for the manufacturer." He paused. "Particularly if the recovery of the documents is, um," he stopped, looking at Sir Roger.

"You have my word, Jonathan that this is all above board. Unfortunately, the manufacturer is no longer in business, casualty of the war, you know."

Jonathan was immediately interested; it must be a Champion.

"Is it a Champion safe, sir?"

Glances were again exchanged.

"Yes it is; how did you know?"

Sir Roger had the familiar twinkle in his eye. Jonathan explained that it could hardly be any other, since so few companies could afford to produce the sort of safe that 'these gentlemen would employ to safeguard sensitive documents'.

Edward was about to say something, but Sir Roger held up his quieting hand.

Jonathan asked, "Do you have a model number?"

Paul had made sure that Edward brought it with him. He passed it to Jonathan who was startled to see the "X" prefix because Champion had only used this for special designs to unique specifications. He decided to keep this to himself.

"I understand the problem, sir," he said, "but without the design details I may not be able to master this quickly, if at all. I'll need to see it for myself."

Sir Roger raised his eyebrows at Edward, who took this to mean that he should speak.

"Mr. Hare, this matter needs the most urgent attention. How soon can you start?"

Jonathan explained that his schedule was full for the next day or two, but after that he might be available. He looked at Sir Roger. "I'll need cover from Harry, sir."

Sir Roger laughed and told Jonathan to leave that to him.

The food arrived. The other men looked at it and agreed that Jonathan had had a good idea. The blue suited man was sent off. There was an air of relief in the room.

Edward had been examining Jonathan. "You look very young to have this sort of reputation, Mr. Hare, how did you acquire it?"

Jonathan explained that mechanical puzzles of all sorts had always fascinated him.

"Actually, sir, once you understand the internal design structures, most locks can be opened. Combination locks can be more challenging, but again there are techniques."

"Good Lord," said Edward, "is nothing sacred?"

There was some laughter.

"Did I hear you're up for a scholarship at Oxford?" Edward asked.

Jonathan looked at Sir Roger, who nodded.

"Indeed, sir, but I haven't got it yet."

"Which College?"

Jonathan looked at Sir Roger again, who explained that Jonathan's science and mathematical skills matched the charter of the newly founded Abingdon College.

"Bit of a boffin, eh?" Edward was smiling. "Wanted to go up myself, you know, but things got in the way."

Paul was surprised at the ease with which Edward admitted this.

Edward had moved closer to Jonathan. "Know anything about steam engines?"

Jonathan told him that he knew the theory, and would have liked to build some models. "But they're a bit too pricey for me."

"You must see mine at Mountbeck," said Edward.

They carried on an animated conversation about the merits of inside versus outside cylinders while Paul looked on in pleased surprise. First Maria this afternoon, when Edward had been gravely courteous but newly overcome by Maria's beauty, and now his easy manner with this young man whose intelligence seemed to shine out of him whenever he wasn't on his guard.

In Paul's world assessing character was essential; Jonathan's real self was normally well hidden behind his mask, but Paul sensed that this stoicism was really a cover for a determination to chart his own course. He decided that Jonathan presented a most interesting challenge; he would see what he could find out about the lad. And, he thought, if his skills are as good as Sir Roger thinks, I may have a use for him. Another thought emerged. Why had Sir Roger reacted that way when the lad first came into the room? Yes, Paul thought, I need to find out more about this young man, he might carry a secret with him that could be useful someday.

Sir Roger's feelings were far more complex. He was glad to see Jonathan's technical competence at play, but was unsettled by his appearance – Antonia had been so right about that – and the ease with which he was talking with Edward. Of course, he hadn't introduced either of the men by their titles.

When the food had been disposed of, they reconvened. Sir Roger summed up; he would inform Edward as soon as Jonathan could make himself available. He reminded Jonathan that this was a delicate operation and that the fewer that knew of it the better. He introduced Edward as Edward Bellestream and Paul as Paul Passaglietti. He did not include their titles.

As Jonathan left the suite, he was in high spirits because of the confidence they had placed in him and his heart-to-heart with Edward Bellestream. He collected his hat, and, putting it on in front of the mirror, he smiled at Dick Powell. As he entered the foyer, a door in the grand entrance was held open and a tall fair-haired young woman strode in. She was dressed in full evening attire, with a long flowing dress and a waist length fur jacket; she was quite strikingly pretty. It was Victoria.

As soon as he recognised her, he ducked his head and she swept past. He was breathing a sigh of relief when he heard her voice.

"Jonathan? Jonathan Hare?"

Still feeling good about the evening, he turned and, looking from under the brim of the hat, said, "Sorry, ma'am, my name is Dick Powell."

She responded with that irritating tone of superiority, "Stop it Jonathan, I'd know you anywhere. What are you doing here? Oh, meeting my father I suppose."

He was horrified and took her by the arm.

"Be quiet, Victoria, please, not here."

He steered them from the foyer into a corner of the lounge. She was looking at him in astonishment.

"Please bear with me for just a moment longer, Victoria," he asked.

She heard a note of command in his voice and was surprised that she didn't find it annoying.

He told her in an undertone that she must speak to her father as soon as possible. "He'll tell you that it would be better if you didn't recognise me if we should meet again."

She looked shocked. "But, Jonathan, why not?"

He got up. "You really must ask your father."

He turned away and hurried out of the hotel.

Had he looked back, he would have seen Victoria staring after him wide-eyed. Had he been close enough he would have been surprised by the tiny smile at the corner of her mouth.

Into the Jaws of Death

The next morning Jonathan arrived early at Paddington Station and took a walk along Platform One, which one could walk onto from the street without a ticket. Such apparent generosity was rather spoiled by the fact that all the named expresses left from there and all carried ticket inspectors. This morning the carriages had the Cornish Riviera Express headboards.

When he got to the far end of the platform he took a moment to admire the great King-class engine, sizzling with heat. It would head the train all the way to Plymouth over the difficult terrain west of Exeter. The train would then cross the Tamar Bridge into Cornwall and continue all the way to Penzance.

He walked back through the ticket office into the street where the taxis were dropping off passengers in a steady stream. A black Wolsley Ten was parked rather awkwardly. He strolled past it and saw that the mark above the wheel housing had been recently touched up, but the brush strokes gave it away.

When he entered the Main Buffet, Harry was already there. Jonathan was hungry – Rita hadn't offered to make breakfast – so he took a couple of unappetizing buns and a cup of evil-looking coffee over to Harry's table.

"Mind if I join you?" he asked in his best upper class accent.

Harry looked up with a start. "You're good, Jonathan, fool me every time, you do!"

110 / PASSE PARTOUT

Jonathan took a sip of the coffee and found it to be a disgusting lukewarm concoction made from essence of chicory. He pushed it to one side.

"Fussy bugger!" said Harry, "I'll drink it."

Then he nudged Jonathan. "In a minute, look to your left, see a small man, flat cap, carting a big suitcase."

Jonathan smiled and nodded, "Seen him, case must be empty."

Harry scowled, "Too smart for your own good, ain't yer?"

Jonathan moved his chair slightly. The small man was walking around apparently looking for a place to sit. A woman in a black coat was drinking tea at a nearby table; she had a small suitcase by her side. As she raised the cup to her mouth, the small man dropped his case over the woman's, picked it up and moved aimlessly away.

Harry grinned, "Neat oppo, eh?"

Jonathan was amazed, "He stole her case, Harry!"

Harry laughed, "That's Andy Capp, well known case artist. If he's lucky, the bluebottles[8] won't spot him."

Jonathan didn't know what to do; Harry seemed to think it was all in a day's business.

"How does it work?" Jonathan asked, playing for time.

"No bottom to Andy's case. Two spring-loaded prongs grab the case, easy as pie, takes a bit of face, mind," Harry explained.

Just then Andy appeared with two uniformed men on either side.

"Anyone lost a case in here?" demanded one of them.

The woman in the black coat jumped up, "My case, it's gone!" she shrieked.

"That's all right, dear, we have it."

The woman was "ever so grateful"; Andy was taken away by his escort.

Harry muttered, "Getting too old for it, is Andy." He didn't seem at all concerned about the woman. Jonathan decided not to tell Harry about the black Wolsley.

---

8   A derogatory term for the Railway Police

When Count Paolo woke in his luxurious bedroom in the Isis suite that morning, he had at the front of his mind a startling imagery. It was not unusual for his brain to work on problems during the night and the Count had gone to sleep with a disquiet that he had been unable to pinpoint. There had been something he had missed about the meeting with the young man, and this in itself was irritating.

The image he was now presented with was Sir Roger's reaction when Jonathan entered the reception room. But, he thought, I have already stored that away for future reference. Then the thought hit home. What was Roger doing there in the first place? Surely a man of his stature should have delegated such a trivial matter? And since he had not, it would be just too flattering to suppose that Edward and he warranted such personal attention. So the importance must centre on the lad. He sat up with a sudden keen interest, hearing his father's stern but loving reprimand to "Look beyond, Paolo, look beyond!" The lad must have some other value to Roger, and it must rank high in importance. He thought back to his initial investigation into Edward's problem and recalled that there were other interests in the Mountbeck landholdings – Abercorn, that was it – and it must be the Bessemer people behind that. But even this hardly justified Roger's personal interest. The lad simply had to be part of something bigger, something "beyond". He recalled an odd request from Jonathan, "I'll need cover from Harry, sir." He lay back with a smile. This would be a test for his agents in London. They were used to uncovering commercial intrigue and identifying cracks and weaknesses in other institutions, let them have a go at this, he grinned.

Harry and Jonathan took a train to Reading and changed to a stopping train serving a number of small country stations. They were the only passengers to the market town on the Thames that Jonathan knew quite well. Only one other passenger got off, a blue suited man who disappeared into the ticket office. A car was waiting for them and took them down a series of country lanes, where the hedgerows seemed to brush the sides of the car. They turned into a long tree-lined driveway that stretched away to a castellated gatehouse.

Harry spoke to a porter there, and they continued to a great Tudor house with timber beams and herringbone brickwork.

Inside the grand entrance was a panelled reception room.

"Wait here," said Harry.

He returned with a massively built older man who exuded more power than Jonathan had ever previously experienced.

"You may leave us now, Sparrow," the huge man said, without looking at Harry.

His eyes were fixed on Jonathan. Harry almost bowed as he left the room. The man sat down at a small table and opened a file. He didn't ask Jonathan to sit. His voice carried a North Country accent, perhaps Northumberland, thought Jonathan.

"So, you are Jonathan Hare, father deceased in the war, mother working to support house and home, educated at Standish College and recently at St. Eligius."

Jonathan was stunned; 'Father deceased in the war' rang entirely false.

He was about to protest when the man continued.

"Excellent academic progress, impressive 'A' levels, outstanding supplemental skills – I see that you opened the old Champion safe. Harry's reports are uniformly excellent also. You don't seem to have done so well at social studies, no record of activism, few demonstrations, you don't read "The Worker" or any other socialist literature, more interested in Tatler, are you?"

Jonathan was feeling bombarded by these staccato utterances.

The man didn't seem to want any answers and continued, "Excellent ear for languages, able to assimilate local accents, when dressed appropriately can pass himself off as of a much higher class, is at ease with the gentry, has a charm that women find attractive, although he is apparently unaware of this."

Jonathan was feeling faint.

"Up for a Galdraith Scholarship, probably get it."

The man stopped. He had reduced Jonathan to an entry in a file. Jonathan was dismayed and angry, but maintained his stone face.

"Well, Hare, I'm pleased to say that you have amply justified our investment in you and now you can begin to repay us. We have an assignment for you. You will have to use all the skills that you practised at St. Eligius."

Jonathan was feeling like a slave in a market whose owner was laying claim to him. As far as he was concerned, he had gone to St. Eligius on a Scholarship and owed them nothing. He recalled some of the more left wing speakers going on about 'worker solidarity' and 'bringing the aristocracy to its knees' but he had never felt it applied to him. And Charles had often seemed uneasy with his responses, he recalled.

The big man went on to explain that the movement needed to examine some documents. "We believe the papers are in a safe and the combination has been lost. If they are what we think they are, you will have to bring them to us; if not, they can remain in the safe. We have the owner's confidence, and you will be provided every facility. Nice place, too, you'll probably find it to your liking." This appeared to be an attempt at humour, which Jonathan couldn't share.

"When can you go?"

The man hadn't left him the option of refusing.

"Can you tell me more about the safe, please?" Jonathan asked.

He didn't feel any urge to add "sir"; if they didn't need his expertise they wouldn't have set up this elaborate interview.

The man opened another file. "An older safe, made by Champion, previous attempts have failed, no factory representatives available. Last used a couple of years ago. That enough?" Jonathan thought that there must be more Champion safes around than he had imagined.

"I can't say until I've examined it, I'm afraid."

The man sat back. "Then you will go," he said; he had not left Jonathan any room for manoeuvre.

He took out an envelope from the second file and tipped the contents onto the table. Jonathan spotted a roll of bank notes, some of them that special dark blue that meant they were five pounds in value. Before he had extracted the money from Harry, he had never had one in his possession.

"Here is the address. You will contact Mr. Travis, the Butler, who is expecting you. You will tell him that Mr. Hawthorne has arranged your house call. The owner is titled, Lord Erinmore, soon to be Duke of Hawksmoore."

"What about Harry, will he be my support?"

"Ah, good point, Hare, he'll be there just to bail you out if there's trouble. The sensitivity of the documents is such that the fewer that see them the better. Harry is also too well known in certain circles, you understand."

"So I will be on my own on this job?"

"And more to your credit when you succeed!" the big man said with a smile. The prospect of failure was apparently not to be mentioned.

"Keep what we have discussed entirely to yourself. You will endanger Sparrow if you tell him anything. Take these papers with you, they contain all the instructions; do not show them to anyone, you understand."

The unspoken threat of dire consequences hung over the big man's words.

Jonathan seemed to have few options. He picked up the papers and was putting them back into the envelope when he spotted the address; it was "Mountbeck, Heckmondsley, Yorkshire." The name "Mountbeck" rang a faint bell.

The train was just pulling in to Paddington when he recalled that Edward had his steam engines at a place called Mountbeck.

Victoria was sitting in her father's study. She had told him what Jonathan had said to her in the Savoy. Her father was as indecisive as she had ever seen him. He was drumming his fingers on the desk, another unusual thing.

Finally he said, "Jonathan was right to ask you to talk to me and yes, Victoria, if you run into him again, it would be better not to acknowledge him."

She was astonished. "But why, what has he done, is he in trouble?"

Sir Roger swivelled his chair and looked out of the window so Victoria couldn't see his face. Antonia had burdened him with her concern that Victoria and Jonathan were too close, and it now seemed worse than that, for she had deeper feelings for the lad than a recently engaged young woman should. He decided that Antonia would have to carry out the corrective, for he felt quite unable to deal with Victoria. He decided that it was time for some misdirection.

"Jonathan is a special young man. You have met him in circumstances that don't reflect his particular abilities. He is gifted academically – he is just about to enter Oxford with one of the most prestigious scholarships that can be awarded. But, Victoria, he has other gifts that I am cultivating for the future benefit of the Society."

"He's going to be a watchmaker?" she asked with disbelief.

Sir Roger groaned inwardly. "Victoria, the Society provides a consultation service that is famous throughout the world. We deal with other national bodies, privately with heads of state and with some of the richest people in the world. We need to have someone with his talents groomed to take over; I won't last forever."

She seemed more persuaded. Then she launched another attack. "But, father, he has no social position, no contacts, no mentors." She stopped with her hand over her mouth.

"Oh, I'm such a fool! You're mentoring him aren't you?"

He silently thanked his Lord for rescuing him.

But she was in full stride. "If you are so taken with him, why is mother so against him. I told her about the last time at the Society and she was almost in tears."

He tried to smile at her. "You know your mother, she wants you to have a successful marriage and won't let anything get in the way of that."

All she could manage was, "I suppose you're right, father," and left the room.

It was a bitter moment for him. It had always been assumed that the family would be blessed with male heirs, but Sir Roger had not managed that. The Baronetcy could only be passed down through the oldest son, who for generations had been registered at birth for the family's traditional school, and introduced at the appropriate age to all the protocols that would affect his life of service. None of that had been possible.

Charles Barnes was sitting in Grey Central. It had acquired some more maps and photographs. More coloured pins had been added and ribbons ran from place to place.

Sir Hubert was chairing the meeting.

"There have been some interesting developments since we last met. I have consulted with the heads of certain services. It seems that there is another line of interest that runs through this young doppelganger, Ward or Hare. Miss Montpelier, you have been keeping close to him, what should we call him?"

She shifted awkwardly, sensitive to the expression 'keeping close to him'.

"I suggest, sir, that we forget about the Ward alias, he certainly doesn't use it. I think we can accept that it was just one of Harry Sparrow's economies."

Sir Hubert grunted. "That may be so, but my instinct tells me that there is some connection to the Grey gang that we are missing. Tell us what you have found out, Miss Montpelier."

She consulted her notes. "The team watching his movements reports that all his work has been with Harry, with one exception, when he returned to the Royal Horological Society on his own. We have no contacts there, and it seems as if he was just invited for lunch. All his assignments have been during normal business hours, with one exception that you may feel justifies your instincts, sir. He and Harry opened an office safe in a warehouse owned by an Arthur Salmon. Apparently his manager, Bert Coleman, had forgotten the combination and called Harry in urgently. Arthur Salmon owns other property along the river, some derelict. Arthur is married to Ronnie Grey's sister." Sir Hubert looked pleased.

"Thank you."

But Charmaine was not finished.

"You asked me to take on Mr. Hare as a special assignment" – there was some suppressed laughter that earned a glare from Sir Hubert – "I have had the opportunity to talk to him at reasonable length. He is difficult to pigeonhole; he seems exceptionally gifted in some areas and very naïve in other ways. He seems to me to be hiding behind a façade, to be honest, sir."

Sir Hubert was looking at Charmaine with a noticeably more appreciative smile.

The superintendent cleared his throat. "There is one report on Hare's movements that you should know about, sir. We kept a watch on Bronsky's, bearing in mind the part it played before the capture. Hare stopped in the other night, very well dressed, sir, my man nearly didn't recognize him. When he left he was wearing a hat, brim pulled down hiding his face. My man was nearly fooled again, but called it in to be safe. Hare went to the Tube station, where he bought a ticket, paid with a pound note. Got off at Charing Cross, walked to the Savoy. We put another man in the lobby. We lost sight of Hare for about an hour. When my man next saw him, he was involved in a quite forceful exchange with a young woman, dressed to the nines, so my man reports, fur jacket, evening dress. Hare took her arm and almost dragged her into the lounge, out of sight of my man. Hare left in a hurry, sir, on his own. My man followed Hare, nothing to report, returned to Harry Sparrow's."

Charmaine was stunned, wondering what on earth he was up to, going to the Savoy, dressed in disguise, meeting a society girl there, with whom he was obviously acquainted. She was surprised to find that she was a little hurt.

Charles couldn't imagine Jonathan mixing in society circles. He was supposed to be opening safes and practising the supplementals. Another thought surfaced; was this a misdirection exercise? Could Jonathan have picked up the watchers and set up a smoke screen? But where did he get the clothes and the money? And why was he not working with Harry?

It began to worry Charles; he hoped Jonathan hadn't lost his way, he never seemed at ease with the lectures at St. Eligius, and, now that he thought about it, never went on any of the field trips and demonstrations.

Back at Harry's after the Tudor House experience, Jonathan picked up a letter that carried a crest and the words "Galdraith Foundation."

He was to attend a selection interview in Oxford to determine the recipient of the 1954 award. The date was set for later in August.

"Plenty of time for Mountbeck, then," he said to himself.

He lay in bed that night, thinking over the day's events. He was excited with the challenge of the experimental Champion safe, but couldn't understand why both Sir Roger and the big man in the Tudor mansion had the same interest. He wondered why the powerful, blunt executive never gave his name. And he was offended that he should have to report to the Butler.

"They'll want me to come in the tradesman's entrance, I expect!" he snorted. And Harry had been, well, different on the return journey, not his usual cocky self at all. He thought about the contents of the safe. All he had to do was give them to the owner, surely? Then he remembered he had his instructions in the envelope. He fell asleep thinking he'd better read them tomorrow.

Victoria, on the other hand, couldn't sleep at all. She kept replaying what her father had said, "Your mother wants you to have a successful marriage and won't let anything get in the way of that."

But successful for whom? The available men during the Season had been nice enough and her mother hadn't pushed her too hard at first, but, as the days went by, she found herself partnered more often with Robbie.

Robert Erskine Dunne, the Earl of Dornoch to be, was good-looking, almost handsome, wealthy and most considerate towards her. She had only to lift an eyebrow and he would be there, asking if he could be of assistance. His estate was wild and beautiful in a remote sort of way, certainly a long way from London. They had danced and exchanged the expected kisses at the end of the social functions. His proposal had been socially correct and their engagement had had a sense of inevitability. Her mother had been ecstatic, had even asked her how she felt about it, but, as Victoria now realised, had hardly listened to her reply.

Her father had always deferred to her mother and she understood why. Certainly it would be a good marriage, even by the exalted standards of the Tatler. But there was no challenge there. She had an image of riding an old mare, plod, plod, she thought, and asked herself where was the pounding, blood-boiling excitement of the full gallop, hooves drumming on the turf, the wind bringing tears to the eyes? She had a vision of the Ridgeway, running along the crest of the Berkshire downs, so lonely yet so dramatic, so wonderful to ride along.

She finally fell asleep, and dreamt that she was in a Hollywood film. A 'private eye' in a hat with the brim pulled down was pulling her away from the edge of a cliff, saying, "Be quiet, Victoria, stop screaming!"

SIXTEEN

Coming to Mountbeck

Jonathan woke early and opened the Tudor House envelope, finding the roll of notes labelled 'for expenses only'. He read the instructions; there may be nothing in the safe, or there may be family papers. Should there be any financial papers including bearer bonds, certificates or bank records of accounts, particularly overseas accounts, he was to retrieve them and telephone for further instructions.

When the number answered, he was to say, "This is Hare and it is exactly 12:12."

So, he thought, until I get the safe open and know what's in it, I don't have any decisions to make. He felt more settled.

When he heard Harry downstairs, Jonathan got up. He explained about the Galdraith interview, and suggested they set a date for the Mountbeck operation.

Harry said, "Sooner the better," but seemed a lot less than enthusiastic.

He told Harry that he had to confirm the Galdraith interview and used the telephone. He reached the Society switchboard and told the operator that it was Mr. Harrison for Sir Roger. There was a click and when he heard Sir Roger's rounded tones, he said, "I can be available for the interview. But I shall be away at Edward's home from tomorrow evening. If you need me, please call me there."

He put down the phone, hoping Sir Roger would interpret the message correctly.

Harry had been studying timetables. "There's a good train from Kings Cross. Change at York, go on to Thirsk. I'll find a hotel there. We'll have to play it by ear from there." They packed their suitcases accompanied by Rita's whining, "Why can't I come, just going away like that, bloody mystery men!"

Harry didn't look up. "Good to get away sometimes," he whispered, whether to Jonathan or to himself it was hard to know.

A little later there was a knock at the front door. When Jonathan opened it, the man in the blue suit was standing there with a bulky envelope in his hand.

"I am to give you this personally, Mr. Hare," he said in a voice that carried a certain authority.

The envelope was addressed to Jonathan, so he took it up to his room. There was a large package of banknotes, and a small supply of calling cards. They were of a very high quality and announced that he was Jonathan Hare, Special Advisor to the Royal Horological Society.

He thought they were a distinct improvement on Harry's and this time the name was his own. He felt rather flattered that he now had a title, even if it was a myth.

He read the accompanying note that explained that he was to telephone Mountbeck. The Butler, Mr. Travis would answer and Jonathan was to ask to speak to Edward Bellestream, who would be expecting the call. There was a strange final demand that he couldn't understand. Before he arrived at Mountbeck he was to chain the small case carrying his special equipment to his wrist.

He told Harry that he was going to the library to get something to read on the train. When he got there he asked the librarian for a copy of Debrett, the reference volume on the Aristocracy. He quickly located Bellestream and found that Edward was in fact Erinmore, Lord, a title used within the family of Hawksmoore, Duke of, and found that the family seat was indeed Mountbeck. He sat back, wondering what to do.

"One step at a time, I'll have to open the safe first," he said to himself.

He asked for the reference section, found a financial glossary and looked up the meaning of a bearer bond. He read:

'The owner of a bearer bond is not registered anywhere. The interest and principal go to the holder of the bearer bond upon physical presentation of the bond or of the coupons that are attached representing the interest payments'.

He thought these must be as good as cash, just as much risk, but untraceable, all the more reason for keeping them in a safe. As he was leaving he remembered to get something to read on the train.

He stumbled across a rather battered volume on navigation aids. It contained an account of the Harrison longitude timepiece.

On his way back, he passed Bronsky's. Something new in the window caught his eye. It was a more modern stethoscope with a combination bell-diaphragm contact piece in a nearly new box. As usual, Bronsky was overjoyed to see him, and it was all he could do to pay for the stethoscope. He thought this would be a reasonable charge to expenses.

The next day at Kings Cross, he wouldn't let Harry go to the buffet, telling him that there was a dining car on the train. Harry snorted that the buffet food was good enough for him. To cheer him up, Jonathan offered to pay, which put Harry in a better mood. They had a good breakfast and when Jonathan paid, he carefully used the money from the Tudor House roll.

Harry sniffed when he saw the roll. "Come up in the world, ain't yer?"

Jonathan, worried about Harry, said, "It's just a job, Harry."

Back in the carriage, he was reading the account of the Harrisons' attempts to construct and test their longitude timepiece, and the vested Establishment interests that they ran into. Committee after committee sided with less accurate models presented by better connected inventors.

As the story unfolded, Jonathan felt the stirring of some anger that science should have been so politicised. He caught himself thinking that he'd soon be like one of those lefties, all long hair and wire-rimmed glasses.

When he got to the end of the chapter, he found a museum photograph of the timepiece. It was not what he had worked on, which was a reasonable facsimile certainly, but definitely not the original.

He put the book down and started to replay in his mind the episode with Harry and the Curator. Luxurious facilities; one way mirror; false identification of the timepiece; Sir Roger's interest in him. Had he been under scrutiny? And then there was that time when Victoria was there. Had they wanted him to spot the staged identification? They had certainly seemed pleased when he challenged them. And what had Victoria's role been? She had seemed so emotional in the garden. He remembered that her mother was an actress and thought he had better look Lady Antonia up in a stage directory; perhaps Mountbeck would have a library.

He realised that he was carrying a lot of money. Harry knew about the Tudor house roll, but not the other. And why had Sir Roger been so free with his money, offering to support him at Oxford? A suite at the Savoy must cost a lot just for a meeting. It was all too confusing, and really nothing that he could do but carry out the job.

They got off at York and took a local train to Thirsk. Harry signed in at the Station Hotel, while Jonathan rang the Mountbeck number. When a voice answered, he asked for Edward Bellestream.

"I beg your pardon," the voice answered, full of indignation.

"I am to ask for Edward Bellestream, he is expecting me," said Jonathan in his best and smoothest voice. There was a series of clicks and he heard Edward's voice.

"Mr. Hare, where are you?"

Jonathan explained that he was in Thirsk, at the Station Hotel.

"Wait there, I'll have the car sent. Good of you to come so quickly!"

The car was a huge pre-war model Rolls Royce, which transported Jonathan smoothly along small roads between gaunt drystone walls, turning into a winding driveway lined with untidy laurels, and eventually coming to a stop in front of a grimly proper entrance. He chained his tool case to his wrist.

Someone was waiting for him at the top of some rather neglected steps.

Travis was eyeing Jonathan's case. Gentleman did not carry luggage in through the front entrance at Mountbeck. Jonathan sensed the disapproval, and allowed Travis to see the wrist chain.

Travis sniffed. "Please follow me, sir."

Jonathan thought that Travis could be a problem. They entered the Small Drawing Room where Travis presented a silver tray, obviously expecting some response.

"Your card, sir, please?" Travis prompted.

"Yes, indeed, Travis, one moment please, this case is so awkward."

He made a show of searching for his card, and pulled out one of the elegant productions that Sir Roger had sent. It seemed to impress Travis.

"If you would wait here a moment, sir," he said, perhaps with less disdain than before.

SEVENTEEN

What You See Is What You Get

The Headmaster of St. Eligius was wondering whether to pass on the strange information he had received from young Charles Barnes. The police assumed that Jonathan had some connection to the Grey gang and had him under watch. The Headmaster thought this was preposterous. But Charles had also said that Jonathan appeared to have been taken up by another Service, although he had no idea which; this had resulted in him associating with society people in the Savoy Hotel.

The Headmaster was struggling to resolve these absurdities. He opened Jonathan's file and noted that several masters had complained, "Hare does not seem to be involved with much beyond his 'A' levels." And yet his skills in supplementals were beyond praise.

The Headmaster decided that this was the usual friction between the School's academics and practitioners. He turned to the section covering political activity and demonstrations and discovered that almost nothing was recorded. At first he thought this must be sloppy record keeping.

One entry caught his eye, a disgruntled lecturer complaining, "Hare spent his time looking at a book of fascist photographs." The Headmaster could find very few occasions when Jonathan attended the mass demonstrations, or subscribed to any socialist publication. He recalled that Charles had suggested that Hare had 'charted his own course', and had been particularly reluctant to attend the frequent political lectures. He would sit quietly reading something that interested him, like the art of disguise.

The Headmaster was also thinking about Charles, who had been one of the brighter stars in the management disciplines. Good 'A' level results; might get a decent University place. Charles had left the impression of having a sound head on his shoulders and would not have telephoned him without careful thought. He sighed, at a loss to think what action he could take based on this skimpy evidence.

He decided to call Harry, and Rita answered. As soon as he mentioned his concerns regarding Jonathan, there was a strange silence at the other end. Finally Rita laughed.

"There's a lot more to this lad than I thought. I never felt right about him, Headmaster, woman's intuition perhaps. He doesn't fit with the pattern of the others we've had here. Harry is really impressed, but says that Hare has abilities that enable him to work both sides of the street, not quite sure what Harry meant by that. And he had a Chaseman suit, said he was given it, but I don't know.

"Then he can look after himself in a rough house, brought down Ronnie Grey in a pub, next thing the police have him. Grey's people think he's a police operator sent to flush Ronnie out, but that doesn't seem right to me. The Grey people are really after his blood; you can understand their point of view. Another thing, they suspect that Hare has a case that may contain the diamonds stolen from Hatton Garden recently. I told them that was nonsense, Harry knows what's in the case, just tools for the supplementals, as you call them. But they're dead set on finding out, going to put Sailor Wilson on it, I suspect."

The Headmaster was getting nervous.

"Hare has achieved all this in just a few weeks, Rita?" he asked, "And where's Harry?"

Rita told him that both Harry and Jonathan were away on a job. "Wouldn't tell me anything, said to call you if things went off the rails."

At last the Headmaster began to see a pattern. "We may have to ask you to get involved in this job that they're on. It's not one that we can afford to go wrong; we certainly don't want the Grey people involved. Let me ring you as soon as I know." The line went dead.

Rita chewed her lip for a while. This Jonathan was a constant irritation to her; he presented an image that she couldn't accept. No one coming for supplementals should arrive with a Chaseman suit; it was a symbol of the class she had had to put behind her. What a story Jonathan had told, that Bronsky gave it to him for saving the old man from some sort of trouble with Ronnie. But that seemed to be borne out by the attack in the King's Head. Then he simply wouldn't respond to any name other than Jonathan, not "Johnny boy" or "Jon", stuck up little bugger. What was it that Harry had told her about the Transport café? Jonathan wouldn't go in, 'thought it beneath him' that was it. When she thought of his charming greeting to Charmaine, she found herself blushing. She had almost given herself away warning him about getting involved. Surely she wasn't jealous? His French had been academically sound, but his manner was definitely continental, he seemed quite comfortable raising her hand to his face. She had noted that he had not actually allowed his lips to touch her hand, so he must be well practised. And Harry had commented that the Curator at the Royal Horological Society had taken a liking to Jonathan, and that Jonathan had seemed quite comfortable with him; 'gave as good as he got' was what Harry had said. But Harry had also noticed that Jonathan could put on a pretty good cockney lingo, didn't know all the slang, but had the accent down to a tee. She shook her head; better watch her step, she could get caught playing both sides of the fence.

Jonathan had been looking around the Small Drawing Room. It was a charming room, decorated with a woman's touch, he thought. There was a decidedly Mediterranean flavour; several small paintings caught his eye. He thought he recognised one as a Van Gogh, not one in the usual books; the other was definitely a Sisley. He was standing close to it wondering if it was original when he heard a cough behind him. It was Travis. There was a moment of silence before he escorted Jonathan to the Study. Edward's greeting was genuine and this seemed to unsettle Travis, who was a bit late announcing Jonathan.

"Mr. Hare is going to help us with the old Champion safe, Travis, he comes directly to us from the Royal Horological Society in London, a great favour, what? Is his room made up, fire going?"

"Indeed it is, my Lord," Travis said as he slid out of the room.

Edward was looking at the case chained to Jonathan's wrist. "You look a bit sinister, got piles of money in there then?" he laughed.

Jonathan told him it was his special toolkit. "Can't do anything without it, really, sir."

They chatted for a while. Edward seemed even friendlier than at the Savoy.

Jonathan had heard Travis use the phrase "my Lord", and thought he had better face the issue.

"Sir Roger introduced you as Edward Bellestream, but Debrett refers to you as Lord Erinmore. Should I call you that?"

Edward sucked his teeth.

"Actually, when we're together like this, there's no need, but," he paused, "Well, Lady Jane is rather conscious of such things, so perhaps in her company. Been a bit of a hiatus here since my brother and his wife died, tragedy you know, lost at sea on their way to Biarritz. Clarence was with them as well. So just Jane, their daughter, and me left in the Bellestream line," he continued in a rush.

This was obviously of greater concern to Edward than Jonathan could fathom. He had read enough about the importance of maintaining the line of succession, but had no personal understanding of it. His mother never talked about his father at all. He suddenly remembered that ugly old bully at the Tudor House, what had he said, "Father killed in the War", that was it.

Edward was chatting away, "Jane is here on holidays with her friend Germaine, out riding just now, back for dinner, you will join us? Balance the table, for once."

Jonathan, always concerned that he may be left to get his own meals, expressed his thanks.

"When would you like me to look at the safe, sir," he asked when he could get a word in. Edward got up and led him to the huge bank of bookshelves.

"Never could understand why it had to be in here, ugly old thing, pretty useless if you can't open it, what?" he said, sliding a section of the bookshelves to one side. Jonathan was looking at the safe, eyes wide. It was definitely an experimental model, but not one in any of the books he had read. It had the standard central dial, this with one hundred gradations and a better quality handle than usual.

"Have you ever opened it yourself, sir?" he asked.

Edward shook his head vigorously, "Oh, no, domain of William, you know."

"So it hasn't been opened for about two years?"

Edward concurred.

"I'll need several hours of concentrated work, very boring, I'm afraid," Jonathan said, preparing the way ahead.

"Well, no point starting before dinner, then; I'll get Travis to show you your room. Listen for the gong, what?"

Travis appeared and shepherded Jonathan up the main staircase, which was surprisingly plain. Rather uninspiring portraits hung on the walls. As he passed one of a young woman, he stopped and read the plaque. "Marguerite, Duchess of Hawksmoore", it read. He thought she looked a bit like Charmaine. They travelled down a corridor and into the end room. It was well furnished, but in a heavy Victorian style that Jonathan found depressing, although a fire was burning in the handsome grate. His luggage had been placed on a stand at the end of the bed.

Travis was looking at him with a small smile. "Dinner will be in one hour, sir. You will want to dress, of course. The bathroom is just next door." He turned to go. Jonathan had read enough Tatlers and Strand Magazines in the Standish Library to realise what dressing for dinner implied.

"Bit of a problem there, Travis, I'm afraid." Jonathan had adopted Edward's clipped enunciation.

Travis' raised eyebrows prolonged the agony.

"Didn't come prepared for anything formal." Jonathan was trying not to blush, struggling to maintain his stone face.

Travis relented. "I think I can find something suitable, not a

Chaseman's, of course," he smiled with a knowing glance at Jonathan's suit. Jonathan tried to stop laughing; these people and their clothes, even the Butler could recognise them!

He unpacked his things, and was preparing for a bath when he heard distant voices in the corridor. Feet were hurrying towards his room. Wondering what was happening, he looked out of the door. A girl was a few feet away, dressed in riding clothes. She reminded him a bit of Victoria at Frodsham.

"Who the hell are you?" she demanded with that same annoying superiority.

He was instantly irritated, and responded with "I'm a guest of Edward's."

She glared at him. "Do you mean Lord Erinmore?"

"If you prefer."

"I do and please remember that in future."

He was so astonished that he laughed. "You must be Lady Jane, my name is Jonathan Hare," he said, holding out his hand.

She gave him a withering look and turned abruptly, disappearing into a room the other side of the bathroom.

He shrugged and went into the bathroom. He was hardly into the bathwater when there was a rattling at the door.

"Is that you in there, Mr. Hare? What are you doing in my bathroom?"

He thought it was rather obvious, so he said nothing. There was an exasperated sigh from outside the door.

"I need the bathroom, *now!*"

He imagined he heard a foot being stamped. His mother's saying came to him. 'Always respect a lady's wishes, then she may respect yours'. At the time it had sounded like yet another Victorian epithet.

He sighed and got out of the bath. "Give me two minutes and I'll call you," he shouted through the door.

But when he emerged, she was standing there with her arms crossed.

"I don't want you in this room again!" she snapped as she pushed past him. Out of her riding outfit she was not exactly pretty and certainly not attractive.

He found a dinner jacket laid out for him together with a semi-stiff white shirt and a double-ended bow tie.

"Oops," he said to himself, "How do I tie this thing?"

He had plenty of time, thanks to the hurried bath, so he dressed and used the brush on the stand to smooth his hair. He slipped into the trousers and jacket and examined himself in the mirror. He saw not a bad likeness to the men pictured in the pages of Tatler. It was a pity about the tie. Nothing for it but to get some help, he thought, so he walked down the corridor towards the stairs.

As he did so, he heard a girl's voice calling, "Is that you, Jane?"

A door opened and a young and very pretty girl came out. She stopped when she saw Jonathan.

"Oh, are you the guest for the dinner? Lord Erinmore was telling me. I am Germaine Boisin, Jane's friend."

He heard the French overlay. "Vous avez raison, ma'mselle. Je m'appelle Jonathan Hare."

They shook hands, she was laughing. "But excuse me, I am to speak English when I am here. Did you know that your tie, she is not done yet?"

Jonathan shrugged in the Gallic fashion. "I never could get it to look right."

She looked at him for a moment, and decided with a grin.

"Come in here," she said, leading him into the room.

"Better leave the door open!" she laughed, but there was a teasing undertone there. She stood him in front of her mirror and performed a minor miracle on the tie.

She was just doing the final adjustment, standing close to him, when they heard a voice at the door, "Really, Germaine, must you always be making up to the men!"

Lady Jane disappeared in the direction of the stairs.

Germaine laughed. "She is so very English, she thinks men are just for marrying!"

They talked for a while; she mentioned that they were on holidays from Oxenham.

"I know someone who was there, Victoria de Quincy," said Jonathan.

"Oh, yes, but she was a Senior Girl, she has left now. Very nice, but we didn't meet very much."

Jonathan told her that it was the same at College; juniors didn't mix with seniors. Just then the gong went and they walked down together. As they approached the dining room, she slipped her arm through his, which seemed to Jonathan to be the natural thing to do.

Lord Erinmore and Lady Jane (Jonathan was practising his titles) were waiting. While Germaine at fifteen had a young woman's figure and was dressed in a flatteringly simple dress, Lady Jane was almost painfully thin and was wearing a fussy satin evening dress that looked too big for her. As they entered, Jonathan noticed that Edward was looking at him with a frown.

Edward was thinking that Jonathan reminded him of someone; at School perhaps? He thought it was quite unnerving how a dinner jacket could transform a man. He stood up rather abruptly and welcomed them.

Edward sat at the head of the table with Lady Jane on his right; Jonathan was next to Germaine, which suited him well.

Travis supervised the meal with help from a waitress called Daisy. They were the only servants. The conversation centred on Germaine, who sparkled with the attention from the two men. Lady Jane sat morosely staring down at the table, even though Germaine tried to encourage her.

"Mr. Hare knows one of the girls who was at Oxenham, Jane, Victoria de Quincy, fancy that!"

Jane showed no interest, but Edward looked up sharply. The meal progressed with a fish course followed by roast beef. Everything reminded him of lunch with Sir Roger; the food was good but uninspired. For a moment he recalled the effect on his palate of Charmaine's cheese and pâté.

Two wines were served, which seemed to overpower the food. The dessert was called "summer pudding", which, when his mother made it, was a tasty way of using up left-over cake and fruit.

As the meal ended, Germaine said, "We had such a good ride, didn't we Jane?"

Jane, who had been mostly silent, said, "You may have done, but it just made my legs stiff. And I didn't get much of a bath, either!" She was glaring at Jonathan.

Germaine hastened to fill the gap. "And do you ride, yourself, Jonathan?"

Jonathan wondered why these girls seem so fascinated with horses. He had drunk more wine than he ever had before, and Germaine's exuberance had loosened his tongue.

"The only thing I can do with a horse is to plough a straight furrow."

There was a silence.

Lady Jane sniggered, "Well, Germaine, no wonder you like him, he's just like your stable boys in France."

Edward had seen this coming. "I think that's enough Jane, perhaps you and Germaine will leave us now."

He rose, as did Jonathan. Lady Jane was blushing, whether with rage or embarrassment, it was hard to say. She and Germaine hurried out of the room. Edward sat down and motioned to Jonathan to do the same. "Shall we have some port?"

Jonathan declined. "I want to do a preliminary examination of the safe after dinner, sir," he said.

Edward cleared his throat. "I should tell you something about Jane; she seems to have taken such a dislike to you and was rather a bore tonight. Rude to you, I'm afraid."

Jonathan appreciated Edward's empathy. "We didn't get off to a very good start, sir, I think I stole her bath!"

Edward laughed, "Oh dear, you really crossed her path, then. But you should know this; she was only thirteen when her parents died, her Nanny had looked after her, did a good job, far as I know. There was nothing much for her here, so I sent to her to Oxenham. She hates it there, apparently. Actually, she doesn't even like horses much, only goes out because Germaine is here. Sad really."

There didn't seem much that Jonathan could say.

There was another silence; Edward suddenly asked, "Related somehow to Sir Roger, are you?"

Jonathan spluttered. "Related, sir? Hardly!"

"How do you know Victoria, then?"

Jonathan found himself thinking that Edward was smarter than he had first thought. A version of the truth would have to do.

"Do you know their place at Frodsham, sir?"

Edward shook his head. Jonathan felt on safer ground. "Helped her out of a spot of bother there a couple of years ago now, ran into her at the Society again, not long ago."

"Met her mother, have you?"

Jonathan grimaced.

"Enough said," smiled Edward, "Formidable lady, very beautiful but, well, too much of the dramatic persona for me. Could have been a major star, but ran into some scandal, forget what. Married Sir Roger on the rebound, apparently."

Jonathan was fidgeting, which Edward noticed.

"Oh, you're right, getting late, let's have a look at the damn safe then! Leave the girls to themselves, better that way." He winked, pouring himself a hefty glass of port.

Jonathan needed his tool case. He excused himself and trotted up the stairs to his room. As he passed Lady Jane's room, he heard voices. Germaine was saying something soothing, but Lady Jane's voice was raised.

"I won't apologise, ever!"

He shrugged, and got his case. To his amazement, when he went past the room again, he could have sworn that he heard crying.

In the study, Edward was sitting at the desk. "Now, how do you go about this sort of job, Jonathan?"

"Normally, sir, it's pretty straightforward with a production safe. They're made to a pattern that only varies slightly with the manufacturer. Once you know the internal structure, it's really trial and error. Can be time consuming, though." It was another bit of preparation to get Edward out of the way.

"Fascinating!" said Edward, leaning forward.

Jonathan went to his case and extracted his new stethoscope. Edward had just about finished his port. He got up.

"What on earth do you have there?"

Jonathan explained that a stethoscope was a standard tool for safe opening. "Used all over the world, sir, it's surprising how many people forget combinations! This one is more sensitive than others."

"Can I try it?" Edward asked.

Jonathan wasn't ready for this, so he took the foam safety pad and fitted it over the contact piece.

"In a moment, I have one test to do." He applied the contact piece and listened as he moved the dial. As he expected, the safety pad had damped down the sound; there were no clicks. He offered the earpieces to Edward, who listened with interest. "Can't hear a thing!"

"Exactly, no wonder the previous attempts all failed."

He tried some misdirection. "Here is our problem, sir – the dial mechanism seems to have disconnected itself. Very unusual, but as things are now, we have a major problem. And you wouldn't want a gelignite solution!"

"Certainly not, blow the whole house down, what!"

Jonathan decided to play another card. "I may be a while here, sir."

Edward went back behind the desk and finished his port. "Have to stay with you, rules of the game."

Jonathan put down the stethoscope, wondering whose game was being played. It was clear to him now that he was not going to have the option of assessing the contents of the safe, so there was not much point trying to outstay Edward.

"Perhaps we should call it a night, sir, the wine has made me a bit slow."

Edward seemed relieved and got up, jingling some keys. "Have to lock up, keep out the bogey men, you know," Edward grinned at him, "I always feel like a jailor carrying these around. Shall we start again after breakfast?"

Jonathan nodded and said good night, carrying his case up the stairs.

As he passed Germaine's door, he saw that the light was still on. He was at his door when he heard her behind him. He turned to see her holding a finger to her lips and nodding in the direction of Lady Jane's room. She waited, so he opened his door; she followed him in, pushing the door quietly closed. She hurried over to the bay window, motioning him to join her. Jonathan was very uncomfortable, her hair was down and she was in a dressing gown. And what was that about her and stable boys, what a snide comment from Lady Jane. He sighed, wondering what this was all about.

Germaine was looking at him appraisingly. "Do you like me, Jonathan?" she asked.

He tried a smile. "Bit young for me, aren't you?"

She giggled, "Not that way, silly! I mean will you aid me?" He waited.

She chose her words carefully, "If you don't like Jane, I would have understanding; she is always so awkward, and she was upset with you."

He waited with his eyebrows raised.

"There is no one here to love her for herself," she whispered.

He sighed, "We all have to get through life somehow, even if there isn't any love, it doesn't mean you can treat other people like dirt. She was rude to you as well."

"She was just jealous, you looked so nice in your smoking and you didn't even try to talk to her, you and Edward. But you liked to talk to me, yes?"

Jonathan smiled. "It's a pity she doesn't have your, um, élan."

"Oh, Jonathan, I have the élan, you think?" She was flirting again.

He thought it was time to change course.

"Now, what did you want me to do?" he said pointedly.

She pouted, but it seemed to be in good humour.

"If Jane makes the apology tomorrow, be 'gentil', would you do that for me?"

"Me, 'gentil'?"

"Oh yes, Jonathan, it would mean a lot to me!"

He gave in. "Just for you, Germaine. Now you must go."

They moved towards the door. She turned suddenly and put her arms round him. Before he could protest, she had kissed him demurely.

"I thank you for your kindness," she breathed.

He was exhausted, and tried to sleep, but couldn't resolve the conflicting demands. He thought of that massive old bully ordering him around. Then there was Sir Roger, playing such games. What did they want with him? He was just trying to earn some money for University, and, if he had the special skill needed, why not use it? He fell asleep and dreamed of running down the main street of his home town stark naked.

EIGHTEEN

Caught in the Middle

The next morning Jonathan woke feeling hungry, so he dressed and went down to the dining room.

"Good morning, Mr. Hare," said the ever-present Travis. It wasn't a particularly warm greeting.

Jonathan shrugged mentally; Edward had treated him well so whatever Travis felt didn't really matter. But there Jonathan was wrong.

He had no idea what to do, breakfast in a grand house was a new experience. To buy some time he walked over and stood to one side of the great window. It provided a view of a rather dilapidated formal garden, surrounded by low balustrades. Every now and then a statue adopted a classic pose. It left him with the impression that it had once been a grand sight, but had been neglected for some time.

He heard a door open and the rustle of skirts. He could see Jane, well Lady Jane, he supposed, reflected in the window. She didn't sit down but approached a side table bearing a number of silver dishes. Remembering the first principle of camouflage, he kept quite still and watched as she helped herself from the dishes, setting the lids to one side. Travis hurried over and replaced the lids. She didn't appear to acknowledge Travis, but sat down and started to eat.

Jonathan's hunger got the better of him, so he walked over to the side table.

Lady Jane was startled.

"How dare you come in here and spy on me? Travis, perhaps Mister Hare would feel more comfortable in the servants' quarters."

Lady Jane's voice carried that superior tone that instantly raised Jonathan's heckles, but before he could respond Travis was at Lady Jane's side and was saying something in a low voice. She threw down her fork, pushed back her chair and stomped out of the room.

Jonathan was left standing in no man's land, not knowing what to do.

Travis approached him, murmuring, "Lady Jane is not at her best in the morning, perhaps you should take your breakfast now."

It was a broad enough hint so he carefully followed what Jane had done at the side table.

He was finishing the scrambled eggs and something that Travis called 'kedgeree' when Edward and Germaine entered hurriedly. They looked alarmed.

Edward was red in the face. "I say, what ever happened in here, Jane is in a terrible state!"

Jonathan detected an antagonism that hadn't been there last night at dinner.

"Actually, sir, I didn't even speak to her, she objected to me being in here and, well sir, she just left the room."

Edward was clearly having a difficult time controlling himself. Germaine said something quietly that Jonathan couldn't hear.

"We'll talk about this later," said Edward, grumpily.

It was an awkward moment so Jonathan decided to leave the room. As he did so, Germaine came alongside.

"Was she rude to you again, Jonathan?" There was no animosity there, so he felt able to be frank.

"Well, she seems to resent everything I do or say. You asked me to be 'gentil', but I never got a chance, I don't know what Travis said but she just exploded and ran out of the room."

"Travis, he spoke with her?" Germaine's pretty eyebrows were well elevated.

"Yes, but I didn't hear what he said."

"You must be careful, Jonathan, Jane is the only Bellestream left to carry on the line, you know, and Lord Erinmore must take care for her."

"I did nothing, said nothing to make her so angry."

They walked together out through a side door, and towards the stables. In the distance they spotted a paddock with Jane standing at the fence. Germaine grabbed his arm.

"She mustn't see us together, she takes it so personally. Try to be 'gentil', Jonathan."

And she disappeared back into the house.

As he watched her go, he noticed a black Wolsley parked near the stables and out of sight of the main house. He found the touched-up spot above the rear wheel. So, he thought, it *was* me they were watching. He didn't know what to think; he had done nothing wrong, perhaps it was another part of Sir Roger's game, or Sir Hubert's. He was deep in thought, wondering why Sir Roger was the more powerful of the two, when he heard Lady Jane.

"Are you still spying on me, Mr. Hare?" she snapped. The superior tone was very apparent.

He was immediately irritated, but heard Germaine's plea, 'Be gentil!'

He shrugged, "I needed some fresh air after last night."

"Not used to wine at dinner, I suppose."

He had no idea what she meant. 'Be gentil!' he heard again.

"Do you mind if I walk on the bridle path?" he tried.

She turned to look at him. Her face was red. She seemed about to speak, then turned away.

He gave gentility one more try.

"How are your legs this morning, still stiff?"

She turned on him, her eyes flashing with anger.

"How dare you remind me of last night, you, you *ploughman*!"

He raised his hands in mock surrender. She strode away from him. He decided to go on with his walk. Gentility was proving to be too treacherous, he thought.

But when he came back towards the great house, she was still there, nervously feeding a horse with fresh grass. He stopped and reached the back of his hand out to the horse. It fluttered its nostrils and moved towards him. He cupped his hand above the nose; the horse pushed upwards into his hand with some snorting. He gave it a bit more attention, speaking softly to it, and then moved away. It followed him along the railing.

"Am I supposed to be impressed?" she asked.

He was about to respond angrily, when it dawned on him that she had used boarding school code. No one in such an environment could issue praise or compliments; they always used a negative protocol. "Not bad!" for instance, might have been considered too effusive.

What Lady Jane meant by her expression was actually, "I am impressed, but can't acknowledge it."

He laughed, and said, "I was ten years old when I learnt to plough, scared to death of the great beasts. I learned quickly that they only respond to a certain kind of treatment. If you're scared, they know it. You can show them who's the boss all day and they'll still give you trouble. But talk to them and show them some affection, and they'll respond. Once you've learnt that, any horse recognises it."

She was staring at him. "Then why don't you ride?"

He smiled at her. "You can't ride a Clydesdale, and we lived on a working farm."

"Where was this?"

"In Cornwall."

She asked him where.

He used some misdirection, "How well do you know it? Our place was out in the wilds."

"We have a place on the Camel River, but we haven't been there since," she stopped, unable to continue.

He decided to give gentility another try. "Your uncle told me about your tragedy. It must have been awful for you."

She seemed calmer. "Yes. Shall we go in now?" They walked towards the house.

She broke the silence. "Mr. Hare, my uncle will only tell me that you are here as a great favour to the family."

He looked at her, refusing to be drawn.

"Why *are* you, here?"

"You will have to ask your uncle, I'm afraid," he said.

She stamped her foot. "What's the big secret? I'm not a child, something's going on, I know it, first my uncle comes back from London all starry-eyed, then you arrive!"

She had turned towards him; he was once more the object of her wrath.

He grinned at her, looking pointedly at her foot.

She turned and ran away from him into the great house.

Edward was in the Study. Travis was expecting to be summoned, so he was able to appear from nowhere as soon as Edward rang.

"Travis, I understand that you were in the dining room and observed the scene?"

"Indeed, sir"

"Was Mr. Hare rude to Lady Jane?"

"Perhaps Mr. Hare startled her ladyship. I understand she had not noticed him standing by the window."

Over the years, Travis had become considerably more than a Butler. He had seen the family through several disasters and had found a way to cope with Edward's frailties. Edward had come to rely on him for advice, but carefully respected the difference in status that Travis expected.

"Got to be more to it than that, Travis, she was fit to be tied when we saw her."

"She certainly objected to his presence, sir; I had to remind her that Mr. Hare is a guest of your Lordship."

"She was rude to him, like last night at dinner?"

Travis raised his eyebrows to indicate that Edward should assume that he was correct.

Edward sighed; Jane and her moods were simply more than he could deal with. His knowledge of young girls was so inadequate that he failed to realise how far Jane's behaviour was beyond the norm.

"What do we know about him, anyway? Surely Sir Roger wouldn't have recommended him if there was any doubt about him?"

This put Travis in a difficult position. He had been thrown out of his usual calm demeanour when Jonathan arrived. It is a Butler's duty to 'place' a visitor, a procedure that requires years of study and must be put into practice almost immediately the door is opened. It is an acquired skill, consisting of assimilating the clothes, personal grooming, manner of speech, and social behaviour of the visitor.

Travis had at first been annoyed at the visitor's temerity in carrying luggage through the grand door, something that no-one with any social graces would have attempted. But Mr. Hare had been wearing a very acceptable suit, a Chaseman's if ever he saw one, wore a hat and had presented a more than decent card. He seemed comfortable with being met by a Butler and had used all the right protocols.

But Travis remembered that when he returned to the Small Drawing Room to escort Mr. Hare to the Study, the visitor was standing rather too close to the pictures, as if he was appraising them. All in all, Travis was unable to come to a conclusion, particularly because his Lordship had been, well, a trifle too welcoming. Another thought struck him.

"You will recall, sir, that Mr. Hare did not respond when Lady Jane spoke so rudely to him at dinner, and restrained himself when she did the same this morning. There will be those in your Lordship's experience who might have been less forbearing."

Edward looked up sharply at this pointed remark; rather unusual for Travis, he thought. But Travis was right. He sighed, thinking that Jane had once more created an unnecessary crisis. He would have to speak to her, he realised, not welcoming the task.

"Thank you, Travis, I shall bear that in mind."

When Jonathan came back into the house, Travis escorted him to Edward's study. He felt it was too much like being taken to the Headmaster's study for discipline. Perhaps he could pre-empt Edward's anger.

"I met Lady Jane on my walk this morning. I think I upset her again."

Edward didn't immediately reply. He was anxious not to upset the young man, his skills were so vital to the future of Mountbeck. And the lad had indeed been remarkably accommodating when Jane had been rude. He would have to buy some time.

"It's easy to do. Don't take it to heart."

Jonathan decided to try some more misdirection.

"Sir, I need to get some more technical data on the safe, may I telephone Sir Roger?" he said quickly.

The moment passed as Edward gestured towards the telephone.

When he got through, Sir Roger was anxious for his news.

"I'm afraid, sir, that I'm having certain difficulties."

"Safe too complicated?"

"No, sir, it's my instructions, they need, um, clarification."

"In what way?"

"It's difficult to explain over the telephone, sir, security you understand."

He hoped Edward – or anyone else for that matter – wasn't listening too closely.

Sir Roger seemed to have anticipated all this.

"Conflicts, Jonathan?"

"Yes, sir, which need to be sorted out before I can proceed."

"Give me a moment, please." There was a muffled conversation at Sir Roger's end.

"A car will pick you up and take you to York. There are several fast trains. Ring me here when you know which one. Someone will meet you at King's Cross. Come as you are, we will provide overnight things. I appreciate your confidence, Jonathan."

The telephone clicked off, leaving Jonathan to wonder what confidence Sir Roger was talking about.

He told Edward that Sir Roger wanted him in London. Edward seemed upset at the delay, but Jonathan promised he would be back as soon as possible.

Travis entered. "A car has arrived for Mr. Hare, my Lord."

Edward looked at Jonathan with astonishment.

So, Jonathan thought, the black Wolsley must be there by command of Sir Roger.

He explained this to Edward, who said, "Sir Roger must be mightily impressed with your talents, Jonathan!"

He ran up to his room to collect his money, saw his hat and remem-

bered old Bronsky's edict, so he took it with him. As he came out of
the room, Lady Jane was standing in her doorway.

"Are you leaving?" she asked.

He told her he had to go to London.

"Will you be coming back?"

"Tomorrow, I think, but I must rush, Lady Jane!"

She turned away with a rather obvious shrug and went into her room.

He ran down the stairs wondering why girls had to be this complicated.

At the great door, the black Wolsley was waiting; the man behind the
wheel was Sergeant Davies. As they drove away, he said, "Well, Mr.
Hare, we meet again, quite a chase you've led me, if I may say so!"

Jonathan was determined not to show his hand until he had spoken to Sir Roger.

"I have to get to York as quickly as possible, please."

Sergeant Davies laughed, "Wait 'til I show you what this thing
can do."

By the time they had navigated the hill roads and narrow streets of
York and arrived at the great arched station, Jonathan had had his
first experience of a police-trained driver on a hurry-up mission.

"Quick enough for you, Mr. Hare?" the sergeant asked.

Jonathan was unable to answer; he fled from the car into the station and took several deep breaths before he could look up the first
fast train. He rang Sir Roger and told him the arrival time at King's
Cross.

"How will the person recognise me, sir?" he asked.

Sir Roger laughed out loud. "Don't worry, Jonathan, they'll know
who you are!"

Travis was sitting in the kitchen, enjoying a cup of tea with the Steward, who seemed unusually fidgety to Travis.

"Has the expert for the safe arrived yet?" the Steward asked.

Travis told him about Jonathan's arrival, "I thought he should
have come to the tradesman's entrance, but his Lordship vouched for
him; very posh card he had, too."

The Steward looked perplexed. "What card would that be, Mr. Travis?"

Travis, whose job it was to remember such things, told him about the Royal Horological Society.

The Steward shrugged, "Well, I don't know, thought he was freelance, myself. Anyway, he's here now, so I can tell my contacts, you remember, the firm down south?"

The express train moved out of York and picked up speed, the telegraph poles flashing by. When they passed a train going in the opposite direction, the carriage rocked from side to side and the noise was deafening.

All the way to London, he prepared himself for the meeting with Sir Roger. There must be more to this than opening a safe. When Edward had heard that it was Sir Roger that wanted him in London, he hadn't seemed anxious about opening the safe, disappointed, but not angry.

It seemed strange that two powerful people had called on him to perform the same task. Perhaps the 'game', as Edward had called it, was between the Tudor House bully and Sir Roger. But they had nothing in common, opposites, in fact. He thought about that strange scene at the Tudor house; what was someone like that ugly bully doing in a beautiful, historic house in an estate with a gatehouse? He didn't *belong* there, not like the de Quincy's at Frodsham, or the Bellestreams at Mountbeck.

Lectures from his time at St. Eligius floated back into his consciousness. Some had been almost hysterical tirades about 'exploitation of the working class' and the absolute necessity for 'worker solidarity' in order to 'bring the aristocracy to its knees'.

He hadn't paid any attention and had ignored most invitations to join field trips to demonstrate against the Establishment. It hadn't seemed to matter to the demonstrators what idiotic logic was being pushed forward, like British communists protesting the NATO nuclear program, when it was there to protect us against Communist Russia. Jonathan sighed.

A thought emerged; what if the aristocracy *was* being brought to its knees? What would they do about it? They could hardly sit around waiting for the end; they had the French experience to alert them. Acquiring the Tudor house must have been a victory for the socialists. And what a victory! Compared to Mountbeck, it was a showcase. In fact, he realised, Mountbeck was hardly a good advertisement for the 'obscene wealth of the ruling classes'. One wing closed up, hardly enough servants, plain food, no central heating, neglected appearance, huge stables and few horses. Travis was everywhere, doing everything. Why would it be a target for the socialists? And, he thought, if I do what the bully expects, I would contribute to their success. The last piece of the puzzle seemed to fall into place; Sir Roger must be trying to prevent the opposition having his skills to use. Perhaps that was why he outranked Sir Hubert.

NINETEEN
I'll Take the High Road

The train weaved and jolted its way into the great London terminus. He put on the brown hat and adjusted the brim and suddenly felt more confident. He jumped down and walked past the huge engine, a lot bigger than the King at Paddington, but not so powerful, or so the Great Western propaganda said.

Once through the ticket barrier, he paused, looking around.

"Mr. Hare?"

It was the man in the shiny blue suit.

"Come with me, sir, good job they told me about the hat, I mightn't have recognised you."

They moved briskly through the crowd and out to the forecourt where a Rolls Royce was waiting. The man opened the back door for Jonathan to get in and, as he sank into the luxurious seat, a voice said, "Good evening, Jonathan." It was Lady Antonia.

For a moment he was too surprised to speak. He wondered what this part of the game was about, and played for time.

"I wasn't expecting anyone to be in the car, ma'am."

She lavished a smile on him, making him even more alarmed.

"Did you think the car was for you?" she asked.

Her beautiful eyes contained another message that he remembered from her antagonism at Frodsham. He wondered how much she knew about his work with Sir Roger, and realised that he had never seen them together. Alarm bells rang. He tried some misdirection.

"Did your man make a mistake, then?"

She sighed with frustration.

"I'm going to the Savoy, to dinner. The car will take you on to meet my husband."

There was an uncomfortable silence.

"Victoria and I are dining with her fiancé, Robert. Oh, did you know that she is now engaged?"

There it is, he thought, another barb, she just couldn't wait. He refused to be drawn.

"Wasn't it announced in Tatler a while back?"

She tried to hide her surprise.

He went on the attack, "Please convey my very best wishes to Victoria."

He sat back and looked at his watch, as if to say that he had other things on his mind.

As the car drew up at the great hotel, she gathered up her things and said, "Good night, Jonathan," in a tone of exasperated dismissal.

When he arrived at the Society he felt nervous. Sir Roger was his usual affable self, but Jonathan now understood it to be part of the game. They went into the study, but Sir Roger didn't seem to be in any hurry.

"How are things at Mountbeck? Have you met Lady Jane yet?"

Jonathan parried this with, "I seem to get on well with Lord Erinmore, sir."

Sir Roger smiled, "I expect Lady Jane tested your patience, she can be quite difficult at times. Did Edward tell you about her misfortune?"

Jonathan nodded. "Yes, sir, but however tragic it was, if she goes on treating people the way she treated Germaine and me, no one will ever like her, will they?"

Sir Roger sat back in his chair. "So you think that we only get in life what we deserve?"

Jonathan shrugged. "We get dealt a hand and have to play it the best we can. Very few of the boys at my first school had fathers, so we learned to do without."

Sir Roger seemed to be having trouble breathing.

"What about these conflicts you reported from Mountbeck?" he said, in a noticeably different tone of voice.

"Well, sir, when we met at the Savoy, you introduced the two people as Edward and Paul. I didn't talk much to Paul, but had a good chat with Edward. He talked about his steam engines at Mountbeck. My schedule required me to go to a meeting that Harry had arranged with someone I had never met before, a big man, very powerful. He never gave his name, but I won't forget his face. He seemed to think that he could order me around, sir. He gave me an assignment that began to sound similar to the one you gave me. He said it was for a Lord Erinmore, who had approved it. I didn't connect the two until later, when I looked up Edward Bellestream in Debrett and saw that he lives at Mountbeck. Anyway, the assignment was to find out if the contents of the safe were valuable, I think he mentioned bank instruments and some sort of bonds, and if so to take possession and let him know. But there's no way I can do so, even if I felt it was, um, above board, sir."

"Why can't you?" Sir Roger asked.

"Because Lord Erinmore is following the 'rules of the game' and is there with me at all times. They're your rules aren't they, sir?"

"Yes, they are. You have just finished at St. Eligius, haven't you?"

Jonathan agreed.

Sir Roger smiled, "On a scholarship, of course. Did you never wonder what St. Eligius expected in return?"

"When I was sent there from Standish, it just seemed like another school for sixth formers where I could focus on my subjects. My "A" levels results are a credit to St. Eligius, at least Harry thinks so!"

"And what about the other subjects, don't they call them 'supplementals'?"

Jonathan realised that Sir Roger knew a lot about St. Eligius. "They were practical things, mostly the kind that have always interested me."

"Like opening safes and breaking into places?"

Jonathan felt a bit betrayed.

"But, sir, it was just an exercise of skills, we never broke any laws, in fact, they were very firm that we must always avoid that. And your own Sergeant Davies knows that Harry and I only opened safes as a service to others."

"But surely you can't have been blind to the socialist indoctrination. They attract the most radical speakers there, you know."

Jonathan had to admit to a degree of stupidity.

"I thought about that coming here in the train, sir."

He stopped, unsure of his next words.

"They tried very hard to interest me in their point of view, but I hardly ever listened. It all seemed a bit too emotional for me!"

Sir Roger smiled.

Jonathan chewed his lip for a moment. "Some of my friends did seem persuaded, now that I think about it, they went on demonstrations, I remember. My friend Charles dragged me along to a few evening lectures, but I was bored."

"You are a very focused young man, Jonathan, too focused perhaps, there's more to life than passing exams and enjoying one's hobbies. Tell me something about your home life."

Jonathan blanched. Surely he wasn't going to have to open that door? Perhaps he could tell Sir Roger a version of the truth.

"I live not far from Frodsham, sir, when I'm at home, that is, but that's not often, just school holidays. This assignment means that I'm home even less. My mother is a teacher, and I try to work whenever I'm home, to help out."

Sir Roger shifted uncomfortably.

"No father at home, then?"

"No, sir." Jonathan didn't want to offer any information.

"So not much social life, dinner parties, dances, travel?"

Jonathan agreed, reluctantly.

Sir Roger was finding this quietly depressing. His own upbringing had been a repetition of a pattern that had been established generations ago. When a family serves the nation faithfully for several hundred years, most domestic events become entrenched in family ritual. A boy's interests may be indulged for a while, but must give way to the development of those attributes that such service requires. Girls, of course were a different matter, they must be prepared for the Season and a suitable husband found for them, preferably one who furthered the family's interests.

"You start at University this September?"

Jonathan nodded.

"What do you see as your future?"

Jonathan didn't want to admit that he hadn't got a plan. His life so far had been dictated by the consequences of winning scholarships. Win a scholarship, go to this school, do well and keep your nose clean, pass enough Ordinary levels to go on to the next school and take Advanced levels, do well and go to University.

I'm a bit like a train on rails, he thought, other people decide where I go. But he couldn't admit this to Sir Roger. He had to say something.

"I suspect the people at St. Eligius will have things for me to do. At least, that's what I understood the other day."

"As I thought, Jonathan, but is that what *you* want to do?"

"Perhaps something will open up while I'm at Oxford, sir."

Sir Roger wondered whether this was the time to suggest a career in his service. He shied away from it and decided that there was plenty of time for that; meanwhile he had to keep Jonathan out of harm's way.

"Well, let's see what we can do about these conflicts. Your St. Eligius man expects you to produce financial documents and bonds, that sort of thing?"

Jonathan nodded, "If they are there, sir."

"Quite," Sir Roger mused, "And he told you that Lord Erinmore approves?"

Jonathan thought for a while. "Perhaps he meant that Lord Erinmore approves of me opening the safe."

"I would think that's more likely. Lord Erinmore would certainly not approve of you taking anything that belongs to the family."

"I believe the phrase was 'returned to their rightful owners', sir, whatever that means."

Sir Roger smiled. "Sounds like a piece of socialist propaganda to me! When is your Galdraith interview?"

"Next week, sir."

"And you have a minder at Mountbeck?"

Jonathan was confused.

"Minder, sir?"

Sir Roger laughed, "Oh, excuse me, Jonathan, I meant is there anyone supporting you from the St. Eligius camp?"

"Just Harry, sir, he's at Thirsk in the Station Hotel, seemed a bit put out about it to me."

Sir Roger nodded. "I'll talk to Lord Erinmore. We will provide you with some documents to satisfy your other assignment. It'll take a while to put them together, so you'll have to spin out the safe opening."

"That won't be difficult, sir, this is going to be a bigger challenge than I expected. The safe has a greater level of protection than I've come across before, it's not a model described in any of the literature."

With that, the interview ended. Jonathan stayed the night at the Society and left the next day for York.

Lady Antonia did not grace the Society with her presence often, but Sir Roger had learned that whenever she did there would be trouble. She stormed into his study without the courtesy of an announcement, trampling over the accepted protocols he had put in place.

"I have told you before, Roger," she announced without preamble, "that I will not have Victoria's future jeopardised."

This came across as a line delivered badly in a third rate theatre.

Sir Roger tried to contain his anger, "And what tragedy has befallen Victoria now?"

"Don't play the innocent with me, Roger, it's that Hare boy that you have such an interest in, he is once more exerting his influence upon Victoria!"

Sir Roger was lost. "Please explain how this could be so, Antonia, he was only here for an hour or two and is certainly not here now. How on earth did Victoria even know about his visit."

"You know very well that I had dinner with Robbie and her at the Savoy, and I suppose it just came up that he was on his way to see you. Victoria almost forgot that Robbie was there, wanted to know all about it, not that I could say much of anything, for all you ever tell me."

"So you were the one who started the fire?"

"Don't evade the issue, Roger, I demand that you put an end to this relationship. Quite why she finds him so fascinating is beyond me, but, no matter, Victoria will marry Robbie and I will permit nothing to get in the way."

Sir Roger sighed. He knew that he dared not push her too far. She was the keeper of a secret that could not be allowed to see the light of day, and she would expose it if he frustrated her. She had played this advantage to the hilt throughout their life together, demanding her own way in every circumstance. She had been initially grateful for his intervention, but had understood with cold calculation that one word from her could bring about a scandal in the highest social circles.

He would have to buy her off once more.

"Hare has a most important task to carry out, Antonia, and I will not jeopardise that. He is now far from here and I can see no way that he will run into Victoria again. Perhaps you can avoid mentioning his name to her and get her away from here. I'm sure that there are arrangements to be made at Robbie's place."

This was a masterstroke, for he knew that she would extract a fearsome settlement from the Dornoch family, using all her guile and charm. If she and Victoria could be persuaded to spend some time in that remote Scottish estate, it would give him the opportunity to dispense with Hare's services.

For all his unique repertoire of skills, Hare was, of course, a quite unsuitable person, with no family and no money. He thought about the lad's reaction when he had dangled that carrot of a monthly stipend in front of him. He had had no intention of actually paying it, of course, but Hare had bitten on the bait and he had stored away the fact that the lad was susceptible to the lure of money.

But behind this pragmatic thought there was another, deeper concern. He was reluctant to admit it, but the lad carried with him some special quality. His appearance and mannerisms seemed to contradict the circumstances in which he found himself. Even Antonia had noticed that that the lad could easily pass for a socially acceptable young man, and Victoria had obviously found some form of friendship with him. Sir Roger recalled her anxiety when the lad had set her straight in the Savoy.

He would have to stop this line of thinking, he realised, his responsibilities weighed far too heavily for any personal concerns to intervene. He must get Antonia out of there before she compromised more of his operation.

Rita had heard from the Headmaster; she was to monitor the gang's intentions closely, preferably acting as a minder for Jonathan. She had asked to meet with Arthur and Sailor Wilson. They were in an upstairs room in one of the Billiard Halls. The meeting wasn't going well, because Arthur was adamant that he was going to demonstrate to the manor that Jonathan had been dealt with and, if he had the case of diamonds, to get it back.

Rita was furious.

"You're making a big mistake here, Arthur, the lad hasn't got the diamonds, and he had nothing to do with Ronnie's capture."

Arthur didn't care, "Not what it looks like to the manor, Rita," he snapped.

"What you don't understand, Arthur, is that my people have a special interest in him, and have him on a high profile job right now. If you bugger them around, there'll be consequences."

There was a stony silence. Rita played her trump card.

"Well, I know where he is right now. Tell you what, Arthur; I'll take Sailor to meet him, he can check on the case first. That will clear that up. Then Sailor can question him and find out what you want to know. Believe me, Arthur, you don't want to mess with our interests in the lad, it'll be far worse than losing the manor."

Arthur was spluttering with rage. "You threatening me, Rita?"

Rita laughed, "Only if you try and strong arm your way out of this."

Arthur brooded for a while. "What do you think, Sailor?" he asked.

Sailor Wilson had risen to his lofty position more on brawn than on brain, but he thought this was a low risk opportunity to get out of the manor for a while. Things had been a bit too hot lately, outside of Dockland there were rozzers round every corner, he needed a small army of watchers to move about.

"Can't see how we can go wrong, Arthur, have to go by car. Me and Rita can go by the cab route to Watford, pick up a limo there." Arthur understood by this that Sailor would be dressed as a taxi driver with Rita as his passenger, and that they would transfer to one of the gang's larger cars at their depot in Watford.

Mr. Frederick Broomhead, a name he had had to live with for far too long, was debriefing the Count. The investigation had been frustrating at first, and it wasn't until someone had put the name de Quincy into play that it dawned on them that Jonathan must have some part in police activities. A troll through press releases eventually gave them the connection to the phrase "I'll need cover from Harry, sir." It was easy enough to pick up Harry Sparrow's name from reports of Ronnie Grey's arrest. But even the Count, for all his experience in the games played in the higher circles of commercial and political power, couldn't initially see why that should place Jonathan into such a key position.

When Jonathan arrived at York, Sergeant Davies was waiting, and drove them at a reasonable speed through the moors towards Mountbeck. He seemed amused about something.

"Seems you've got Sir Roger's confidence, surprise to me. He's a hard man to please is Sir Roger."

Jonathan waited.

"Good man to keep the right side of, I'd say!" prompted the Sergeant.

Jonathan thought this wasn't exactly how he saw Sir Roger, so he said nothing.

"Good boss though, as he ought to be, bred for it, like his whole family."

This finally interested Jonathan. "What do you mean?"

"Been de Quincy's in that sort of job for generations, pity it'll end with Sir Roger. No son and heir, you see."

Jonathan nodded, but couldn't think of anything to say.

TWENTY

Softly, Softly Catchee Monkey

As Jonathan entered the Great Hall, Travis greeted him with pointed reserve.

"A Mr. Sparrow telephoned and asked you to ring him. And I should tell you that Miss Germaine left us this morning. I understand there is a family emergency."

But Jonathan sensed that Travis was sending another message, perhaps a warning that Germaine's absence might create a problem.

"Thank you, Travis. Oh, and thank you for finding the dinner jacket."

Travis inclined his head, led him to the Study and opened the door.

"Mr. Hare has returned, my Lord."

"Good of you to hurry back," Edward said. "I have heard from Sir Roger. Take a seat. How long will you be here, do you think?"

Jonathan heard another sentiment behind this question, as if Edward wanted to get rid of him. He explained that he had to be in Oxford for the Galdraith interview the next week.

Edward nodded. There was an uncomfortable silence.

"Did Sir Roger mention the package he is sending?" Jonathan asked.

"I have to give it to you unopened. Roger said something about a safety play, but it's all too cloak and dagger for me."

There was another silence while Edward sat drumming his fingers on the huge desk.

"I don't know what happened, but Germaine has rushed off. She's been a good friend to Jane, you know, keeps her company. Pity there aren't more young people of Jane's age here. Bit difficult to keep her amused all summer as things are."

Jonathan thought he saw what was coming.

"Does Jane have any interests other than horses?"

Edward looked uncomfortable. "Darned if I know, Jonathan, I rather relied on Germaine to fill in the time. Oh, I suppose Jane does have a rather grand collection of dolls in her room, but she won't let anyone near them."

Another uncomfortable silence settled on the two of them. Jonathan put on his stone face.

"Look, Jonathan, even if Jane has taken a dislike to you, you two will be bound to run into each other. Perhaps there is something I can do?"

Jonathan sat back, racking his brains. The last conversation with Jane came back to him; she had wanted to know why he was staying at Mountbeck.

"Sir, is there any reason why she shouldn't be told why I am here. She asked me, but I thought it better to keep quiet."

Edward looked concerned. "Good point, it is her future after all. Roger did say that the fewer who know the better, but I shall put that to him."

Harry Sparrow thought that Thirsk wasn't a bad little place, but it was a desert compared to the Smoke. He missed the liveliness of the East End, with its pubs and its determination to have a good time come what may. He was angry at being relegated to supporting Jonathan even if he did understand the explanation. He had to admit that Jonathan was a wiz at safes. He was green as grass when it came to living in the real world, but the lad could hold his own with the toffs. Harry had become quite fond of him, for all his snotty ways. He'd certainly boosted Harry's standing around Dockland.

He had done some spotting for Jonathan, taken the bus out to the village of Heckmondsley and sorted out the situation at Mountbeck. The local pub had been a revelation; great ale and food enough to sink a battleship. Edith the middle-aged barmaid was nice; she'd made him welcome, hadn't she? She was a chatterbox, though, nearly talked his ear off!

She knew everything that was going on at Mountbeck; the disappearance of the young Duke and Duchess, the steady decline in the estate with no one in charge. That Abercorn property would make a lovely estate on its own and would solve all their problems, wouldn't it? Her daughter Daisy was in service there, not that there was much to do, most of the great house was boarded up, wasn't it? Daisy had told her about the new man, some sort of expert there to help his lordship. He was young and attractive but had no eyes for Daisy, more's the pity. He'd arrived with a case chained to his wrist, hadn't he?

Harry picked up on this and probed gently at the story. Apparently there was much coming and going, the young man had rushed off to London, had a car drive him to York, but he was back the next day, though.

"Oh!" said Edith, "and he's always upsetting Lady Jane, not that that's difficult, according to Daisy."

Harry had smiled to himself; he could just see Jonathan's face if anyone tried to play hoity-toity with him.

Jonathan went up to his room, passing Jane's door, well, Lady Jane's door, he supposed with a sigh. He heard some noises like a small animal in distress. He shrugged; he might as well accept what Edward had said and try to avoid any confrontations with her.

Going in to his room he closed the door firmly; he wanted to check that his tool case hadn't been compromised while he was away. Everything was in order; he had placed the end of a match under one of the hasps and it was still there. Then he noticed a small envelope on his dresser. The writing was unfamiliar, but there was a tiny fragrance which reminded him of Victoria's letters.

There was a note that read:
'*Cher Jonathan:*

When you read this billet I will have absented myself. It is better that Jane can not see us together anymore, she thinks we are enamoured and it will cause a brouhaha. It would give to me pleasure if you will be amicable to her.'

It was signed 'Germaine Boisin, your friend' and she had underlined the word 'friend'.

He smiled, thinking that Germaine was special; he wouldn't mind being friends with her. She was pretty and certainly had élan, not like some English girls who were so, what was the word, 'wooden' perhaps? Couldn't say that about Jane, though, he thought, she was certainly quick to show dislike. In a way, though, even that was better than dumb indifference.

Suddenly he heard a series of crashes from Jane's room, the noise getting disturbingly louder. He ran down to her door and shouted "Are you alright in there?"

The noises stopped and the sound of an animal in distress began. He tried the door handle and pushed the door open. He went in and found the room in turmoil, broken dolls and pieces of china were everywhere. All he could see of Jane was a prostrate figure wrapped in a blanket on the bed.

"Lady Jane," he began.

She sat up violently, her face streaked with tears, her hair undone and straggling around her face.

"Get out, get out," she shrieked, "Leave me alone, I hate you!"

He realised that he ought not to be in her room alone and she seemed unharmed, physically at least. He had no idea what to do or say, so he raised his hands in a gesture of surrender. As he turned he stumbled on a doll, its head lolling to one side and an eye out of its socket dangling on a piece of elastic. Without any conscious thought he picked it up and went back to his room.

He listened for a while but could only hear the small whimpers. He couldn't decide whether such excess of rage and despair was normal for a girl of her age. He'd better get some help anyway.

He went downstairs and found Travis and explained; Travis

looked at him with alarm. It was the first time Jonathan had seen Travis show any emotion.

Travis was wondering what this young man was doing interfering in family affairs; he mustn't discover the weakness shared by the two remaining Bellestreams, the extreme mood swings and dark depressions. He thanked Jonathan politely and said he would see to Lady Jane. It was a rather abrupt dismissal, thought Jonathan, but was glad Travis had taken the responsibility off his shoulders.

Sailor and Rita were on their way up the AI road in the gang's limousine. Sailor had got rid of the taxi driver's clothes and was wearing a loud off-white jacket and brown trousers that he thought made him look 'real swish'. He'd made Rita sit with him in front of the glass partition. A young stuck-up bit like her alone in a nice big car, it was going to be easy pickings, he thought. He drove well and fast, barging less expert drivers off to the side with a blaring horn. Rita pretended not to be scared but was biting her lips by the time they got to Peterborough.

Sailor sent her into a pub to get sandwiches and bottled beer. She started to object, until she remembered that Sailor was a wanted man. While they ate, she slowly became aware of his demanding little eyes running over her body. It wasn't flattering and her alarm bells went off. When they had finished their food, she rummaged in her handbag, pulled out her manicure set and started to examine her nails in some detail. She extracted a cuticle tool with a sharp enough edge, and held it hidden in her hand.

Sure enough, Sailor started his approach run, telling her he had always fancied her, nice girl that she was, beautiful legs, all the men thought so, blah, blah. His hand strayed across and started to massage her knee, the fingers sliding under the hem of her skirt. She let him get under way for an inch or so, then dropped the pointed end of the tool onto the back of his hand.

Sailors let out a few incoherent swear words, amongst which she heard the word 'bitch'. She kept a light pressure on the tool until he took the hand away.

She looked at him with a smile.

"Come on, Sailor, you're old enough to know better. Don't forget who I report to – you wouldn't want to cross my people!"

Sailor grunted and started the car. They drove up the A1 for some time without speaking. Sailor tried again,

"Don't know what you're so fussy about, shacked up with that wide-boy Harry, not enough meat on his bones to give a girl like you a good time. Look at me, all man and then some!"

Rita was caught; she couldn't tell Sailor what her real relationship was with Harry; that would have blown her cover. And she certainly knew better than to enter into a discussion about Harry's performance compared to Sailor's. So she played another card.

"Darlene at the Ship is all the advertisement you need, Sailor!"

Sailor actually blushed and started to say, "How did," and then realised that Rita had the gen on him and Darlene. If Ronnie got to know, there would be hell to pay.

Sailor decided to play for time, "Come on, Rita, can't blame a man for trying, good looking girl like you, no harm done, eh?"

Rita tossed her head and said, "Just behave and all will be well."

Back in his room Jonathan was aware of comings and goings, some loud voices from Jane's room and then silence. He shrugged, it wasn't his business, but he found himself more shaken by Jane's behaviour than he expected.

Presently his eyes fell on the broken doll; he thought it might be an interesting repair job. The doll was quite large, dressed in elaborate clothing. He turned it upside down; as he expected, there was a fabrication hole in the lower back. He opened his case and took out the torch and some metal probes. Shining the torch into the hole he could see the intricate arrangement of strings and elastic that kept all the movable parts together.

It must be an expensive doll, he thought, the quality of the mechanism was excellent. He slid in a probe, hooked the elastic connected to the eye and attached it to the mechanism.

As he worked on the doll's head he grew more concerned about Jane's behaviour. Surely it wasn't normal, no-one could live with a person who flew into such rages. And she was at Oxenham, so she ought to have been disciplined into better control of her emotions; that's if Oxenham was anything like Standish, he thought.

He had restored the head to its usual angle and was examining the doll thinking that it now looked to be in remarkably good condition when he remembered Harry's phone call. He picked up his tool case and went downstairs to find Edward in his Study

Edward was reading a magazine on steam engines.

"May I use the telephone, sir?"

Edward waved at the telephone and moved to an armchair. Jonathan detected another shift of mood.

He rang the Station Hotel and eventually got through to Harry, who was a bit curt.

"Took yer time, mate; but I'm just the hired help here, ain't I?"

"Sorry, I had to do some research, never seen anything like it. Talk about Fort Knox! Not in the main gate, yet. I'll ring you when I've made progress."

He hoped Harry would get the message.

Harry grunted, "I'll pass that on then, shall I?"

Jonathan agreed and hung up.

Edward cleared his throat.

"Do I understand that you went into Lady Jane's room?"

Jonathan was taken aback at Edward's sudden return to formality, but could only nod.

"That wasn't a good idea, you should have asked for help."

"Yes, sir," said Jonathan, "but I thought she may have fallen, there were several loud crashes that I heard even from my room."

"And what did you see when you went in?" Edward was sounding like a master about to administer discipline.

Jonathan felt a little irritated; he had gone to Jane's assistance and now was being given the Spanish Inquisition.

"Sir, Lady Jane was upset and her room was in a mess. I didn't know what to do, so I spoke to Travis."

"So you felt that Lady Jane was in need of help?"

Jonathan decided to play safe.

"Yes, sir, she was not her usual self."

"You know Germaine has left us?"

Jonathan nodded, watching Edward closely, looking for some clue. Perhaps Edward was suggesting that it was Germaine's sudden departure that had set off Lady Jane. But that didn't explain Jane's words to him, why would she hate him so violently?

Edward sighed, thinking that the effort to keep Jonathan away from the family secrets without antagonizing him was too draining. He simply had to get that damn safe open or the family would never recover. He would have to present something of the truth; the lad was too intelligent to be fobbed off with a smokescreen.

"Jonathan, Lady Jane has a disposition to such turns. The doctor is treating her, she will be better tomorrow."

Jonathan sensed that Edward was putting a brave face on what had happened. He recalled Travis' reaction, so unusual for him. Jane's problem was obviously of deeper concern than Edward had divulged.

"I'm glad Lady Jane is in good hands, sir," was all he could think to say.

Edward took this to be as good a result as he could expect. Time to change the subject, he thought, surprised at his decisiveness.

"Perhaps we should tackle the safe?"

The Mountbeck safe's central dial had a hundred gradations, and moved easily. Jonathan applied the stethoscope and to his amazement couldn't hear the expected clicks. He realised that, while this explained the failure of the previous experts, it left him with a doubly embarrassing problem. How could he explain this to Edward? He cast a sideways glance at Edward, who was deep into his magazine, so he sat back on his haunches and tried to unravel the mystery.

Those with any knowledge of combination locks know that the cylinder is one integral unit and can't disengage from the tumblers. Unless, of course, it was designed that way, he thought. Perhaps it had a sort of clutch to make and break the connection? So where would the clutch lever be positioned? He got up and examined the safe from all angles. It was as solid as a safe could be. He was getting desperate when he remembered a line from Sherlock Holmes, something about 'when you have eliminated all the possibilities except one, that is the solution, however improbable'.

Staring insolently at him was the handle, resplendent in its silver sheen. It was made of a white metal, coated with varnish. He pushed it downwards, expecting to meet resistance, but it moved easily. Something must be wrong, there was supposed to be a locking bar that only released when the combination was set. He put on the stethoscope again and moved the handle up and down. There was nothing to hear. Frustrated, he was trying to get the handle back to its original position when he heard a noise in the earpieces, and felt resistance. He pushed upwards and heard a loud metallic sound. The handle moved steadily upwards until there was a similar sound. The handle wouldn't go any further. He transferred the contact piece to the cylinder and turned the dial. The clicking started immediately. He took a deep breath and rotated the dial fully. He heard the welcome sound of the first gate closing which told him that the sequence started clockwise.

He sat back on his haunches and found that he was sweating. His reading on combination safes had never included this type of additional security, but it did account for the 'X" prefix. He recalled Tweedy's description of the effect of the Blitz on the Champion factory, this particular specification must have been destroyed in the explosion. Well, he thought, there was no hurry because the package from Sir Roger hadn't arrived yet.

He packed up his gear and said, "Well, sir, I've made some progress, but the next phase will take time. We both need to be fresh, so perhaps we should start when the package arrives?"

Edward had been watching, remembering Roger's warning. So the lad had solved the first problem, good for him. One of the hurdles had been negotiated and the problem with Jane suddenly didn't seem so serious. He felt surprisingly relieved.

"Good idea! What d'you say I invite Paul and Maria – that's his sister, you know – to come and stay for a while."

Jonathan frowned, "Paul, sir?"

"You met him at the Savoy. His name is Paolo, Count Passaglietti, actually, but we've known each other for years, so I just call him Paul."

"His sister is a real beauty," he added in a voice that Jonathan hardly recognized.

The next morning Edward joined Jonathan at breakfast. The mood was a bit brighter than the day before.

"Jane is feeling better this morning," announced Edward, "She is upset over her dolls, though, apparently she can't find her favourite, the one she calls Amelia. Bit of a mystery, really." Edward didn't seem unduly upset.

Jonathan had a stab of guilt; it would be just his luck that the doll he had picked up would be her favourite. He would just have to face the music when the time was right. He went up to his room and as he passed Jane's door, the maid called Daisy came out carrying a tray.

She gave him a look of disgust and tossed her head as she turned away from him. He was taken aback, thinking that Jane must have put Daisy against him as well. But when he went into his room he found the bed made and Amelia the doll placed carefully against his pillows. He felt himself tense; he would have to be careful. Perhaps a walk would clear his head.

On his way downstairs he met Travis.

"Lord Erinmore would like to see you, sir," he said, looking straight ahead.

Something was up, thought Jonathan; Travis had spoken with hardly concealed disdain.

What Daisy had said to Travis was, "Sitting right there on Mr. Hare's desk, Amelia was, nasty metal spikes next to her, Mr. Travis, I don't dare think what he might want to do to her!"

Travis had relayed this to Edward, who had received the news with exasperation, feeling once more under assault. He would have to get to the bottom of it without offending the lad; what on earth was he doing with one of her dolls at all, let alone Jane's favourite. He could accept that Jane's behaviour warranted some reaction, but this seemed excessively spiteful. But then why would Jonathan take the doll and let Daisy find it?

Edward was not looking forward to yet another test of his self-control.

When Jonathan entered the Study, he again felt a different atmosphere; it was beginning to annoy him. He had at first felt at home at Mountbeck, genuinely welcomed by Edward, and had assumed that the servants would take their cue from him. Instead he had begun to feel that the household had him under a microscope, with suspicion and hostility not far away. And Edward had changed his attitude several times. Jonathan realised that he held the strong hand, well, at least until the safe was opened, and that would have to wait until the package arrived.

Edward found that his hands were trembling slightly, never a good sign. He would have to control them; stiff upper lip and all that. He grimaced, remembering that awful Wall Game and the need to pretend that he enjoyed it. There was an idiotic epithet about some War being won on the playing fields of Eton, fat lot of good it had done him.

He looked at Jonathan and saw a young man who had gifts beyond his comprehension. Roger had said that the scholarship was pretty well in Jonathan's hands, and that presaged a stellar future with lots of doors opening for him. It was strange though that the lad also had these skills that properly belonged to the lower classes. He sighed, choosing his words carefully.

"Jonathan, I have been told that Jane's favourite doll is at present in your room. Can you explain that?"

Jonathan was prepared, but growing angry. He decided to be awkward.

"Yes, I can, sir," he said as lightly as he could.

Edward groaned inwardly, the lad was ahead of him.

"I'm sure you can, Jonathan, but would you please enlighten me?"

Jonathan had been observing Edward and had spotted that his hands were not quite steady and his face was a little flushed.

He shrugged. "It was broken and I repaired it. I just haven't been able to return it."

Edward was once again thwarted. Now, instead of protecting Jane, he had to acknowledge that Jonathan had done a kindness. And he must maintain the relationship with the lad at all costs.

"I see," he said, buying time, "so you're a doll doctor as well?"

Jonathan understood the reference to a Doll's Hospital, a fancy name for a repair shop for the playthings.

"Not really, sir, but they do have some interesting internal working parts."

"So I can tell Jane that Amelia is safe and sound?"

Jonathan nodded. It was becoming increasingly clear that he was never going to be accepted in the Bellestream circle, nor in any other like it. He recalled Lady Antonia's efforts to cut him out of that relationship with Victoria, not that it would have ever amounted to anything anyway. As he thought about it, he decided that he didn't need these people; he would just have to win this new Scholarship and make his own way in the world. It was then that he remembered Victoria's outburst, what was it, something about hating her life because it was so arranged? But arranged by whom? The thought of anyone arranging his life sent shivers up Jonathan's spine.

That night at dinner, he was taken aback when Jane appeared. It was inevitable, he supposed, but it made him feel uneasy. She was wearing a different dress that suited her more. She was subdued, and on the few occasions when she looked up, he noticed that her eyes were somewhat unfocused.

Edward was hoping that the dinner would go smoothly. He would have to be on his toes to keep the conversation away from dangerous subjects.

"Jonathan had to go to London on an emergency, Jane, he needed some assistance with the safe that he is here to open, you know, the monster in the Study?"

Jane looked up.

"So that's why you are here, Mr. Hare, to open the Mountbeck safe?"

Jonathan detected some emphasis on the word 'Mountbeck'.

Edward rushed in.

"Jonathan is an expert, Jane, he comes with the highest credentials."

She sniffed.

Jonathan told them about the car ride to York and the speed of the express train to London. Edward wanted to know about the great engine.

To Jonathan's surprise, Jane wanted to know about London and what he saw there.

"Oh, I ran into Victoria's mother, Lady Antonia, on her way to the Savoy, she was having dinner there with Victoria and her fiancé."

Jane was looking at him with a new, more focused expression.

"I thought it was strange when you said Victoria was your friend."

The implication was there; Victoria came from a different class and wouldn't associate with someone like Jonathan. He decided to ignore the barb.

"Yes, she's just an acquaintance. She moves in rather exalted circles these days," he said.

"You mean the Season, I suppose?" she said.

He thought he'd better draw the line somewhere.

"Yes, Lady Jane," he said forcefully, "Lady Antonia did explain that to me. It sounds awfully like a marriage market, doesn't it?"

He was expecting a fiery response, but was shocked to see tears in her eyes. She got up abruptly and left the room clutching a handkerchief.

Jonathan glanced at Edward, who shrugged.

"I'm sorry, sir, I shouldn't have said that."

"Oh, I think you restrained yourself, Jonathan. Perhaps this would be a good time to tell her about the doll?"

When he left the dining room, he could hear restrained sobbing. She was sitting on a hall chair. She got up as he approached.

"I suppose you thought that was clever," she began.

He held up his hand hoping it would have the same effect as when Sir Roger did it. To his surprise, she stopped and waited.

"No, it was unkind. I apologise, Lady Jane. And another thing, I have something of yours, a doll that I trod on in your room. I thought I had broken it so I repaired it."

He was proud of this version of the truth.

"You mean Amelia? So you had her all the time?"

She had stopped crying.

"Yes, she's very well made, she looks as good as new now."

She sat down rather abruptly. She wouldn't look at him.

"Can I have her now, please?"

He started up the stairs only to find her almost running behind him. She stopped at her door and he fetched the doll. When he gave it to her, she started to cry again and rushed into her room. But she didn't slam the door.

He went back into his room, but before he could do anything, there was a knock at the door. When he opened it, Jane was standing there with a different doll in one hand. The limbs dangled loosely and she was holding the head in the other hand.

"Show me," she said. There was a pause then she added "please." She was looking at him with some intensity, although her eyes still didn't look quite right.

"Come in, then," he said, "and leave the door open." After a deliberate pause he added, "please."

He put the pieces of the doll on his desk and opened his tool case.

"Do you know how dolls are made?" he asked.

She shook her head.

"The good ones have a hole so that if they get broken, you can get inside with a probe and repair them," he said.

Without saying anything she sat down next to him and watched as he re-attached the head first, pointing out to her that it was furthest from the access hole and impossible to work on when the other strings and elastics were in place. Eventually the doll was restored to working order.

She said nothing for a while.

"You know a lot about dolls."

He listened for some sarcasm, but it appeared to be a simple statement.

"Only the working parts, Lady Jane," he said, "I'm interested in mechanical puzzles of all sorts."

She stood and picked up the doll.

"Lucky for me, then," she said, and walked to the open door. She hesitated for a long moment.

"Thank you," she muttered, and hurried to her room.

TWENTY-ONE

The Craftsmen

Sailor and Rita arrived in Thirsk late at night. Harry put on a show for Rita's benefit, "Been a long couple of days, love" he said, winking at Sailor, who couldn't do more than grunt.

When Rita told Harry what she had agreed to do for Arthur, he was horrified. Jonathan might be a snotty little bugger, but he didn't deserve to be blamed for the capture of Ronnie. Harry had never got on with Arthur, never trusted him; he was up to something behind the gang's back, although Harry had no idea what.

And Rita was a dope; he had been forced to take her on by those Bessemer folk; they seemed to think she was a star, told him she was an aristocrat turned socialist, more like a stage-door whore, he thought.

As for having Sailor anywhere near Jonathan, what was Rita thinking? Sailor was as likely to use his fists as what little brain he had and would be briefed to carry out what Arthur wanted, regardless of what Rita had in mind.

He told her what he thought of her plan. As he'd expected, she defended it ardently. She told him it was just a way of keeping Arthur quiet, and when Sailor saw that Jonathan's tool case wasn't the one that Ronnie carried the diamonds in, the fuss would blow over.

It dawned on Harry that he was wasting his time. He considered his own position, which lay somewhere in the shadow between legitimate businessman and opportunist. His knowledge of that arcane world where everyone was a mug to be fleeced as effortlessly as possible was legendary. He was against all forms of violence, it just 'upped the ante' when there was no need.

Ronnie and Reggie enjoyed nothing more than intimidation; the manor had lost count of the number of jaws Ronnie had broken with that sucker punch, and all just for his sick pleasure.

Harry thought that the next gang might even resort to using guns. There had always been an agreement in the underworld that firearms would not be used, since it would only bring an armed response from the police, which was to nobody's benefit.

Not like those crazy Yanks, he thought, they solve every problem with a bullet; no wonder the murder rate was so high there. He thought of the number of times he had heard of the underworld disciplining their own when guns were used against 'the code', but had a premonition that this might not last much longer, there was too much at stake, with big money moving in and out through the warehouses, and Arthur was one of the chief operators.

Harry did well enough in the shadows, the consulting fees from St. Eligius were handy, but his main income was from providing expertise to those learning the 'trade'. He thought back to the film of Leather Lane and the 'paste special', one of his favourites. Jonathan had seen right through that scam, not the only one to do so, mind, but he had got the psychology right as well. He would have liked to take Jonathan to see the 'packaged goods' scam, perhaps the most profitable and most interesting.

He took a moment to relish the scene of a lorry loaded with goods, the 'pusher' standing on top touting the goods, "Unbelievable bargains, ladies, see these stockings, five bob a pair in Harrods, yours for only two bob, but wait, I'll throw in these six tea towels, just come in from India, love, really. And not only that, what about these socks, just right for that man in your life, ducks, three pairs, and now watch this! Bath towels, his and hers, beautiful quality!"

All the time the pile was growing in the pusher's hands, and all good merchandise, in case anyone checked. The pusher offered the whole pile for a pound, "First pound note, let me see them"; the shill waving the pound note got the pile, which was moved back behind the scenes all in good time. Now came the switch; the pusher slapped more and more piles together, grabbing pound notes as fast as he could until everything was gone. The mugs wouldn't discover that the stockings were cotton ones for nurses and everything else pretty obvious seconds until much later, and if they did, well a few replacements were just the cost of doing business. Harry wondered how many pushers he had trained, must be scores of them, that old warehouse echoing with the pitch script, Harry correcting the timing and throwing in some harassment to try and throw the pusher off. Just street theatre really, was how he saw it, old as the hills, bet the Frogs and Iti's did it just the same.

Jonathan was in the Study with Edward, telling him about the incident with Jane and the doll.

"Jane has decided that you're a magician with dolls," said Edward.

He was looking at Jonathan with unusual intensity.

"You went to boarding school, Jonathan, so you'll understand that she has had little opportunity to mix with boys of her own age. Germaine is the only friend she has, really. I feel we've let her down a bit, you know, not much social life here. So she probably has no idea how to relate to you. She can be difficult, as you've found."

"Yes, sir, but I know what you mean, my mother disapproved of the girls around where I live, so I didn't have many girl friends."

Edward pulled a face, as though to say "Mothers!"

Jonathan was encouraged. "Germaine is a good friend to Jane, sir, she asked me to try to be 'gentil', in the French sense, of course."

Edward smiled, "Languages not my strong point, but I recall that from Nanny, source of 'gentleman', as I recall. She needs a lot of gentility, I would think."

"Unfortunately, sir, I'm too short tempered, haven't given her much chance, really."

Edward laughed, "I don't think Jane would agree, from what she said last night."

Jonathan tried to contain his surprise. He thought he would never get the hang of the way girls behave, best to change the subject.

"Sir, there is something else. Did Sir Roger tell you about the, um, conflicts?"

Edward looked blank. "Conflicts? Concerning what exactly?"

Jonathan decided that he must face up to the situation.

"Another party has an interest in the contents of your safe, sir, I didn't realise it until too late. I thought I had two separate assignments, didn't connect the two until I was on my way here. I thought I could combine the two jobs, but I realised that wasn't, well, above board, sir." He waited.

"Go on," said Edward.

Jonathan groaned inwardly; he would have to tell the whole truth this time.

"I started out thinking that, if I knew what was in there, I could satisfy both Sir Roger and the other party, so I misled you into thinking that the dial mechanism was disconnected, trying to buy some time. But you didn't give me that chance, 'rules of the game', you said."

Edward was looking out of the great window. "Yes, I knew."

Jonathan was stunned.

"No man can serve two masters, Jonathan, so you had to choose, what? Can't sit on the fence all the time. Sir Roger told you about the other side?"

Another sporting analogy, thought Jonathan. He tried to remember exactly what Sir Roger had said. Mostly questions about St. Eligius, but he had used a phrase, 'socialist indoctrination', that was it.

"I went to a sixth form school called St. Eligius, on a scholarship. They were good to me and excellent in getting me through "A" levels, sir, but there were all these lectures and pressure to accept, um, socialist indoctrination. It never seemed convincing to me, although many of the other courses helped me to develop skills, like stagecraft and locksmithing."

Edward turned from the window. "Stagecraft, Jonathan?"

"Oh, yes sir, magician's tricks, misdirection, tricks of that trade, sir."

"Like the foam pad over the stethoscope head?"

Jonathan gulped, "Yes, I'm sorry about that, sir!"

Edward smiled, "You forget that Sir Roger had warned me! Tell me some more."

"People mostly see what they want to see, so it's not hard to misdirect people."

He thought for a while and remembered the Dick Powell hat.

"Clothes and hats change a person's external appearance, you don't need elaborate disguises, sir, that's why I find some of Sherlock Holmes a bit far-fetched."

Edward found this fascinating.

"Yes, when you came down in the dinner jacket, you reminded me of somebody I knew years ago, been trying to remember, but I'm not good with names. But what about all those Music Hall acts, gals in tights locked inside cabinets, swords thrust through, not a damn scratch on 'em!"

Jonathan laughed and explained how it was done.

"I think it's cheating really, sir, lots of variations, but just one basic ploy."

They talked about some of the acts that Edward had seen and Jonathan explained the various techniques.

"Actually, sir, what I like is the purely manual, the sleights of hand, although most of that is misdirection, the magician is always getting you to focus on something in one hand while he uses the other to extract a new scarf or pigeon. The tailcoat is usually a giveaway, that's where the props are stowed. Watch for things like the finger snap, because that's just to get you looking there."

"You'd better stop before you spoil all the fun. Though to tell the truth, Jonathan, we haven't been to a show in ages."

The Count's agents had found it difficult at first to penetrate the secrecy surrounding Scotland Yard. They had quasi-official connections with those police sections dealing with commercial fraud and particularly with the evasion of the Sterling Control Regulations and it was a chance comment in the canteen concerning the unusual number of meetings between Sir Roger and Sir Hubert de Quincy that was passed on as a matter of routine. As soon as the Count received that news, he made the connection to the Grey gang. He had been made aware of Arthur Salmon's arrangement to get round the payment problems associated with the gang's business interests, but he had considered this merely an unrelated piece of commercial intercourse. He had never thought about where Arthur would safeguard the bonds, but it would be in a special safe somewhere, and Arthur would be sensitive about it. So a safe breaker like Jonathan would be a major weapon in the police arsenal. Exactly how they would use him was still a mystery, but use him they would. The Count smiled. An investment in some increased surveillance might present some interesting longer term opportunities. His chest swelled; he was certainly 'looking beyond' this time.

The 'war council' that met that morning in Harry's room at the Station Hotel consisted of Harry, Rita and Sailor. It had not been a convivial meeting.

Rita was anxious to get the thing over with and pushed Harry into the spotlight.

"You're his minder, Harry, ring him and set up a meeting. All we need is for Sailor to see the case. You know it's not Ronnie's, so that will be that."

Harry held up his hand. "Wait a minute, Rita, how do we get Jonathan out of the house with his case? It'll look too suspicious."

There was a dull silence.

Sailor said, "Arthur ain't going to like this!"

Harry decided it was Rita's problem, and shook his head. She got up and strode around the room, thinking.

"Let me see that map, Harry," she said pointing to his Ordnance Survey. She ran her finger over it until she found what she wanted; she had a solution but it was not one she relished explaining to the men.

"Come on downstairs to the telephone," she snapped. When she got through, she said in a voice of some authority and certainly with nothing of the East End coarseness that she had recently adopted, "Travis, this is Annabel Winstanley, Lady Brockhurst's niece."

There were muffled sounds from the earpiece.

"Thank you, Travis, I will pass that on to my aunt. May I speak to Lord Erinmore?"

After a short delay, she continued in a voice full of social lubrication, "Lord Erinmore, good morning, I'm here in Thirsk hoping to be able to help my aunt. She is distraught; the lock on her Jacobean portmanteau has jammed. It's a family heirloom, my aunt feels responsible for its safekeeping, she can't bear to see it out of her sight. She has taken to her bed, poor thing."

She held the earpiece away from her head and smirked at them.

She responded, "Yes, you could help actually. I understand that you have an expert there who might be competent."

She listened.

"Well, if you could spare him, I will pick him up as soon as he can leave. I have a car and driver here."

There was a short delay.

"Noon would be excellent, Lord Erinmore, we can be in Beningham for luncheon."

Harry and Sailor were looking at Rita as if she had grown two heads.

Sailor was the most impressed. "And just how did you pull that off, Rita?"

Rita's voice returned to the familiar. She sighed, "You think you're the only people who know how to pull a scam? I went to school with the Brockhurst's daughter, awful little snot actually, but they have a place just outside York, so Lord Erinmore is bound to know them."

Harry laughed, "And who is Annabel whatever her name is?"

Rita smiled triumphantly, "See, Harry you don't even remember her name; 'Lady Brockhurst' is all that Travis would recognize and relay to Lord Erinmore and after that it's all good neighbourly relationships. Who cares who Annabel is?"

"Did Sir Roger explain about the documents that he is preparing?" Jonathan asked.

"Yes, apparently we shouldn't rush to open the safe, best to wait until the package arrives."

"Do you know what we will find in the safe, sir?"

"I know what we hope to find." Edward seemed reticent.

"It's just that the package from Sir Roger has to be credible when it gets to the other party."

Edward looked glum. "I wish Paul was here, he'd be able to tell you. Let me see, he said something about "sequestered assets," whatever that means."

Jonathan was astonished that Edward was so unprepared.

Edward cleared his throat. "I've never been at all good with figures, can't make head nor tail of the stuff the Steward gives me, pages of assets and figures, graphs and whatevers, they make my head spin!"

Jonathan decided that further questions would embarrass Edward. Then a thought struck him.

"Can you remember whether the assets list any works of art, paintings in particular?"

Edward frowned. "Only the family portraits, boring old duty paintings, most of them are hanging in the stairway."

Jonathan told Edward about the time he had waited in the Small Drawing Room.

"Oh, that was Marguerite's favourite room, did the décor herself, went up to Town and chose everything. She wanted something to remind her of France."

"There are two wonderful paintings, sir, if they're originals, they would be worth a small fortune."

"Yes, but really they will belong to Jane, you know."

Edward looked harder at Jonathan. "Don't tell me you're an art expert, too!"

Jonathan laughed, "No, but we had a good library at my first school, plenty of pictures. These two are French Impressionist, one may be a Van Gogh, the other a Sisley."

Edward grunted, "The Van Gogh that cut off his ear, went mad, painted sunflowers?"

Jonathan thought that was about as much as most people knew of him.

"Yes, sir, that's the one. The other painter is much less well known, but highly thought of, much more 'presentable', if you know what I mean?"

Edward laughed, "Not everyone wants pictures that dominate the room, eh?"

"What about the closed wing, sir?"

Edward looked apprehensively at Jonathan, wondering whether to disclose more family business.

"Why do you ask?"

Jonathan considered how to continue; an indirect approach would be best. "Perhaps the contents of the safe would be less important if there were some other assets. If the two paintings in the Small Drawing Room were originals, sir, they could fetch several hundreds of thousands of pounds at auction."

"How on earth do you know that?" Edward was leaning forward.

Jonathan blushed. "Our Librarian let me read some of the magazines reserved for the schoolmasters, sir, Tatler and Country Life and they carried articles on fine art, so I suppose I just absorbed the prices. Just seemed like another world to me."

He paused and remembered Frodsham.

"Actually the de Quincy's have a Sisley at Frodsham, not one of the better known ones, of course, they're all in Museums, but I'm sure it's genuine."

Edward was shaking his head. He got up and found a Country Life. "Show me!" he commanded.

Jonathan thumbed through to the advertisements. Sure enough there were several discreet advertisements of pictures for sale and an article on recent auctions at Sotheby's. A Stradivarius violin with provenance had sold for over half a million pounds.

"And that's not a particularly famous one, sir, not like the Lady Blount, if that came up for sale it would fetch a world record price!"

At that moment, the telephone rang.

TWENTY-TWO

Down the Rabbit Hole

Edward put down the telephone and smiled.

"Seems as if your fame is spreading; that was a call to help Lady Brockhurst. She has a wonderful place north of York, early Tudor, a national treasure, full of Jacobean furniture. We really ought to help her, she takes her position seriously, you know, protector of the heritage, what? Her niece said she is upset over a jammed lock. Just your ticket, I should think. Nothing we can do here for a while, anyway."

Jonathan wondered how others so far from London could know of his skills. Perhaps this Lady Brockhurst was a friend of Sir Roger's; if that were so, why wouldn't Sir Roger have rung? He shrugged, thinking that Edward wouldn't have agreed unless it was genuine. He had an idea.

"Perhaps Jane would like to come?"

Edward thought that was a grand idea and sent for her. She arrived in a sulky mood. Edward suggested that she might like to go with Jonathan to visit Lady Brockhurst's place.

Lady Jane chewed her lip for a moment then sighed.

"At least that will get me out of here, there's no one to talk to, now that Germaine has gone to visit her family."

Jonathan smiled to himself, thinking it would be too much to expect any graciousness.

Edward told her to be ready at noon; apparently lunch would be served at Beningham.

Rita was in full command and Harry was glad to let her have her head.

"Sailor, wear your taxi driver gear, make sure you have the cap on. I can't be in the car or Jonathan will recognize me. So drop me at the pub and pick me up as soon as you have Jonathan."

Travis entered the Study. "A limousine has arrived for Mr. Hare, my Lord."

Lady Jane and Jonathan went down the steps. Jonathan held the rear door open for her; she entered without any acknowledgement. He slid the tool case against the partition, under the folding seat. The chauffeur, a big man wearing a rather strange cap, was looking in his mirror. As soon as Jonathan was settled in the seat behind him, the car moved off rather faster than was usual in a stately driveway. They went quickly through the village, past the pub. A woman was standing in the forecourt, waving. The chauffeur waved back, but didn't stop. Jonathan thought the woman looked a lot like Rita.

Lady Jane was talking about Lady Brockhurst and her sad family history, all the line had perished in two World Wars, and only she was left.

Jonathan was nodding and grunting, giving the impression of listening, but thinking about the speed of the car. Perhaps not as hair-raising as when Sergeant Davies drove him to York, but not wasting any time either. Lady Brockhurst must be in a terrible lather, he thought.

It wasn't until he realised that they were passing through York that he began to worry. He had understood that they were going to an estate north of York. He tapped on the dividing glass. The driver pulled the car over and slid back the glass.

"Well, Mr. Hare, fancy meeting you, last time I saw you, you was in the Loaf, throwing Ronnie around like a sack of spuds!" Sailor was enjoying himself.

Lady Jane was not amused. "How impertinent!" she said loudly, "Kindly remember your place, my man!"

Sailor laughed out loud, "And who is this hoity-toity miss?"

Jonathan's worst fears were now a reality. He mustn't panic, he thought.

He turned to Lady Jane and said, "Be quiet, please, Jane, let me deal with this."

He looked at Sailor. "You must be Sailor, sorry, I don't think I know your last name?"

Sailor laughed again, "Save the smart stuff for Arthur, it's him what wants to see you. We're going to the Smoke for a nice visit."

Jonathan had been trying the door handle, but Sailor had spotted this, "Don't try it, doors are controlled from here, security comes in handy in our line of work."

Lady Jane was bouncing with annoyance. "I demand to know what is going on!"

Sailor raised a massive hand. "Listen little lady, your Mr. Hare is going to have a nice cup of tea with my boss in London. We didn't know you would be a couple of lovebirds, did we? Never mind, enjoy the trip."

He closed the glass and moved the car away. Once on the open A1 road, the car rocketed along, heading towards London.

Lady Jane was crying into a handkerchief, while Jonathan was thinking hard. Arthur must be the gang's boss now that the Grey twins were behind bars. He recalled the time he and Harry went to help poor old Bert, what had he said, "Arthur would sack me, soon as look at me." Anyway, he thought, there's nothing to be done until later. He became aware that Lady Jane was still sobbing. He reached over and took her hand, but she tried to snatch it away. He pulled her closer and said as softly as he could, "Come on, play the game, we're lovebirds, as far as Sailor knows."

She stopped crying and looked at him in alarm.

"What do you mean?"

He put his left arm round her shoulder and whispered in her ear, "I need to get into the tool case, so just play along. You have to help me or we may be in even more trouble."

"What do you want me what to do?" she said. She had stopped struggling.

"Do some cuddling. Make it convincing, for goodness sake."

She was blushing, "What am I supposed to do, make up to you like Germaine did?"

"Good idea, but take it slowly, come closer now."

He thought he sounded a bit like Charmaine giving that dancing lesson. He felt her moving closer, and to his surprise, she leaned her head on his shoulder, whispering, "Is this right?"

He moved his right arm round her; she was painfully thin and shivering. After a while, she felt warmer, so he decided to try the next stage.

"You have to pretend to kiss me, Sailor won't know, your head will be in front of mine."

He pulled her shoulder gently so that she had to lie across his chest, with her face close to his. He leaned back, reached out his foot and hooked the tool case so that it slid closer. As far as he could tell, he was shielded from Sailor's view. He was holding Jane close with his left arm, and as he moved forward again, he felt her lips brush his. She jerked her head away with a gasp, but remained close to him. He had the case's first cantilever clasp open and was concentrating on slipping the second free, when he realised that she was holding him quite fiercely. He looked at her and was amazed to see that her eyes were closed and she was smiling.

He was now able to lift the lid off the case and feel around inside. He located the picklocks and removed them, sliding them into his pocket. He closed the lid and engaged the cantilevered hasps.

He was breathing a sigh of relief when he realised that Jane was very close to him. He suddenly felt guilty that he had used her in this way.

"You can relax now, I've got what I needed," he whispered.

But she pressed closer to him.

"Perhaps we shouldn't move too quickly," she murmured, "it might make the chauffeur suspicious."

Jonathan relaxed for a while. It wasn't unpleasant holding Jane and he realised that it could be the first time that she had been this close to an older man. He was really only being 'gentil' wasn't he?

She seemed to be breathing regularly now, so he looked down at her. He was surprised that, relaxed like this, she had a certain potential beauty. Suddenly she came awake and pushed herself away. She sat in her corner, glancing at him sideways.

"Was that what you wanted?" she said.

He smiled at her. "Oh yes, Germaine couldn't have done it better!"

He had meant this as a compliment, but she didn't laugh.

Rita had taken the bus back to Thirsk and was explaining to a grim-faced Harry what Sailor had done. Harry had never seen her so shaken. He was fighting the temptation to say that he'd warned her. Instead he picked up the telephone and asked about trains to London.

"Look, Rita, if we let Jonathan get rubbed out by Arthur, you and me are in big trouble, so we'd better get down there, round up some help. I know a few tricks we might be able to pull."

Rita simply nodded.

Jonathan was trying to work out just how Sailor had been able to convince Edward to allow them to leave. Must have been someone well known with connections to the aristocracy, he thought. And that person must have known that he was at Mountbeck. Eventually, when he had reduced the list of candidates to Sir Roger, a shiver ran down his spine. Surely not, why would Sir Roger want him to leave the Mountbeck assignment? And would he be a party to kidnapping Lady Jane?

Then he recalled the interview at the Society, Sir Hubert grunting in the corner, not at all friendly, if anyone wanted to use him to get at the gang it would be him; and Sir Roger was his brother. Jonathan could make no sense of it, so he would have to wait to see what Arthur had to say.

It was evening when Sailor's car got to Watford. He drove the limousine into a covered garage, where several men were looking after the gang's cars. A taxi was waiting, and Jonathan and Jane were shepherded into it by a couple of the men. Sailor got into the back with them, took the tool case and looked at it carefully. He seemed puzzled.

"Open it," he said to Jonathan, who slipped the cantilever catches open and showed Sailor the inside. The stethoscope fascinated Sailor.

"What are you, a doctor?" he grinned.

Jonathan tried to conceal his nervousness, "A safe doctor, Sailor," he explained.

Sailor turned the case upside down and all the tools dropped onto the floor of the taxi. He grabbed the foam lining and ripped it out. It came away intact except for some small chunks of foam still glued to the case. There was nothing else in there.

Sailor scratched his head. "Well, chum, at least Arthur won't take it out on you for the diamonds."

Jonathan was lost again, wondering what diamonds Sailor was talking about.

Sailor threw the case to Jonathan. "You can put your stuff back in there. Come on, let's go and see Arthur."

He went round to the driver's seat and one of his men got in the back.

Sailor drove the taxi expertly, taking a number of smaller roads eastwards through Barnet and Hackney and then south into Dockland. Jane asked where they were, but Jonathan told her firmly to be quiet. She didn't complain much, and didn't seem to mind being jammed close to him in the back seat.

He took her hand and said, "It's just me they want to talk to; they have no interest in you. Sorry I got you into this." She didn't take her hand from his.

TWENTY-THREE

Hare and Hounds

W hen Travis got back to his Pantry, he was still annoyed that chauffeurs were so badly trained these days that they would actually disturb the gravel when departing from the front entrance. And there had been something about the cap that hadn't seemed proper. It was so unusual for Lady Jane to go anywhere without a chaperone that his sense of order had been somewhat disturbed.

The brandy eased his concern for a moment, but eventually he decided to make a discreet enquiry and telephoned Jardine at Lady Brockhurst's. Jardine was courtesy itself, and was pleased to hear from a fellow Butler, but when Travis introduced the subject of the jammed lock, there were several moments of confusion. Jardine was more interested in Annabel Winstanley, and it was some time before Travis could be sure that there was no need for assistance. He learned that Miss Annabel Winstanley had not been heard from for several years and Jardine was sure that Lady Brockhurst would be anxious to find out where she was. Travis said that he was unable to assist, since all he could recall was that Miss Annabel was perhaps in Thirsk.

Travis thought about the last few days at Mountbeck while he decided what he should do. The arrival of the young man with the silver case had been unsettling; he had thought that he was dealing with a presumptuous tradesman, carrying luggage indeed, even if it was chained to his wrist. But surely not in a Chaseman suit? He had been quite shocked at his Lordship's happiness when he saw Mr. Hare's card. Then, when he had returned to the Small Drawing Room, he had had the impression that he was only just in time to prevent the young man making off with the Duchess's paintings. He had been so disturbed that he had nearly forgotten to introduce the young man, he thought with a grimace.

But Mr. Hare had conducted himself with a natural grace, and his appearance at dinner had been so in keeping that Travis had begun to think that he was losing touch with the younger generation. The changes brought about by the two Wars and all the social upheaval recently had altered the established patterns completely. He thought of Daisy and the difficulty he had had teaching her to serve with any commitment. All she wanted was her pay and her days off, and she pouted whenever he asked her to stay late for even an hour. He sighed.

His thoughts returned to Mr. Hare, and the effect he had had on Lady Jane. She was sometimes the most unrewarding young lady, but what chance had she had, still stuck in her sadness after her whole family had been lost so tragically. She had been so rude to the young man at the table; he hadn't understood the words, but, judging by his Lordship's sharpness, they must have been quite unacceptable. What had caught his attention was that it was the first sign of jealousy he had witnessed in Lady Jane.

He had understood his Lordship's difficulty; it was vital to get that hideous safe open. He had guarded the secret of its contents as any Butler should, but the steady decline of the household with so little income was a constant challenge. So Mountbeck's future depended on Mr. Hare's ability to open the safe.

And yet Travis couldn't quite resolve his difficulty in placing the young man. He had none of the spoiled arrogance displayed by some of the titled members who had graced Mountbeck in the old days. He dressed appropriately and held his own with his Lordship. But the young man's technical prowess placed him in a class well outside any that Travis could relate to.

He had been most disturbed when Mr. Hare reported on Lady Jane's attack, for it opened a most unfortunate door into the present Bellestream difficulties. It simply wouldn't do for an outsider to know about their illnesses. And he had been initially shocked beyond words when Daisy reported that the young man had stolen Amelia and was about to destroy her.

Later, he had overheard the conversation in the Study when the real story came out, and later when she had expressed her admiration for the young man's ability to repair her dolls. So he hadn't been too worried when the two of them went off in the car, glad in fact that she was having some form of outing.

But what if he had been wrong all along and this stranger was a confidence man, who would take Lady Jane for ransom? He was so shocked at this thought that he downed the rest of the brandy, washed out his mouth and set out for the Study.

Edward listened with increasing alarm to Travis, who was more emotional than he could remember.

"But, Travis, surely Miss Winstanley can't be mixed up in anything so sinister?" Travis explained that Annabel had not been close to Lady Brockhurst for several years. Edward paced around the Study, wondering what to do.

Travis took the bull by the horns, "Perhaps you should alert Sergeant Davies, my Lord?" Edward brightened, "Of course, thank you, Travis, have him come in immediately."

The telephone call that Sergeant Davies made to Sir Roger set in motion a chain of events that involved the Commissioner of the Metropolitan Police and several sections of different Services that normally did not work together. Sailor's absence had been noticed and routine watches posted on several safe houses. As soon as the intelligence came in that the kidnapping had began north of York, a squad of specially equipped men set up watch at the gang's Watford depot. They were issued with cards setting out their conditions of service – to a man the squad had been told that this was a national emergency requiring an unusually high level of delicacy.

The urgent meeting between Sir Roger and Sir Hubert that Sergeant Davies' message had brought about was not a convivial one. It was all very well to throw the Hare lad to the wolves, but when Jane Bellestream got involved the situation changed entirely for the worst.

Both men understood the increased risk to them. Roger remembered the concern on the Messenger's face only too well.

Hubert noticed Roger's nervousness, unusual for him, normally so unflappable.

"We'll have to get someone into Dockland", he announced, and they quickly agreed that Sergeant Davies was best suited to work there, bearing in mind his report on the meeting with Harry and Jonathan. Sir Hubert invoked a procedure rarely used by the Met. It required the explicit approval of the duty Deputy Chief Constable for each County. Sergeant Davies drove from Mountbeck along main roads cleared by county police using barriers and cars travelling at high speed with headlights flashing and bells ringing. Scores of motorists lodged complaints afterwards about being rudely shunted off the road.

Arthur Salmon had heard from Sailor when he arrived in Watford. Looking at his watch, he decided to give directions to the gang bosses.

"Too late tonight, go home, be back here eight o'clock tomorrow."

He turned to Sailor's friend Freddy.

"Get a room ready, the store room next to the office will do. I want a guard on the door. Don't harm them. We'll deal with Hare tomorrow. Get some foam slabs from the warehouse, they can sleep on those. Freddy, stay and take a watch, give Sailor a hand."

The taxi driven by Sailor left Watford in a fleet of four identical vehicles. The surveillance squad had tailed two of them but these turned out to be West End taxis specially hired and paid for with instructions to pick up passengers at Watford; when they got there, the passengers had apparently found other transport. The drivers had shrugged, "Got paid anyway, didn't we?"

The squad reported this failure, but were quickly dispersed to cover the A11 road south of Hackney and north of Dockland. Sailor's taxi was spotted but not quickly enough to jam it before it crossed into Dockland.

TWENTY-FOUR

Gone to Earth

Sailor shepherded Jonathan and Jane up the stairs where they came face to face with Arthur.

Sailor grinned, "Here he is, Arthur, and his girly friend too!"

Jonathan felt Jane's hand stiffen and he squeezed it hard enough to stop any outburst. To his surprise, it kept her quiet.

Arthur stepped in front of them, his face several shades of red.

"Well, well," he said, "the nark and his little whore, eh?"

Jonathan said, very softly, "I don't know who you are, but there's no need for that!"

Arthur exploded, "I'll say whatever I feel like, you fink."

He moved threateningly towards them, but to Jonathan's surprise, Sailor stepped in front.

"Arthur, don't go making a mistake here, the lad may just be what Rita said, she was straight with us about him. He doesn't have the case we thought Ronnie used. And I'm up for kidnapping, not you."

Arthur stepped back and snarled, "Oh, very nice, Sailor, are you in this too?"

There was a moment of complete silence.

Arthur seized the moment. "We'll find out tomorrow, all the manor bosses will be here – bet you I'm right. Put them in the storeroom."

Sailor said, "They'll need food, been on the road since noon."

Arthur shrugged, "You think so much of them, you feed them," and walked away, leaving Sailor clenching his fists. Jonathan took note but kept a straight face. He was holding Jane's hand protectively.

"Jane will need a toilet," he said.

A voice from the back of the room said, "She can use the lavvy, not very swish, but it'll do."

Jonathan looked up and saw another version of Sailor, heavily built with a face that looked like a suet pudding.

Jane whispered, "I want to know what's going on." She was shivering.

Jonathan said, "Wait until we're alone. Don't worry, it's got nothing to do with you."

Sailor said, "Come on Freddy, take the little lady to the lavvy, then." He went out to get the food.

Freddy came forward, avoiding Jonathan's eyes and escorted Jane to the 'lavvy'.

When he returned he took Jonathan into the storeroom and pointed at the foam slabs.

"You'll be fine on those, better than most mattresses."

He looked at Jonathan, "You the one from the Loaf?"

Jonathan nodded.

Freddy shook his head, "Never thought I'd see the day when Ronnie got beat by a shrimp like you!" There was a hint of admiration behind the frown.

Freddy didn't seem threatening, so Jonathan said, "Just self defence, if Ronnie hadn't been so angry he wouldn't have been off-balance."

Freddy scratched his head, "You wrestle then?"

Jonathan started to explain about the Cornish variety, but Freddy stopped him. "You used the flying hip on him!"

Jonathan laughed, "Never heard it called that, but we practised it all the time at school!"

Freddy peered more closely at Jonathan, "Hey, you ain't got too bad a build after all, low centre of gravity, you should try Judo, Yanks brought it over, didn't they?"

This didn't appear to require an answer.

Freddy puffed out his chest and said, "Might have me black belt soon."

Jonathan had some idea what that meant, so he was expressing admiration when Sailor returned with some pub food.

Sir Hubert de Quincy had been in the Operations Room for several hours, reading the files put together in Grey Central, where Clive Atkins and Charles Barnes had been brought in to correlate the data.

"Somewhere in Dockland," mused Sir Hubert out loud, "Could be anywhere, place is a rabbit warren, been a disgrace for years."

Charles was reading his own notes from the second meeting. He nudged Clive and pointed to the passage describing the night visit to open the safe for Bert. Clive read it and cleared his throat, "I wonder Commissioner, whether you would turn to the second set of minutes and paragraph 13?"

Sir Hubert glared at Clive, "Well?"

"We think that there may be more to this account from Sir Roger's agent. If this Hare person is so skilled, why would he be called in to open just any safe? We would like to suggest that this warehouse might actually be Arthur Salmon's centre of operations. It's certainly large enough and has offices and a loading jetty. Actually, we think from this photograph that it may have a Dutch crane, sir."

The Commissioner said, "Show me."

Clive nudged Charles and said, "Actually, it was young Barnes here that spotted it. Show the Commissioner the photograph, please."

Charles placed the print in front of Sir Hubert and pointed to a pulley at the end of an arm high above a large double door let into the second storey.

"Quite a few of these were introduced as a result of the trade with Holland, sir. Very convenient for off-loading smaller loads, and discreet too, a person would have to be on the river to spot it. We got this from the Thames Police."

Sir Hubert grunted, "Good work, shows initiative."

He turned to the Superintendent, "Get onto the Thames Police. I want a patrol launch within striking distance of this warehouse. Got to be out of sight, understand?"

The Superintendent managed not to smile because he had had the Thames Police on special alert for several hours.

Sir Hubert looked at Charles. "You seem to have invested a lot of energy on this case, special interest is it?"

Clive recognized, once again, Sir Hubert's intuition at work and stepped in hurriedly, "Barnes has taken the view from the beginning that Hare isn't in league with the gang. If I may say so, Commissioner, the files can be interpreted to support that view. We think it worth considering that Hare is being made a scapegoat by Arthur Salmon for his own purposes, filling a command void, perhaps?"

Sir Hubert had risen to power in part because he had always allowed his officials to give advice without fear of retribution. He thought aloud about how Arthur might fill a command void. "A mock trial perhaps, to demonstrate that he can operate with impunity?"

He nodded to the collators, "Thank you, good idea."

Jane had returned from the "lavvy" with a disgusted look on her face. "Doesn't anyone clean here?" she demanded.

Freddy looked embarrassed, "Best we can do, not exactly Buckingham Palace, is it?"

Jonathan explained to Jane that men aren't as particular as ladies.

Sailor produced some pork pies and some pickled onions, another feast for men, with no allowances for female taste. Hunger got the better of her, however, and she managed to eat half a pie without complaint. She refused the pickled onion and nearly choked on the bottled beer. But, to Jonathan's amazement, she refrained from her usual acidity; whenever he looked up, he caught her looking at him. Eventually, Sailor directed the two of them into the storeroom.

"We'll wake you early, need to prepare for Arthur's little bit of theatre."

Jonathan heard the sarcasm, and wondered whether he could swing Sailor around. This didn't appear likely after Sailor shut the door and they heard a heavy key turn in the lock. Jonathan put his finger to his lips and motioned Jane towards the mattresses. He squatted down and peered through the keyhole. Sailor had taken the key, so he had a tiny view of the room they had just left. He could see Sailor at the table. The key was lying there, and under the table he could see his tool case.

He turned back and looked around the storeroom. Some light was filtering in through a half-moon window. Must be from a street lamp, he supposed. The room was full of abandoned steel shelving and some flat panels covered in fabric. When he looked closer, he saw that the panels were joined to form a screen. He opened them slowly and pulled the screen between the mattresses. Lady Jane was standing with her hands on her hips.

"What are you doing?" she whispered.

"Giving you some privacy," he answered with a grin. She nodded, but made no move and said, "I want to know what's going on, are we in danger?"

He took her hand. "Look, it's just me they want, although I don't know what for. It was just bad luck that you came with me. Sailor couldn't do anything but take you as well. It's Arthur that wants to question me. Perhaps it's because he found out that I opened his safe, but that was just to get Bert out of a jam. Really, I don't know."

She looked at him and said, "I'm frightened, Jonathan, I don't like these men, they're criminals aren't they?"

He nodded, not knowing what to say, then he realised that she needed some comfort, so he put his arms round her. She stiffened for a moment and he was sure she would push him away, but she slowly relaxed. After a while, he said, "You need to rest."

She sighed against his chest then broke free and went behind the screen.

As soon as she was out of sight, he started to search the room in earnest. His eyes had adjusted to the half-light and he could just see between the steel shelving. It was several sections deep against the outside wall. He crawled under the lowest shelf, until he had gone as far as he could go. He touched the wall and found that it was made of a heavy-grained wood. For a moment he was surprised. The wood was cold and moved slightly under his pressure. He felt along it until he sensed a small gap, which meant it must be a door. As he moved past the gap in the wood, he smelled the river.

He backed out of the shelving, trying to work out why there should be a door just there. He remembered how he and Harry were let in when he came to open the safe, and realised that this must be a loading door from the old days of barges on the Thames. If he could move the shelving, he might be able to open the door. He would need Jane, he decided. When he turned towards the screen, she was standing just behind him.

"What are you doing?" she whispered.

He explained, and together they started to move each section of shelving. As they did so, he had an idea. They carefully positioned each section in a pattern that developed as they went. It took them a long time, moving slowly, but finally he could see the loading doors through the last section. There was a long steel bar holding the doors shut. It was locked with a padlock through a large hasp. Moving the last section out of the way, he took out the picklocks. Jane watched with interest as he felt his way through the tumblers. There were five of them and they were stiff with age, but this was a simple task for him. The lock came loose and he was able to remove the bar and push the door slightly ajar.

The origins of the Thames Police can be traced to the eighteenth century when a force was set up by the East India dock merchants to patrol the great river in an attempt to regulate some of the more nefarious activities practised on either bank. It became part of the Metropolitan Police following the Peel Committee deliberations in the early nineteenth century. Over the years it had gained considerable experience in operating on a tidal river at night.

Constable Terry Baker was watching Arthur's warehouse from behind the cover of a jetty across the river. He was using a pair of prototype night vision glasses on loan from the Army. The image was yellowish but clear enough he thought, pity there weren't a few flats in this part of the river, might be able to cop some bird undressing. He panned around once more across the warehouse, and adjusted the focus on the pulley block above the double doors. As he did so he detected some small change. The doors were now slightly ajar. He pressed the alert button and the captain came forward.

"Something going on, guv, doors weren't open a minute ago, now there's a gap, see." He handed over the glasses. A radio message was passed back to Sir Hubert in the Operations Room.

Sergeant Davies arrived at the Operations Room within an hour of Sailor's taxi leaving Watford. He listened carefully to the Commissioner's terse briefing. He scratched his head.

"That's a dreadful place to raid, sir, almost a no-go area." He pointed to the map.

"The area is almost cut off from the rest of London by these docks, sir; access to the warehouse would have to be over either this narrow road on the west side, or this bridge on the other. No chance of surprise."

Sir Hubert glowered, but Sergeant Davies merely shrugged, "Sorry, sir, but I wouldn't venture in there in uniform, and I know a few of the rogues quite well. Some, like Bert Coleman, are harmless, but others seem to have been picked for their muscle. If you mean to send in a force, it had better be a big one, and that's just asking for trouble."

Sir Hubert nodded, "Agreed, but we have to have someone on the ground. I'm not worried about this Hare character so much as Lady Jane, devil to pay if they harm her."

Sergeant Davies said, "Frankly, sir, I don't think she was ever part of the plan. As far as I can tell, she just made a last minute decision to get out of Mountbeck for a while. Whatever you think of Mr. Hare, sir, he wouldn't have involved her."

Sir Hubert got up and motioned Sergeant Davies to the back of the room. He explained that he had two objectives; get Lady Jane out of there, Hare as well if that was possible but he wanted the chance to round up the manor bosses if he could.

"We have no idea how many men they have in the warehouse, but the loading doors appear to be open, they were closed a few minutes ago."

Sergeant Davies nodded, "From what I've found out, sir, young Hare can open just about anything; those doors were for barge traffic, not used for years, probably. Bit of a drop, though to the ground. Let me get down there, sir, best to go alone, I don't think it's on to get any more in from the north."

Sir Hubert grunted, "Got a launch standing by, opposite bank, under cover. Take a torch, use Morse code if you need it."

Sir Hubert left the room; he needed to consult with Roger, the situation with Jane in the hands of the Grey gang was simply too risky, it could bring them both down.

TWENTY-FIVE

People like Us

Roger and Hubert were face to face in Hubert's suite, their personal relationship as prickly as ever. And this time they were both in trouble, and they knew it. They had thought nothing of using the Hare person in any way that would bring a successful end to their current endeavours, but having Lady Jane involved spelt disaster, for the Establishment would never forgive the endangerment of one of their own.

Hubert was not quite as nervous as Roger, for he had developed techniques to fireproof himself, a necessary skill in the political games he had to play. But Roger couldn't get out of his mind the possibility of having to explain their plan to a Certain Person when she was displeased. It would negate all of the personal credit he had earned over the years, and might even see an end to this appointment.

Hubert sat back. "We've finally identified the body in the Thames. It was Bert Coleman. I wonder what he did to warrant that sort of treatment."

Roger looked up sharply and opened the file on Jonathan. Sergeant Davies' report referred to 'old Bert' and the records section had annotated this with 'Bert Coleman, office manager for Arthur Salmon'.

"Hare opened that safe, didn't he?" asked Roger, "There must have been some grisly secrets in there. Arthur wouldn't have disposed of Bert unless he felt threatened. The Greys may be in prison but they can still reach him."

Hubert grunted, "But Bert would have known what was in there, surely, and knew what would happen if he talked about it. There must be another reason."

Roger had often wondered why Arthur would imperil his operation merely to demonstrate who was Boss. Slowly a light dawned.

"But if Hare opened it, perhaps he saw something he shouldn't!"

Hubert snapped, "Stole, more likely, Arthur must have stacks of money in there, otherwise how could he pay for the contraband?"

Roger could hardly breathe. He should have seen it sooner; he'd discovered Hare's fixation on money long ago. And now he was set to open Edward's safe, damn fellow would steal from that too. He found that he had a sudden headache; what more could go wrong, everywhere he turned, Hare had created problems.

And yet lying behind this sudden revelation was a shadow, one that simply wouldn't go away – "Spitting image of you as a young man, Roger." The lad had other qualities, he had held his own with Edward and Paul, although he hadn't known their titles, and, what was it Antonia had said about that time at Frodsham, "I thought at first that he might be from a good family."

Roger had noted Jonathan's adoption of his own manner of speech, and it hadn't sounded false, not like Harry Sparrow's fawning affectation. A decent Public School could have instilled that into him, but Hubert's people had reported that neither Standish nor St. Eligius could claim membership in the higher echelons of the Register.

When he came to, Hubert was staring at him. "Snap out of it, Roger, no time for day dreaming."

Roger nodded. "We'll just have to play this one as it falls, Hubert, there simply has to be a way to get Jane Bellestream out of this mess. And if Hare gets his come-uppance at Arthur's hand –"

Roger shrugged his elegant shoulders.

Hubert was beginning to worry about Roger, making difficult decisions had always been so easy, done so smoothly that it always made him feel a bit inadequate.

He got up and walked briskly out of the room saying, "You may have time to sit around, Roger, but I don't!"

Roger hardly acknowledged his departure, for a new thought had surfaced. Hare was not only a thief but a St. Eligius student directed into Harry Sparrow's care. And Harry was one of the most successful con men around. The Society knew most of what he did, but it was in its interests to avoid bringing this to light; Harry was far too useful as a working go-between, even if the operatives might have become too comfortable using him in that role. It was a two-edged sword, they all knew that.

Was it possible that the Movement was using Hare as a trap to lure Hubert and him into just this situation? Surely not, the lad was too young, too naïve, although, once again, Roger recalled the image of Hare talking so comfortably with the three of them in the Savoy, wearing that suit as if he had the right to wear something so exclusive. What nerve!

Thinking of the Savoy brought another image, what had Victoria said, that Hare had been so commanding, had warned her not to identify him in public, her interest a bit too personal for an engaged young lady. He had thought that Hare was simply taking his assignment a little too seriously, no harm had been done and he could use the situation to put a distance between the two of them. But what if Hare's concern was not to protect the Society, but the Movement? And could it be that the documents that even now were being so scrupulously counterfeited were another trap to ensnare him?

And then he recalled that uncomfortable moment when Antonia had stormed unannounced into his Study, demanding that he put an end to the lad's relationship with Victoria. He had understood Antonia's almost paranoid concern to get Victoria married into the right family and certainly Robbie had all the proper connections. Debrett was all very well, but it was the unwritten relationships that counted. Robbie's father sat on certain boards and an uncle on others. He had discovered that Robbie's family had built up quite a stranglehold on a little known City function and, he recalled, had become unacknowledged advisors to the government on issues to do with the control of the movement of Sterling. He had used that to the Society's advantage and obtained quite a nice 'contribution'.

All in all, an entirely satisfactory match for Victoria, and Antonia would never allow anything to interfere with that! Her intuition about Victoria's feelings for the lad had been, as usual, uncannily right.

Hare's unique skills had to be acknowledged, too. The Society needed them in the short term to resolve the Bellestream's problem, for if that family went down it would be just too big a triumph for the Movement. And no-one in their right mind would leave an operator like Hare free to carry out the Movement's plans.

He sighed, for once unable to strike the balance needed to chart his course ahead. He would have to put a safety play into action, and Hubert would have the necessary tools for that. He switched the telephone to a secure line and asked Hubert's secretary to get him to telephone as soon as he returned to the Yard.

TWENTY-SIX

Slippery Customers

Jonathan and Jane were resting.

"I want to get you out of here," he said, "but it's a terrible place, you'll have nowhere to go. I have a plan, but it's risky."

He explained the plan to Jane. She looked at him in amazement.

"It's called misdirection, Lady Jane," he said.

She sighed, "Look, Jonathan, just call me Jane, it's easier that way. I know why you never used my title when those awful men were around; you were protecting me." Jonathan was surprised that she had worked that out.

He smiled at her. "Well, *Jane w*hat do you think of the plan?"

She frowned, "We have to try, don't we?"

He went over to the locked door and squinted through the key-hole. Freddy was sitting at the table, reading what looked like a nudist magazine. The key was still on the table.

He thought for a while; the storeroom door was hinged so that when Freddy came in, he would push the door to the left. The first thing he would see would be the steel shelving, so he would need to block that so Freddy's eyes would be directed to the loading doors, He took one of the foam mattresses and dropped it through the loading doors. It fell with a soft thud and lay on the cobbles, probably fifteen feet below the doors. Dawn had broken and he could see quite well.

He went back to Jane. "Help me with the screen."

They carried it across the floor and lined it up against the steel shelving that they had positioned earlier. In the half-light it looked like a solid wall immediately inside the door, where the light was streaming in. They stood so that they would be behind the door when it opened and rehearsed their roles.

He knocked on the door. "Sorry, but I need to go to the lavvy," he shouted.

He heard Freddy get up and come to the door. As Freddy came into the room, he yelled, "What the," and then let out a string of profanities as he ran towards the open loading doors.

Jonathan and Jane stepped through the door and into the office. Freddy had left the key in the lock, so Jonathan locked the door. They could just hear Freddy at the loading doors, shouting, "Where the hell are you?"

In the office Jonathan said, "We're safe here for a while, until Sailor comes back, in about an hour, I think. Get as far from the door as you can and don't worry about Freddy."

Jane was looking nervous again and said, "I thought we would be on our way home."

Her lower lip was trembling.

Freddy had made his way back to the door and had found out that it was locked. Another string of blue language came through the door.

Jonathan smiled at Jane and put his finger to his lips.

It was only just getting light when Harry and Rita got back to Limehouse. They had hardly spoken during the overnight run on the milk train. Feeling more secure in his own house, Harry sat Rita down.

"Listen Annabel," he started.

Rita leapt up, "Don't call me that!"

But Harry wouldn't be stopped.

"I know who you are, you damn fool," he snapped, "I know all about working a scam, I knew you had to use your own name to make it work, Travis wouldn't have fallen for a stranger telephoning out of the blue. And when you spoke to the toff, you were just too convincing! And look at the mess you've made, young Jonathan in bloody Arthur's hands, he'll be lucky to get out with his skin!"

Annabel had lost most of her fire, apparently only now realizing how badly she had misread Arthur's motivation. Harry was as angry as she had ever seen him; he pointed out that she was operating out of her element.

"You ain't got what it takes to work two sides of the street, Annabel, you were brought up on one side and should stay there. All this left wing reading you've done didn't help you, did it?"

She shrugged despairingly. Harry thought about her arrival with Sailor; he had sensed what had happened, Sailor would have had to make a pass, and Annabel would have rejected it. Small wonder that Sailor went off without her like he did.

But he had said enough, he thought, no need to rub her nose in it.

She had taken out a handkerchief and was crying quietly. It was the first time he had seen any weakness in her. She left the room and he heard her packing. He sighed, supposing it was all for the best.

Harry was thinking about Jonathan and found himself deeply agitated, the lad might be a snotty bugger, but he didn't deserve this fate. But there wasn't anything he could do about it, he realised.

Across the river, Constable Baker hardly needed the night glasses. He had picked up Jonathan throwing out the mattress and Freddy standing in the doorway. Both incidents had been relayed to the Operations Room and from there to Sergeant Davies in the police van parked just upstream from the West India Docks. Dressed in black, he worked his way through side streets and tiny alleyways to the warehouse jetty. Taking out the torch, he signalled across the river, hoping the launch would read the message correctly.

Jonathan was trying to see how he could get out of the warehouse and sneak Jane away. He found three windows with a view, and it was when he looked out across the Thames that he spotted a police launch drifting towards the landing.

"Come on, Jane," he said, "this is our chance!"

They slid out of the office door and down the steps.

Sergeant Davies heard footsteps coming down the staircase. He pulled back round a corner and watched as the door opened. He saw Jonathan's head come round the door.

"Mr. Hare," he called, "It's me, Sergeant Davies."

Jonathan blinked, sighed with relief and waved Jane out of the door. They were moving towards Sergeant Davies when they heard a car coming fast towards the warehouse. For a moment, they were frozen, and then the Sergeant shepherded them down a set of steps dropping down to the river gurgling below.

Sailor Wilson arrived at the warehouse to prepare for Arthur's meeting. He was not a happy man for he was sure that Arthur was going out on a limb kidnapping the lad just to prove that he was the boss. Still, loyalty to the gang came first; they would all lose a lot if their control broke down. Mind you, he thought, the payouts ought to have been more with all the increase in business. Arthur had been tight with the shares, banging on about contingencies, whatever that meant.

Sailor opened the side door and went up the stairs. The office was empty and quiet until he heard thumping on the door into the store-room. "Be quiet in there!" he roared.

The launch crossed the river under low power and coasted into the jetty. Jonathan asked the Sergeant, "Why are we hiding? That was only Sailor, and Freddy is already locked up."

He took the key out of his pocket and waved it.

Sergeant Davies whispered, "Stay here".

He jumped onto the launch and pulled Jane on with him. There were four men on the launch and the Captain let two go with the Sergeant, took Jane back upstream and reported the new situation to the Operations Room.

Sergeant Davies led the way up the steps. He said to Jonathan, "You stay at the back, don't get involved in any rough stuff, I want you safe, understand. You know the layout, just tell me where to go."

The four of them went softly up the stairs. The door was open and they saw Sailor trying to break down the door to the storeroom. Between him and Freddy, they were making a lot of noise.

The Sergeant shouted, "Stop right there, Sailor, you're under arrest."

Sailor turned and saw three policeman and Jonathan all grinning at him.

The look that spread over Sailor's face was one that was enjoyed in the Met whenever the story was told. He slowly pointed his finger at Jonathan.

"You," he said, "I should have listened to Arthur, he said you'd be trouble."

While Sailor was being handcuffed, Jonathan took the Sergeant on one side.

"Sailor knows something about a meeting later this morning. He's here to get the place ready."

But Sailor wouldn't talk, "Might as well top me right now!" he snarled.

Jonathan took Sergeant Davies to the safe and on a hunch used the number that he had suggested to Bert. It was still the same. When the door came open, Jonathan took one of the certificates out and walked across to Sailor.

"Look, Sailor, this is what Arthur has in his safe."

He showed Sailor the bond. Even to Sailor, it was a lot of money.

"I think Arthur is skimming off money into his own account. There are hundreds of them in that safe. See where they come from, San Marino, bet you didn't know that!"

Sailor squinted at Jonathan, "How in hell did you find that out?"

Sergeant Davies laughed, "Must have been that night when Bert called you in. Sharp eyes you've got, Mr. Hare!"

Sailor was moving his lips and frowning. "How much in the safe?" he asked Jonathan.

Jonathan did some mental arithmetic. "Half a million, I'd say."

"Bastard Arthur, always knew he was a slimy one, fancy cheating his own people."

He stopped and laughed, "Hope you put him in with Ronnie!"

Sailor told them the plan for the meeting. His job was to set up the storeroom. They had about an hour before the manor bosses would arrive. They sat Sailor down and unlocked the storeroom door. Freddy came out in a state of shock. They put handcuffs on him.

Sergeant Davies said, "Time to get you out of here, Mr. Hare."

One of the Thames Police radioed in the latest news. The Commissioner came on and the Sergeant said, "Sir, the meeting is still on. But you'll have to send enough men in by the river, at least twenty more. I'm bringing Mr. Hare to you now."

They started the careful walk to the van. They were half way there before Jonathan realised that he had still had the bearer bond in his inside pocket.

When they got to the Yard, Sergeant Davies and Jonathan were ushered up to Sir Hubert's suite of offices with unusual deference. As they entered, another man stood up. It was Sir Roger.

"Well, here they are, the heroes of the hour!" he said with a generous smile that didn't fool Jonathan.

Sir Hubert grunted, "We got all but Arthur Salmon, he never came, must have been warned off. But this is a major coup, put the gang back years. Congratulations to you both."

Jonathan was fidgeting, "What about Lady Jane, is she alright?"

Sir Roger laughed, "Never seen her so excited, Lady Antonia has taken her away for a bath and some sleep. Good job you weren't here, Jonathan, she kept saying what a genius you were, bit embarrassing, really!"

Sir Hubert was pacing around. "I'm going to make a big splash tomorrow, television coverage, radio, newspapers, pull out all the stops."

He looked at the Sergeant and Jonathan.

"I hope you'll both understand that there'll be many people who'll get recognized. But not you two, got to keep you under wraps."

Jonathan looked at Sir Roger with his eyebrows raised. "I thought I'd be the scapegoat, putting Lady Jane into so much danger. All I did was to get her out, used some stagecraft."

All three men wanted to know what he meant. He explained that he had used the stuff in the storeroom to create an illusion, rather like the cabinet that stage magicians use, only in reverse. Freddy went into the cabinet and they came out. All the men looked at him.

Sir Hubert was the first to laugh, "Like the thing at the Alhambra, when the door was stuck?"

It was Jonathan's turn to gape, "How did you know about that?

Sir Roger intervened, "We have been keeping a watch on you, Jonathan, too many other parties have an interest in you. But you must be tired, come with me and we'll go back to the Society."

The great Rolls Royce slid effortlessly through the streets of London and arrived at the Society just after nine o'clock. Jonathan was feeling the effects of a sleepless night and was hardly prepared for the welcome he received.

Lady Antonia smiled at him, but Jonathan remained wary.

"Jane says that you have been such a good friend to her. We will see you a little later, I expect," she said.

On cue, the man in the blue suit came forward and took him upstairs to a bedroom.

"Well, Mr. Hare, you do get around," he said with a grin. He opened the door for Jonathan, who was more than glad to sleep for a while.

He woke to a knock on the door and heard the man asking if he was awake. He had slept for five hours. The man said, "If you're feeling up to it, Lady Jane is asking to go back to Mountbeck."

A bath revived him and he went downstairs to find Sir Roger waiting for him. They went into the Dining Room, where a selection of food was on the buffet. Jonathan looked around the room and saw Jane talking to a taller blonde girl with her back to him. Jane saw him and waved excitedly. The blonde girl turned. It was Victoria.

Annabel had gone and Harry's house was empty. He was surprised to find that he missed her. Must be getting past it, he thought. He switched on the TV for the Midday News and heard, "Early morning raid on a warehouse deep in Dockland, leadership of a notorious gang captured".

There was a studio map with the Commissioner pointing dramatically with a stick. He watched in amazement as the Commissioner gloated about the capture of the gang.

Harry thought for a moment and decided it was the warehouse he and Jonathan had gone to when they helped out old Bert, fancy that. There was no mention of Jonathan, although the Commissioner stressed that it was a total surprise and the police had suffered no casualties. There was a special tribute to the Thames Police, which had enabled the raid from the river, which caught the gang unawares. Harry shouted at the TV, "Never get there any other way, you ponce, place is a death trap for police, never see them in uniform down there, do you!"

Just then the telephone rang. He picked it up and Sergeant Davies's voice came over the earpiece.

"Harry, Mr. Hare thought you should know that he got out safe with the girl friend."

Harry put down the telephone almost in tears. It was some time before he realised that Sergeant Davies had called Jonathan "Mr. Hare".

TWENTY-SEVEN

A Friend in Need

Jonathan could hardly believe that it was Victoria. Her sunken eyes had dark circles beneath them and her hair was dragged back in an unflattering style. As he started towards her, Lady Antonia floated between them and took Jonathan's arm. She guided him away, saying, "Victoria has had an awful time recently, Jonathan. She isn't at all herself. Don't upset her any more."

He was trying to understand how he could upset her, but before he could say anything, Jane appeared and dragged him towards Sir Roger. She was unnaturally excited, he thought, feeling uncomfortable with the excessive amount of emotion. She seemed determined to relate all the deeds that he had performed. Sir Roger listened gravely, nodding from time to time. Eventually, Jane came to the end of her story. Sir Roger smiled indulgently.

"It seems as if Jonathan has earned his place at the Round Table."

It was an allusion that Jonathan felt was rather forced, as though Sir Roger had to search for something complimentary. Sir Roger looked at his watch.

"It's time for you two to get in the car, long drive ahead of you."

Goodbyes were said, but all Jonathan was able to do was to wave at Victoria, who was sheltered by her mother in a corner. Victoria raised one eyebrow in return.

Charles Barnes was aware of the success of the raid, but not of the part that Jonathan had played. Various sections were hard at work drafting reports and Clive had dispatched him to obtain copies for the files. News of the Commissioner's intention to play up the capture on every available media outlet had spread throughout the Yard. Charles recalled the Press Release drafted when Ronnie was captured and the unfortunate effect on the Records Section. He had been right to question it and was determined that the same mistake wouldn't be made this time. He headed for the Press Section and interrupted Josie Warren in the middle of composing some blurb or other.

She glared at him, "What are you doing in here, this is confidential, out of bounds to you!"

Her desk was littered with discarded drafts. Charles had learned the necessary art of reading upside down, and was surprised to see an official Statement of Offences form, something well outside the mandate of the Press Section. What really jolted him was to see Jonathan's name on the form as the subject. He brought out a handkerchief and blew into it vigorously.

"Sorry, hay fever season you know, look at that pollen blowing out there!" he gasped, nodding at the window. As he hoped, Josie turned to look. He dropped the files onto one of the drafts and blew his nose with both hands. When he had finished, he picked up the files and apologized to Josie. He walked slowly out of the room, then rushed back to the Section making sure no one saw the draft at the bottom of the stack of files.

The journey to Mountbeck passed in a blur. The Rolls Royce, manoeuvred effortlessly by the man in the blue suit, soothed both Jane and Jonathan into a contented stupor. He woke every so often to find Jane slumped against him. He nudged her, but it seemed to have little effect. He decided to be 'gentil' and not push her away. It was getting dark when they arrived to a surprising welcome. Edward was on the steps, accompanied by Paul whom he recognized from the Savoy and a very beautiful, olive complexioned woman. They were introduced as Count Paolo Passaglietti and his sister, Maria. And

Germaine had returned.

Travis was also there, his usual role largely taken over by Edward. As they went in through the great entrance, Travis murmured to Jonathan, "We are glad you have returned safe and sound, sir." He didn't seem at all bothered by Jonathan's tool case.

As they went down the hall to the Dining Room, there was much excited chatter. Jane seemed unable to contain herself and was allowed to be the centre of attention. Jonathan was not comfortable; Jane was being so complimentary that Edward came alongside and murmured with a grin, "Gentility, Jonathan, gentility!"

Sir Roger had travelled up to York with Sergeant Davies. They had stopped at Lady Brockhurst's place at Beningham. Sir Roger was sitting in the Day Room, trying to comfort Annabel Winstanley.

"You did your best, Annabel, it was a difficult situation for you. No one could have foreseen that Jane would decide to come with Hare, but, then, we hadn't reckoned with his stagecraft either. Bit of a shock when he got out so early, nearly foiled the plan."

She was only able to nod.

Sir Roger was thinking privately that he and Hubert had got out of the situation with the skin of their teeth.

He decided that the moment had come. "You realize that your cover can't be used again. As far as I can tell, Harry just thinks that you acted like a silly woman, caught between loyalties. We need Harry to go on doing what he does; he's invaluable as a go-between. Have you cleared your ground with your aunt?"

Annabel nodded again, "She thinks I had an affair, tries to understand, but I suspect she thinks I'm as silly as Harry does. It's strange, though, I had some good times with Harry, it's a different life down there in the East End, more alive than up here." She grimaced.

Sir Roger laughed, "Don't worry, Annabel, someone with your abilities will be needed again. Enjoy yourself while you can, I gather that your aunt is really fond of you. We will have you down to the Society soon, you and Antonia get on so well."

He took his leave. When he got to the car, he took his brief case with the package of counterfeit documents back from Sergeant Davies and directed him to drive to Mountbeck.

After supper, Edward shepherded them all into the Drawing Room. It had not been used for some time and Edward had had to be firm with Travis in order to get it ready on time.

Germaine had cornered Jonathan. "You have made the conquest, I think, Jonathan. Jane is so happy that she has found someone she can look up to."

She paused and looked at him seriously. "She is very naïve, you comprehend?"

Jonathan smiled, "All I did was to work out a plan to keep her safe. She was a good sport, played right along with whatever I had to do."

Germaine sighed, "You men, you don't see what is in front of your noses!"

Travis entered and spoke quietly to Edward, who excused himself and left the room.

Paul had positioned himself within earshot and had heard the name 'Sir Roger'. His instincts were once more aroused. What was Sir Roger doing here? Granted that he had provided the technical expert to open the safe, there simply had to be something more involved for someone as highly positioned as Sir Roger to make the trip from London. The more he thought about it the more he was convinced that the Hare lad represented something more than what he appeared to be. From what he had heard from Jane's babbling, one might have thought that Hare had captured the gang single-handed. But it was clear from the Commissioner's press conference that forces had been positioned well beforehand; which meant that Hare's presence had to have been part of some well thought-out plan. He grew more convinced that a trap had been set and that Hare was the bait. But where did Jane fit in? He knew enough to be sure that Sir Roger would never have authorized that. But he would get to the bottom of it, he thought, surprised that he was more stimulated by the exercise than he had been for several years of somewhat repetitive commercial intrigue.

Edward and Sir Roger were in the Study. Sir Roger was pacing, which was unusual for him. Finally he came to a halt and said, "I think we have a problem, Edward. The Hare lad has dug himself too deeply into Victoria's affections; she has had a terrible experience with her fiancé, least said the better. When Victoria heard Jane's tales about his exploits in Dockland, her reaction really shocked her mother. Antonia is convinced that she will run to Hare, 'on the rebound' as she put it. We may have to take some rather unpleasant measures to put a stop to it; the lad is quite unsuitable, you understand."

Edward looked hard at Roger. He understood the extent of Roger's power and was grateful for his intervention, but something didn't sit right. He had sensed that the lad had begun to have a calming effect on Jane, something that was too important to simply throw away on a whim. Roger's view of unsuitability didn't take into account the realities of modern day England.

"Aren't you allowing personal considerations to intrude in this matter, Roger? The lad has never mentioned any affection for Victoria; he seemed far too focussed on this operation. He could have easily opened the safe and carried out the Movement's plan, but he didn't, he came to you for advice."

Roger was surprised at Edward's forthrightness. He was glad to see it even if it did make his task that much more difficult.

"I'm afraid, Edward, that Hare has a way of lulling us into an easy acceptance of him. We have discovered some distressing character flaws. He comes from an impoverished home life and has a fixation about money; never having had any I suppose that's understandable, but it's had serious consequences for us. We believe that he stole from the gang when he was called in to open a safe, and the authorities now believe that it was the reason for the gang's determination to capture him. I dread to think what they would have done."

Edward expressed amazement, "Stole? How could he steal money, surely he was watched, they wouldn't let him open their safe without supervision, surely?"

Roger asked kindly, "Didn't he ever tell you about his stage magician's tricks? We think he used some sleight of hand, or misdirection, and the gang didn't realise until much later. And he escaped by another trick from his repertoire. Exactly how he got out of that warehouse is still under investigation."

Edward could hardly believe his ears. Then a memory of that strange conversation with Travis about the paintings surfaced; Travis had left Hare on his own in the Small Drawing Room where he had sized up Marguerite's paintings and even had a market value ready. And he'd asked whether there were any other paintings in the closed wing. Then there was the conversation about how the cabinet tricks were all basically the same; he had said something about it being cheating and that he preferred sleight of hand tricks!

It was his turn to pace the Study. Something else was worrying him now, something about Travis and his initial reaction, as though Hare was quite beneath consideration and should have come in through the trade entrance. And then he realised that if Hare opened the safe all the Bellestream difficulties would be over. There would be more than enough to restore the estate and Jane would be a wealthy young girl, on the threshold of womanhood, and a wonderful catch for any young man.

Perhaps things had gone too far between Jane and Jonathan. It was all very well for Jonathan to exercise gentility, but Jane now seemed to have genuinely fallen for him.

He turned with an air of finality.

"I agree, Roger, better to take action now than to have people hurt in the long run. Do you have a suggestion?"

Sir Roger pursed his lips, "I think we have to scare him off."

He produced a slim folder and placed it before Edward.

"This is a smokescreen, Edward, but there is enough truth in it that Hare can't risk it getting into the hands of the wrong people, especially the Galdraith Scholarship committee."

Edward read:

Metropolitan Police – Statement of Offences
Subject – Jonathan Hare alias Samuel Ward

Whereas the subject is an associate of the Grey gang who had fallen out with Ronald Grey, the gang leader, then under surveillance by Task Force 21; and,

Whereas the feud came to a head in the King's Head Public House, when the Task Force was able to capture Ronald Grey while he was exacting revenge on the subject; and,

Whereas the subject is a skilled housebreaker and an expert on safe breaking, having been trained by the gang in these skills; and,

Whereas he is recorded as trying to branch out on his own assuming the name of Samuel Ward; and,

Whereas he is known to frequent the operational headquarters of the gang at a warehouse in the Isle of Dogs; and,

Whereas the subject is skilled at disguise and has a preference for expensive clothes and high society living; and,

Whereas extensive investigation has failed to reveal the source of funds for his lavish lifestyle.

Now therefore he is charged as follows:

Offence 1: kidnapping Lady Jane Bellestream from Mountbeck, Heckmondsley, Yorkshire, in the company of a well-known gang member, Sailor Wilson,

Offence 2: confining the aforesaid in the warehouse at 12 Thames Street, Millwall.

Caution: The suspect has evaded the police and is now at large, whereabouts unknown.

Edward looked up at Sir Roger. "Is this really necessary? It's rather vindictive, the lad was brave enough to rescue Jane, she's none the worse for it. Actually, Roger, it seems to have done her a power of good, jolted her out of her depression, what?"

Sir Roger nodded, "I know, but if we are to deal with the social consequences, I need some strong ammunition. Hare is far too intelligent to fall for anything less. I won't use it officially, of course, I hope the threat will do the trick. If you have any suggestions, this is just an early draft. Oh, and don't let Hare see the inside of the safe in case he tries another sleight of hand. Just get him to tell you the combination numbers. Perhaps you would send Hare to me now?"

Edward entered the Drawing Room and spoke quietly to Jonathan.
"Sir Roger has arrived and would like to see you in the Study."
Jonathan wondered why Sir Roger would come all this way, but it was clear that he was expected to go to the Study.

Paul noted Edward's quiet aside to Jonathan. So Sir Roger wanted to talk privately with the lad? It was another confirmation that something more sinister lay behind this; Paul felt almost as stimulated as waiting for a Juventus home game to get under way.

Sir Roger was at the desk, laying out papers from his brief case.
"This is the package that we have prepared for you to deliver to your St. Eligius people. The documents are all counterfeit, of course."
Jonathan was affronted; there had been no greeting. He sensed the same change of attitude that Edward had displayed on occasion. He shrugged mentally; he would soon be out of this situation, and could focus on his Scholarship interview.
He picked up a portfolio that indicated that there was an unnumbered account at Croffts Bank in London; he had never heard of the Bank, but its title looked very grand. The balance was so large that he found that his hands were shaking.
Sir Roger raised an eyebrow, "Impressive, isn't it?"
Jonathan could only nod, since the thought that people might actually have that much money was quite breathtaking.
He picked up some certificates. They were drawn on the Mercantile and Marine Bank in the Scilly Isles and started with the words "Pay the Bearer the sum of –."

They looked rather like the ones in Arthur's safe, he thought, except that the denominations were many times higher. There were other certificates with the word "Gold" on them.

He looked up to find Sir Roger examining him strangely.

"Are you recovered from your adventure, Jonathan?"

There seemed to be much more to this question than a polite inquiry after his health. Jonathan decided to play for time.

"People are making such a fuss about it, sir, but, to be honest, there wasn't much I could do until we got to the warehouse. And even then I had the feeling that Sailor and the others didn't have their heart in it. Sailor actually stopped Arthur from laying in to me; he didn't appear to like Arthur very much. That was why I had the idea that we could get him to tell us what Arthur's plan was. It's a pity Arthur escaped the net; whoever organized the kidnapping ought to have to pay the price!"

There was a long and unnatural silence.

Sir Roger finally smiled; no one would ever know what emotional price he had had to pay to get that smile to come.

"I shall have to return to London now. You will open the safe tomorrow?" he asked.

Jonathan nodded, "I would like to be a bit fresher than I am tonight, sir."

Sir Roger left the office without a backward glance and it was a few moments before Jonathan realised that Sir Roger had left with no social niceties at all.

He shrugged, and took the package up to his room.

Sir Roger's journey back to London was not a happy one. Hubert and he had agreed that the threat to their standing was too great to allow the Hare person to escape from their control. Hare was the only one who knew what they had done and could expose their cavalier approach. They had assumed from the beginning that sacrificing one person for the sake of capturing the gang was defensible, and the plan was so well designed that it had the potential to be Police Staff College material. But it had gone so wrong, and at every turn it was

Hare who had precipitated the disaster. That it had had a praiseworthy ending was a point in their favour, but Hare could show that they had been reckless and that it was him, of all people, who was responsible for its success.

Then why had he been unable to deliver the threat of the Statement of Offences?

Lurking at the back of his mind was an image of Jonathan at the Savoy, just too much like those photographs of himself as a young man. And what had Antonia remarked? 'Spitting image of you at that age', that was it.

He found himself in yet another indecisive mood when he should have been unwavering. He was unused to such weakness and struggled to understand the reason for this sudden lack of resolve. He began to think that he should take a holiday to get over this stupidity and then immerse himself in his duties.

Had he been able to check his blood pressure he would have been even more unsettled.

As Jonathan was approaching his room, he heard a rustle of skirts, looked back and saw Jane coming up fast behind him.

"Where are you going, Jonathan?" she asked.

"I need to get some sleep, ready for the morning when we open the safe."

She pouted, "But I thought you would stay and talk to me, I've hardly seen you since we got back."

She waited, almost dancing from one foot to the other. She asked him to come back to the Drawing Room. He sighed and then agreed, "I'll be there in a minute."

He went into his room and slid the package of documents under the mattress for safekeeping.

As they entered the Drawing Room, he caught Germaine's eye and sent a signal for help, but she turned away; he could swear there was a small smile on her lips. Jane insisted on parading him around the room, rather like a Shetland pony at a gymkhana, he thought.

When they were alone, she said, "What will you do after you've opened the safe?"

He told her about the Galdraith interview and entering Oxford.

She was quite flustered. "Will we see you here before you go up?"

He thought about it, perhaps for too long. When he looked up, her face had lost the radiance that for a time had made her more attractive. She turned away and ran up the stairs.

TWENTY-EIGHT

What Goes Up Must Come Down

The next morning Jonathan was called into the study for the opening of the Mountbeck safe. Such was the importance of the occasion that Edward had insisted that only Count Paul and Jonathan should be present. Jane made a small fuss, which Germaine was able to quell by explaining how very boring it might be.

Edward's greeting was restrained and Jonathan thought he must be nervous.

"Would you be so kind as to read out the numbers of the combination and allow me to perform the actual opening of the safe?"

Jonathan thought this was a very strange way to speak to him, almost as if he was merely a hired hand. But he shrugged, thinking that Edward had waited so long for this moment that it must have affected his nerves.

He waited for the two men to give him a signal. They sat and Edward nodded. Jonathan took out the stethoscope and applied the contact piece, pushing up the silver handle to engage the clutch. He heard the satisfying clicks and began the process of detecting the minute sounds as the tumblers engaged. He held up one finger when he had the first location and called out the number. Edward wrote it down. The process continued until all five numbers were recorded. Jonathan got up and instructed Edward on the sequence.

"Clockwise to the first number, anti-clockwise to the second, and so on. Then go back to zero and push the handle down."

Edward's hand was trembling as he went through the procedure. The moment came when he had to be push down the handle. He was sweating as he pulled open the door. He looked inside quickly and took a moment to recover from the tension. His face took on a harder and more determined look than Jonathan had ever seen.

He turned to Jonathan and said, "Thank you, Mr. Hare, you have served us well. The Count and I will want to examine the contents privately. I believe you have an important interview in a few days' time?"

Count Paolo had been watching Jonathan closely. He had seen him slip behind a mask of apparent unconcern.

He cleared his throat. "Perhaps I could speak with you, Edward."

He turned to Jonathan, "Wait outside, please, for a moment."

Jonathan was relieved to get out of the Study. He heard voices through the door; Edward's was raised, the Count's barely audible. After several minutes, the Count opened the door and came out. He looked at Jonathan for a long moment. Jonathan was surprised that there seemed to be no animosity there. He took Jonathan by the arm and they walked up the stairs and into his room; the Count closed the door.

"Lord Erinmore has been convinced that you should leave Mountbeck immediately. I have persuaded him to let me drive you to the station at Thirsk. You should pack now." As they drove to the station the Count looked across and smiled.

"May I call you Jonathan, Mr. Hare?"

Jonathan was taken aback for there was respect in the Count's voice.

"Sometimes, Jonathan, we are so busy with immediate business that we are unaware of other things happening. Your service to Edward was only part of another scenario. I am privileged to know how faithfully you did your duty."

When they got to the station, the Count produced a wonderfully understated card.

"If you ever need help, Jonathan, ring that number, they will get a message to me."

Jonathan turned the card over. On the back he read:

Banco Internationale, San Marino.

"Count Paolo," he said, "could you advise me about this?"

He dug out the bearer bond he had taken from Arthur's safe and handed it over.

The Count looked at it with the realisation that Jonathan had indeed been used to open the gang's safe. So that had been the master plan, had it? He would have to have a response ready to answer the inevitable enquiries from Sterling Control regulators. And he should certainly not allow any other loose ends like this to complicate matters.

"Are you planning to visit us in San Marino, Jonathan?" he asked with a smile.

Jonathan shook his head.

"Then allow me to save you any difficulty. I will honour this for you here and now, you will take a cheque?"

He took out a magnificent leather wallet and wrote out a cheque for a thousand pounds. It was drawn on a Bank in London with the same name as he had seen on the fake documents, Croffts, that was it.

They shook hands as the train drew in to the station.

The Headmaster at St. Eligius was trying to make sense of the message young Barnes had sent him. It was to the effect that the police might be targeting Hare as a fugitive criminal, whereabouts unknown.

But Barnes had said that there was no record of the official release of the Statement of Offences, and that that was most unusual. Other information indicated that Jonathan had succeeded brilliantly in furthering the police aims and had received no credit. Barnes had concluded that Jonathan must have run afoul of whatever Service he had been working for and that the document was intended as a threat to keep him in line.

The Headmaster wondered what sort of graduate his school had produced. Hare was certainly not conforming to any pattern that he could comprehend. Clearly however, any information about Mountbeck that Hare provided must be considered suspect. He wondered how he was going to express this at Tudor House; he found himself to be quite agitated at the thought.

All the way to London, Jonathan tried to make sense of what had happened. He had once thought that he had been accepted at Mountbeck and the coldness of his dismissal was an unwelcome shock. He understood that there was no acceptance in the de Quincy family; Lady Antonia had at least been honest in her hostility, but he should have taken it more seriously for Victoria's engagement had demonstrated the values that really motivated the de Quincys.

Sir Roger had pretended friendship in order to make sure that he only used his special skills for the Society and had then used him as a pawn, placing him in danger quite deliberately, like putting a terrier into a badger sett. Jonathan thought Sir Hubert wasn't much better, but he at least had never pretended any empathy.

Edward, though, was another question. Jonathan had thought that there was a better understanding between them, a more level playing field. Yet in the end Edward had only wanted his skills to open the safe and had shown his real feelings with those cold words of dismissal.

He sat back and thought about what sort of life the families led. They had everything, yet were slaves to their positions. Sir Roger served the Establishment and Edward was saddled with the responsibility of Mountbeck. It was in such a state of disrepair that there would have to be enormously valuable assets in that safe.

Lady Jane was a difficult and unhappy girl who was quite unstable. Otherwise, he thought, why would she fall for the first person that showed her any kindness? He sighed, thinking that the world that those families lived in was far too confusing.

His thoughts turned to his own circumstances. The beacon of the Galdraith Scholarship shone brightly in his future. If he won it, as some assumed, he would have a position of his own, and, whatever the duties attached to the appointment, he would be his own man, not beholden to the stifling protocols surrounding those in the Establishment. As for money, which had always presented a problem for him, he had quite a fistful left over from the expenses and then a cheque for a thousand pounds.

He shrugged and by the time he got to Harry's to pick up the rest of his things he had lost the edge of his anger.

Harry seemed genuinely glad to see him.

"Thanks for letting me know that you were safe. What are you going to do now?"

"Go home and relax, I have the interview at Oxford next week."

"What do you want me to tell them at St. Eligius?" Harry asked flatly.

"Give them this," Jonathan said, digging Sir Roger's package out of his suitcase.

On his way out of the door, Harry handed him a small bundle of letters.

"Came while you were lording it up in Mountbeck." he said.

On the top was a blue envelope; the writing was familiar.

Harry said goodbye at the door and turned away rather quickly. For a moment Jonathan thought that there were tears in his eyes.

On the train from Paddington he opened the blue envelope. All it contained was a cutting from the Tatler. It read:

"The marriage arranged between Victoria Penelope de Quincy and Robert Erskine Dunne will not now take place."

There was only the faintest suggestion of her perfume. He took a moment to wonder what disaster had caused Lady Antonia's plans for Victoria to go so wrong. Then he shrugged, thinking again that life in their circles was just too complicated.

When he got home his mother greeted him effusively.

"And did you have a good *time*?" she asked. He recognized the trap.

"Oh, it was only work," he smiled, "I would much rather have been at home with you."

And he was surprised to find that he meant it.